Afterglow

Lily Easton is the pen name for writing duo Katherine and Madeline. Katherine studied English Literature at Wesleyan University and enjoys reality TV in her free time. Madeline studied journalism at New York University and currently works in production. They met in their high school creative writing class and have been writing together ever since.

Also by Lily Easton

Summer of Love
Afterglow

Lily Easton

Afterglow

CANELO

First published in the United Kingdom in 2026 by

Canelo, an imprint of
Canelo Digital Publishing Limited,
20 Vauxhall Bridge Road,
London SW1V 2SA
United Kingdom

A Penguin Random House Company
The authorised representative in the EEA is Dorling Kindersley Verlag GmbH.
Arnulfstr. 124, 80636 Munich, Germany

Copyright © Lily Easton 2026

The moral right of Lily Easton to be identified as the creator of this work has been asserted in accordance with the Copyright, Designs and Patents Act, 1988.
All rights reserved. No part of this publication may be reproduced or transmitted in any form or by any means, electronic or mechanical, including photocopy, recording, or any information storage and retrieval system, without permission in writing from the publisher.
No part of this book may be used or reproduced in any manner for the purpose of training artificial intelligence technologies or systems. In accordance with Article 4(3) of the DSM Directive 2019/790, Canelo expressly reserves this work from the text and data mining exception.

A CIP catalogue record for this book is available from the British Library.

Print ISBN 978 1 83598 098 9
Ebook ISBN 978 1 83598 099 6

This book is a work of fiction. Names, characters, businesses, organizations, places and events are either the product of the author's imagination or are used fictitiously. Any resemblance to actual persons, living or dead, events or locales is entirely coincidental.

Printed and bound in Great Britain by Clays Ltd, Elcograf S.p.A.

Look for more great books at
www.canelo.co | www.dk.com

To anyone looking for a little light in dark times.

Prologue

Alice

'Do you want to know a secret?'

The words coming out of Briar's mouth didn't slur, didn't give away the amount of alcohol they'd drunk that night. Then again, Alice was the one who was usually embarrassing when she was tipsy – she'd always envied that Briar only got cooler, as if that were somehow possible.

Alice laughed, tipping her head back and immediately dizzied by the sight of the stars. 'Is there anything you could tell me that's actually a secret?'

There had never been a more perfect night than this one, the embers of a dying campfire crackling next to them, just her and her best friend squeezed onto one log in her favorite place in the world.

She knew they were shirking their responsibilities – technically, they should have been in their bunks, supervising the campers, but some other counselors were covering for them so they could clean up the final campfire. The other counselors *definitely* knew they weren't just cleaning up. When Briar and Alice were together, work was usually the last thing on their minds. They were famous amongst the campers and counselors for their tight-knit friendship and associated hijinks, which they could get away with on account of Briar being the camp director's daughter and Susan having a soft spot for Alice.

Briar's next words cut through her reverie. 'I don't tell you *everything*, you know.'

When Alice looked back at Briar, she was frowning, her nose scrunched up. It only made her freckles more pronounced, constellations that reminded Alice of the sky. She'd always been jealous of Briar's freckles. Everything about Briar was interesting to her, had captivated her since the day they had met, next to this fire pit, eight years before.

'You don't?'

She was trying to be funny, trying to be the version of herself she felt most when she was at camp and when she was around Briar. Carefree and full of life. Still, maybe because camp was ending the next day and with it the best version of Alice, a hint of anxiety played at the back of her mind. What Briar had said couldn't really be true – Alice was sure she knew everything there was to know about Briar. They spent every moment of every day together. Sometimes Alice thought she knew Briar better than herself. But what if she was wrong?

She couldn't say their relationship hadn't changed over the past few years, first with her boyfriend, Noah, entering the picture and then when Alice had decided to go to college in Scotland. At the time, college had seemed so far away. They'd still had the full summer ahead of them. Now, a part of Alice worried that things wouldn't be the same when Briar came to visit her at St Andrews for fall break.

Briar breathed out slowly. 'I lied about something.' Her accompanying smirk was enough to put Alice at ease.

Alice turned to her. Their thighs were touching now, but Alice didn't feel the need to move away. They were always touching like this, accidentally, or hugging or holding hands on purpose, because that was what friends did. And right now, Alice needed something to anchor her to the earth so she didn't float away.

'What did you lie about?' she asked, focusing in on Briar's hazel eyes, finding the freckle on her left iris. It was a trick she used when she needed to stop her thoughts from racing.

'You know how I said I kissed Trevor Mac at homecoming?'

Alice's eyebrows knit together. 'Yeah…?'

'I didn't,' Briar said simply, and it was only after she leaned away that Alice realized how close their faces had been. 'That's all.'

'Oh.' Alice blinked, and Briar's features realigned in front of her. 'Why did you say you did?'

Briar fiddled with her shorts, and Alice's eyes traced the movement, admiring the smooth skin of Briar's thigh.

'I dunno. I guess I felt like everyone else had done it, and I didn't want it to be like, a *thing* that I hadn't. You know?'

'Yeah,' Alice said, nodding. She had the urge to grab Briar's hand to stop her from messing with her shorts. 'I get lying to everyone else, but why couldn't you tell me the truth?'

Briar looked up again, and Alice struggled to swallow. She glanced over at the fire pit and saw that the smoke was blowing towards them now, making the air more difficult to breathe. At least now she knew the reason. 'It was mostly *for* you.'

'What do you mean?'

'I guess,' Briar started, then chewed her lip as Alice just stared at her, 'it felt weird that you'd done all these things that I hadn't. Because usually we do everything together. And I didn't want you to think... I don't know how to explain it.'

Alice couldn't stop herself from giggling at Briar's skewed logic. 'Oh come on, do you really think it matters to me if you've kissed someone?'

Except suddenly, it seemed to occupy every corner of Alice's mind, and the more she tried to not think about it, the more it repeated itself over and over again. Images of Briar kissing Trevor, or some faceless man, things Alice had never really thought about that deeply before. And it was quickly ruining her good mood. Which didn't make sense, because Briar had just admitted it hadn't even been true.

Briar smiled, oblivious to Alice's thoughts. 'No, of course it doesn't matt—'

Alice didn't let her finish. 'I'll kiss you.'

Briar's mouth gaped, and Alice found herself wondering what it would be like to kiss her. What those images in her head would look like if she got to be the one kissing Briar instead.

'What?'

'I'll kiss you,' Alice said, adopting her bossiest tone. 'So you can go to college having kissed someone.'

'But you just said it didn't matter,' Briar countered.

'It doesn't. But it seems like you want to kiss someone, and I'm here...' Alice was quickly losing steam as Briar stared at her as though she were speaking a foreign language. 'One kiss couldn't hurt.'

'I didn't tell you so that you would kiss me,' Briar said, and her voice sounded strange. For once, Alice had no idea what she was thinking. She suspected Briar was trying to bow out gracefully, but she tried one more time to make her see the benefits of the situation. She knew she could help Briar with this, if she was given the chance. And she wanted to be a good friend to her.

'Obviously,' Alice said. 'I mean, I know I'm not exactly your first choice, but I'm here. So if you want to try, just to see…'

Briar's cheeks went pink. 'Um, oka—'

Alice kissed her before she lost the nerve to. It took a few seconds for her to realize that Briar had probably expected some sort of build-up, like what would normally happen before a first kiss. But for some reason, Alice hadn't been able to wait.

Their mouths were frozen, touching but not moving, for a long moment. And then Alice realized she had done exactly what she'd promised, that she should pull back. So she did. For exactly one second before she leaned in more slowly and kissed her again, harder.

And Briar responded this time, her mouth moving, getting the hang of it quickly. *Very* quickly. Alice got lost in it in a way she hadn't expected, because kissing Noah had never felt this good, this right. It occurred to her that maybe this was how kissing someone was supposed to feel, that maybe Briar had been the missing element from all her previous kisses.

Because of course the person who knew her better than anyone else would also know exactly what she liked, exactly how to suck on her lower lip to get her to moan, in a way Noah never had. It should have occurred to her sooner that kissing your best friend was actually the most sensible way to go about having a good kissing experience. It was only logical.

Alice had never felt better, freer, more herself than she did while kissing Briar.

Chapter 1

Alice

Susan's posthumous instructions had been as forceful as her ones in life. No one ever argued with Susan, not even if they'd received an email like the one Alice had the week before.

> Alice, if you're reading this, it means I'm dead. Excuse the melodrama. I would like you to speak at the funeral — you'll know what to say.

Alice didn't want to argue with a ghost. If she could argue with a ghost, though, she'd have some choice words for her. Primarily, *Actually, I don't know what to say*. She wouldn't have known what passage to choose to represent Susan's life or death under the best of circumstances, and the circumstances weren't the best. The circumstances were possibly the *worst*.

Alice stood behind a podium 3,665.36 miles from her London flat in front of a sea of mourners she didn't want to look at, either because she loved them too much, didn't know them, or was actively estranged from them. In the first row, left side, Susan's children sat with Alice's ex and his new fiancée.

She leaned forward, fixing her eyes on the ends of her friend Freddie's head of floppy hair and reminded herself to tell him to get a haircut later. 'The reading I've chosen is from *The British Scientific Journal of Plants,* a publication Susan cited liberally in my time with her at Camp Lakeside. You may recall her favorite passages the way that I do. This was one of them: "Within the continuum of earth's perfect systems, death is not just death. Through death, nutrients are conserved, often relocated, and may aid in the creation of new resources."' She chanced a glance down at Freddie's eyes, saw they were welling with tears, and quickly looked away. '"Furthermore, scientists have developed evidence to support a hypothesis that some processes of decay are the result of a dynamic cross-kingdom functional succession."' Freddie looked more confused than sad now, which couldn't be a good thing. When she talked about decomposition, Alice was known to digress in ways that most people had trouble following. So she ditched the last part of what she'd spent her red-eye flight writing – honestly, the bit about the distinction between invertebrate and vertebrate species was arcane even for her – and spoke from the heart, something that was never easy for her. 'To conclude, whether you believe death has a meaning, or is simply a necessary part of the creation of new life, we can take from this passage that nothing after death can be done alone. Genesis can only be achieved through the creation of a community. You all are that community for Susan, so thank you for being here today.'

She walked back to her row, sliding past the line of former campers she was sitting with and arriving at her seat between Freddie and Sierra. If they felt like she'd intruded on their group after nearly a decade away, they certainly didn't show it, and Freddie had insisted she sit with them when he'd run into her, disoriented and anxious, in front of the funeral home.

'Nice one,' he muttered now, surreptitiously wiping at his cheeks with the back of his hand. His Welsh accent seemed to only intensify in his grief.

'You really had to remind everyone about decomposition?' Sierra whispered. 'That's morbid, even for me.'

'Quiet,' Alice said. Having been their camp counselor for five years, the line had a nostalgic quality. 'It's Briar's turn. And, anyway, Susan's been cremated.'

'Next we'll hear from Briar Elwood, Susan's eldest,' the funeral director announced.

Briar stood, and Alice allowed herself a first real look at her old best friend. As she walked up to the podium, Alice was struck by the familiarity of her strides, the slightly uneven gait she'd had since childhood. The walk was comforting, because it was the only thing that appeared the same about Briar on the surface.

It was the hair that was most different, Alice reflected, as Briar turned and tucked her overgrown bangs behind her ears. Briar had always had the most beautiful, long strawberry-blonde hair. Alice had run her hands through it and braided it so many times that she could recognize it by touch. She wondered if it still felt the same, even though it was cut into a bob slightly below her ears now.

'She looks good for her mother's funeral,' Sierra mumbled, and Alice cut her eyes sideways in an approximation of a glare. 'Okay, okay, not appropriate.'

Not appropriate, even if everyone in the room was thinking the same thing. Alice certainly was.

Briar rolled her shoulders back slowly, letting out a breath before speaking. 'We're all here because we agree that my mother was an incredible woman. It feels silly to list her accomplishments, the lives she touched, or describe her in simple adjectives. She was not… describable.' She spoke in a low voice. Briar had never been a natural public speaker, but seemed more self-assured than Alice had known her to be. She found herself analyzing Briar's confident posture, wondering how she could be so brave in the face of tragedy. Then again, Briar's whole look screamed *brave*, from the short hair to the stack of ear piercings and the tattoos scattered down her right arm. Alice had been there for her first tattoo, but somehow, even though she'd catalogued the changes through the years on social media, she hadn't expected them to be real. It was like studying the characteristics of a mushroom in a book only to encounter it in the wild and be stunned by the life of it.

'I won't tell you the story of my mother's life, because I assume she held you hostage at some point and told you everything, from her birth in Northumberland to her home in the mountains of Virginia where she passed, and all the places in between. She will have told you about her brief stint in the circus – that one was a hit in our house growing up – and probably also the names she had given to every tree at Camp Lakeside. I won't tell you the story of her life, because I already had to write the obituary and, honestly, I'm tired.' She glanced up, her eyes sweeping across the room, and Alice quickly looked at her hands. 'That was a joke, you can laugh.'

A low rumble of laughter came from the first row, and Alice's eyes bore into the back of her ex's head. Of course, when Briar said to laugh, he laughed. Noah was the type of friend who would persist through the most awkward situation, the type of person who never felt awkward anyway. He always had the right reaction, something Alice had at first admired and then come to resent by the end of their relationship.

'Instead, I'll tell you a story about her you probably haven't heard before, because I was the only one who was there. When I was ten years old, I woke up in the middle of the night to a terrible storm. My brother was six and my sisters were four, all of them sleeping soundly.'

She looked at where they sat in the front row, smiling slightly. 'So, I went and woke my mom, even though I was too old to need comforting at that point. When she was up and understood the situation, she ran around her room like a headless chicken, getting ready, for reasons I didn't understand, to go out in the middle of a storm. It was a distracting enough sight – my mom not calm and collected, but in crisis – that it immediately made me less afraid of what was going on outside.' Briar paused, clearing her throat.

'You might be wondering why she was having a conniption over some rain. Well, it turned out she'd left some of her favorite plants outside of the greenhouse at camp. So in the middle of the night, in the middle of what was basically a hurricane, she got into her truck and took off to save the plants from overwatering.'

There were a few chuckles from the audience, and some nods. Alice watched Briar's siblings, who appeared just as wrapped up in the story as everyone else. It had been a long time since Alice had seen them together, and she was struck by how easily Briar seemed to replace Susan as the matriarch of the family.

'And, of course, that is exactly who my mom was. She was someone who would do anything to help those who couldn't help themselves, who advocated fiercely for trees and plants and campers alike. She wasn't just a mother to me, River John – RJ – Hazel and Laurel. She was a mother to every living being she encountered. If you're here because she touched your life' – Briar looked around the room again – 'you're lucky, because you know she would've dropped anything to help you. Even in the middle of the night, in the middle of a storm.'

Briar resumed her seat in the front row, and Alice watched as Harper, Noah's fiancée, reached over to put a tissue in her lap. Harper *would* do something that was intended to be kind but was actually cruel – the worst thing you could imply about Briar was that she didn't have her act together.

The feeling of being an outsider, the one she'd been suppressing for the past hour, came back in full force. She loved Freddie and Sierra, they were good kids. But there had been a time when she wouldn't have been on the other side of the aisle at this funeral, but in that front row. A time, nearly ten years ago now, when she would have belonged there.

Freddie turned to her. 'How're you holding up?'

'I've been better.'

Sierra nodded. 'It's fucked.'

The funeral director was back at the podium. Alice was getting tired of looking at the sad face of someone who had never met Susan, and she wondered how Briar felt about it.

'The wake will be across the hall. Please give your best wishes to the family on your way out.'

Yet another obligation for Briar. Maybe this new version of Briar didn't mind shaking hands with strangers on one of the worst days of her life, but Alice doubted it.

As the audience began to stir, Sierra turned to Alice with a calculating expression. 'When was the last time you spoke to Briar?'

'Not in a while,' Alice said vaguely, shifting from one foot to the other. The funeral home was starting to feel hot, the afternoon sun slanting through the windows now. 'But Susan and I kept in touch.'

Sierra opened her mouth, doubtless with another question, but Freddie shut her down. Alice watched the Elwood family make their way to the back doors, vaguely listening to Freddie explain to Sierra that actually it was a very sensitive topic for Alice, as she'd been through a tough break-up before university and Briar had taken her ex's side. Which, if well-meaning, wasn't exactly the truth. She'd never talked with Freddie about what had happened – theirs was the sort of relationship where Alice knew every detail of his life and he knew the scant outlines of hers. It seemed he'd concocted a story in his head that painted her in the most flattering light. Well, it was no wonder he'd stayed her friend, then.

'What's happening with camp?' Alice asked abruptly, looking away from where Briar was shaking an elderly woman's hand. 'Did they find someone to run it with only two weeks to go?'

'Well, sort of,' Freddie said. 'Briar volunteered before there could really be any discussion.'

'Briar?' Alice echoed, not knowing why she was surprised. Of course it would be Briar to continue her mother's legacy. She had gone to the camp her whole life, had been a counselor, knew the land better than anyone.

Still, Briar had a life in DC. Alice had watched it online over the years: Briar with Noah and Harper, her coworkers at the bar, a boyfriend or girlfriend featured sporadically. Most people couldn't pack everything up for a summer. Most people wouldn't isolate themselves in the woods with a bunch of screaming children right after their mother's sudden and untimely death. But most people weren't Briar. That was a lesson Alice had learned the hard way.

'I tried to tell her it wasn't a good idea, but she wouldn't listen,' Sierra said. 'Freddie and I offered to be her assistant directors, so she'll have help. But still…'

The memories alone would've been enough to drive Alice away. But maybe Briar was onto something – Alice's instincts had ended with her stranded across an ocean from everyone she loved. Surely that wasn't the healthiest approach to loss. Still, even though she knew Briar would hate her pity, she worried about her spending the summer in a place where she would feel Susan everywhere.

She watched as Briar shook hands with their old biology teacher, unsure if she imagined the slight recoil in response to whatever words of comfort he'd attempted to provide.

Briar would be in Virginia, at their old camp, all summer. It was the place Alice loved most in the world, and a place she hadn't been back to since she'd left for St Andrews. After a decade of not setting foot on American soil, Alice found she couldn't quite remember the feeling of standing in the woods at Camp Lakeside anymore, a memory she hadn't thought it possible to lose.

'When are you back to London?' Freddie asked as the three of them joined the throng headed for the door.

'The day after tomorrow,' Alice said, adjusting her collar self-consciously at the thought of Briar seeing her in person for the first time in years. She was immediately ashamed of her vanity, knowing that Briar had far more important things on her mind and wouldn't spare a thought for Alice or her collar.

She'd considered not coming to the funeral at all, unsure if her being there would make things worse. But Susan had asked her to speak, and ultimately Alice knew that Briar had moved on.

'Back to the lab?' Freddie asked, in an overly-patient tone that made it sound like he'd asked the question once already and been ignored.

She shook her head rapidly. 'No, not until the fall.'

'What's it you do again?' Sierra asked. 'Other than being superior to all of us by studying at Oxford?'

Alice ignored that. 'Mycology, but specifically I'll be defending my dissertation next year on the reclassification of the Basidiomycota division by developing criteria for the unassigned classes across three critical subphyla. If it's finished, that is.'

Sierra blinked. 'Sorry, what?'

'I decide what's a mushroom and what's not.'

'Oh, cool,' Sierra said, sounding like she actually meant it. 'That must be a power trip.'

Alice frowned. 'Not really...'

'You might not, but *I* know a mushroom when I see one,' Freddie said.

'Well, the visible characteristics—' She cut herself off. 'Right, you're joking.'

He winked, then nudged her side with his elbow. 'Nervous?'

'What?' she asked, smoothing a hand down the front of her shirt. Had he picked up on her glances at Briar? Was it normal to be anxious to shake your ex-best friend's hand? Surely it was. 'Do I look nervous?'

'No,' he said, squinting at her thoughtfully. 'You look sad.'

'I *am* sad,' she replied indignantly.

'But it's okay to be nervous, even though you're also sad. Death isn't as simple as just making you sad, it can make you feel a lot of emotions you wouldn't expect.' Alice stared at him and he shrugged. 'I read it in a pamphlet about helping kids through grief when one of the campers lost a parent over the summer.'

'I cussed out a priest at my dad's funeral,' Sierra chimed in.

'All I'm saying is that you can grieve Susan and still want to avoid your ex and the girl who bullied you in high school at her wake.'

Before Alice could respond that she wasn't avoiding anyone, and if she *were* to avoid anyone, she would be prioritizing avoiding Briar over Noah and Harper anyway, they reached the front of the queue.

'I'll take that under advisement,' Alice muttered over her shoulder as she approached the first in the line of family members, Briar's dad. She'd never met him before. He and Susan had divorced, and Tom had absconded home to the UK before Alice had befriended Briar.

'Mr. Elwood,' she said, with a firm handshake. She hadn't seen a picture of him in years, but for some reason she was still startled by how old he looked. In her head, Tom Elwood was younger and more vital than her own father. 'I'm so sorry for your loss.'

'I'm sorry for yours,' he said, staring at her with a disconcertingly earnest expression. 'She loved you very much, Alice.'

'Um, oh.' Tears filled her eyes before she had even processed his words. She couldn't believe Briar's deadbeat dad, of all people, was going to make her cry for the first time in years. She bit the inside of her cheek and managed to mutter out a 'thanks' before moving on to Briar's siblings.

She pulled each of them into a hug in turn, since it would have felt silly to shake any of their hands. Laurel, who had been one of Alice's favorite campers back in the day, squeezed her extra hard before letting go.

And then Alice was in front of Briar, the moment she'd been dreading since she'd decided to come to the funeral. She stuck out her hand, looking Briar in the eye. Close up, Alice could see the signs that Susan's death had taken its toll, but Briar looked radiant even with her hazel eyes ringed in red. The May sun had already started to bring out the freckles on her cheekbones. The two of them used to joke that Briar looked like an elf from a fairytale, and Alice like a princess.

'I'm so sorry for your loss,' Alice said, and Briar took her hand as though just realizing she was there, looking at Alice in an expressionless way that somehow made her feel invisible.

'Thanks for coming,' Briar said, without a hint of emotion, and dropped her hand. Alice felt it like a slap.

Chapter 2

Briar

Briar spent the majority of her mother's funeral wishing she could've culled the guestlist. Ten years later, Alice Hughes was as beautiful as ever. Staring up at her as she delivered her speaking portion, Briar had experienced the same flip in her stomach as she'd once had watching Alice present to the class. Except now, instead of feeling the warmth of friendship, seeing Alice only reminded Briar of betrayal.

At the wake, Briar resisted the urge to look over at the table where she knew Alice was sitting and attempted to listen to her Aunt Charlotte's speech. Until a kick to her shin broke her focus, and she whipped her head around to her sisters. The twins sat with identical expressions of unconcealed contempt.

Stupid cow, Hazel mouthed to Briar, nodding at Aunt Charlotte, and Briar almost smiled. Their mother's sister hadn't lifted a finger to help the family when Susan had first received her diagnosis nearly six years ago. To hear her wax poetic to a room of her sister's closest friends now that she was dead was almost too much to bear.

Laurel leaned over to whisper in Hazel's ear and the two devolved into giggles that they quickly tried to pass off as coughs. Briar was about to tell them off when another kick landed, this one significantly sharper.

'Ow,' she whispered, rubbing her leg.

'Sorry,' RJ said, leaning towards her and keeping his voice low. 'I was aiming for one of them. It's our mother's funeral for God's sake, they should be sad.'

'We're all sad.' Briar sighed, pinning her brother with a sharp look. 'Give them a break.'

A week. Their mom had been dead for a week and it still didn't feel real. Time passed differently than it had before; Briar slept seemingly not at all, spending her nights tossing and turning, a pressing weight on her chest keeping her awake. And yet, every morning when she opened her eyes, for one moment it all felt like it had been a bad dream.

There had been tears, too many to count. It was almost a relief to be in public, around people scrutinizing her every move; it was easier to hold herself together with an audience. Her mother was well-loved, and this day was going to be hard for a lot of people, so the least she could do was not give them another thing to worry about.

'Oh god,' Laurel groaned, 'it's Mr. Teagues. Someone better be ready to grab the mic.'

'Shh.' Their father finally turned to them, frowning. 'Please, darlings, the speeches are nearly over.'

Briar suppressed an eye roll as her siblings straightened and pretended to listen again. It didn't matter that this was her father's first time on American soil in years, and maybe the third time he'd ever worn a suit. If he suddenly wanted to play at being a parent after only ever being one for the sporadic family trip to London, then Briar would let him, even if today of all days she felt her siblings should be given a pass.

Mr. Teagues's homage to their mother dragged on for nearly fifteen minutes. Briar knew because she'd taken to counting the seconds on the clock that hung on the far side of the funeral home's grand hall. The funeral director finally wrestling the mic away from him was Briar's cue to excuse herself to the bathroom. She walked quickly, keeping her head up but also avoiding eye contact with everyone she passed.

She locked the stall door behind her, leaning her body against it, and just stood there. She tried to focus on the pain still thrumming from where she'd been kicked, on where her heel was rubbing a blister along the side of her ankle – anything to ignore the way her body shook.

It took her longer than it should have to realize there was someone in the next stall over, and whatever sobs were about to overtake her died in her throat. She straightened, pushing her shoulders back, and walked out to the bathroom sink.

She stared at her reflection, struck by how she could still look the same when something so fundamental had shifted inside her. Her upper lip, redder than usual and still chapped from the frigid hospital air, was her only souvenir from the whole ordeal.

She began washing her hands, taking care to scrub between her fingers and under her nails, convincing herself that she wasn't stalling. She heard a flush from the occupied stall and her eyes went to it in the mirror.

Alice came out of the stall. Because of course, she was right where Briar didn't want her. Her eyes were red, nose too, the way she'd look after a cry, and Briar hated how she remembered that. Not that she had seen Alice cry all that much in their decade-long friendship. In fact, if Briar had been asked only a few weeks ago, she'd have said that seeing Alice Hughes exhibit a single real emotion was a sign of the apocalypse.

Alice froze as their eyes met in the glass, her hand still poised on the stall door. Briar couldn't stop staring, falling back into her old pattern of cataloguing Alice's every detail. She had spent so many classes watching Alice, memorizing her perfect penmanship, the angle of her fingers as she held a pencil, the way she'd bite her lip in frustration when she didn't know the answer, the smell of vanilla in her long, blonde hair.

Alice's hair now was shorter and darker, her natural color, which Briar hadn't seen since they were children. She had traded her hyper-feminine floral dresses for loose trousers and a button-down. But her eyes were still as blue as ever, still as hypnotic.

'Um,' Alice said, 'hi.'

Briar didn't blink, relishing the way Alice shifted uncomfortably as her words hung between them. Alice *should* be the awkward party here; Briar certainly didn't have anything to feel ashamed about.

'That was a lovely eulogy,' Alice finally managed. 'I'm sure Susan would've appreciated it.'

Some mixture of anger, hurt and regret battled within her, but Briar pressed it all down before any one emotion could win out. She grinned tightly, more of a bearing of teeth than anything resembling friendliness.

'Thanks. Your speech was kind of weird,' she said, flicking water off her hands and stalking out the door.

She braced herself before re-entering the hall but was relieved to see that the speeches had paused as guests lined up for the buffet. Spotting familiar faces in line, she made a beeline for her friends.

'Are we gonna talk about Alice?' Harper said, nodding at where Alice was slinking back into the hall.

Briar was relieved to focus her energy on an easy target. 'I didn't expect her to actually show up.'

She couldn't believe it had taken her mother dying for Alice to come home. That after years of no contact, Alice thought she could just show up and speak to Briar as though they were friends. As though she hadn't abandoned Briar for a better life halfway across the world without so much as a goodbye. She couldn't acknowledge how much it hurt, even to Noah and Harper.

'I know, the esteemed PhD from Oxford,' Harper's voice dipped into a faux posh accent, flicking her long blonde hair dramatically over her shoulder. 'Twice-honored Nobel laureate, and knighted by the King, at this small-town funeral? I'm *so* glad she found time in her busy schedule.'

Noah gave Harper a pointed look. 'She's here for Susan, and she'll be back in London in no time. We don't have to make it a thing.'

Briar glanced over to where Alice was sitting with the former camp counselors, totally engrossed in a conversation with Freddie and Sierra. It was weird to see how naturally she spoke with others after their stilted encounter in the bathroom. Briar couldn't wait for her to go back to London, where she could pretend she didn't exist again.

'Um, obviously,' Harper said, rolling her eyes. 'It's not like I'm jealous. That was a million years ago. And she's a lesbian now.'

Briar winced. Even though it'd been years since Alice had come out in an Instagram post their freshmen year of college, it still felt wrong for Harper to state it so matter-of-factly, as if it hadn't represented a monumental shift in Briar's life. From the Alice she'd known to a stranger. Briar had fixated on it for years. Alice rarely managed to surprise Briar, but her stomach had dropped when she'd seen the post. Nothing could have prepared her to see the girl she'd loved throughout high school fall for seemingly the first girl she'd met at college.

Noah kissed Harper's cheek. 'I mean… if you were jealous, that would be kinda cute.'

'You're impossible,' Harper said fondly.

Briar made a face at them. 'You two are disgusting.'

Noah kissed Harper's cheek harder, smacking his lips loudly.

'God, this summer is going to suck for you guys,' Briar said, blowing her bangs out of her eyes. 'What are you going to do without your third wheel?'

Instead of joining in on the bit, Noah furrowed his brows. Briar mentally steeled herself for his offer of help.

'Hey,' he said, putting a hand on her shoulder. Briar resisted the urge to shake it off. 'If you need an—'

'Nope!' Briar cut him off. 'None of that.'

Even before her mother had been admitted to the hospital a few weeks before, Noah had been by her side through the worst of the illness. But Briar couldn't let him put his life on hold for her. She knew what that did to a person, and she didn't want anyone else to go through it.

Harper frowned. 'But Bri—'

'Uh-uh.' Briar shook her head. 'I know you love me. But you also have jobs and lives and a wedding to plan, so please don't feel like I'm your problem to deal with.' They didn't look convinced, so Briar pressed on. 'Really, I'll be fine this summer. We'll talk on the phone and I'll be back for the Fourth of July party, and just because my mom died doesn't mean that I need you to drop everything. Okay?'

'Okay.'

It was finally their turn, and as Briar looked down the buffet, she silently judged whoever had ordered fettuccine Alfredo to be served with crab cakes before realizing it had been her. She vaguely remembered a call with the funeral director where lunch had been discussed but she couldn't recall any details, only that the talk of food had made her nauseous.

She ended up putting three dinner rolls and a scoop of strawberries on her plate before returning to her table.

Seeing that the twins' plates were equally bare, Briar made a mental note to cook something nutritious for dinner. RJ, ever the odd man out in their family, was shoveling long strands of fettuccine into his mouth.

In any other family, a successful career on Wall Street would have made RJ the golden child, but instead, he was surrounded by eccentrics. The same shrewdness that made him so valuable at work, also isolated him from the family in ways that Briar hadn't worried about until recently, when her texts about him finding a therapist had gone unanswered for several weeks. She resolved to try again tonight.

Then there was the matter of the twins. Susan had first gotten sick when they were still in high school, leaving Briar responsible for them in the formative years of starting college. At least they'd have each other, staying with their father through the summer to ease the transition from university to postgraduate life. She didn't know what she'd do when they all left, how she'd cope.

'Bri?' Briar blinked, turning to her father. He'd taken the seat next to her without her noticing.

She cleared her throat. 'Sorry, what?'

He leaned closer and Briar was struck by the deep-set wrinkles lining his mouth and greying hair at his temples. There was a time she had seen her father every day, and then after the divorce she'd seen him during the summers and at Christmases, but slowly the time between her visits had stretched. She tried to remember the last time she'd seen him, and decided it must have been two years ago, for her twenty-fifth birthday party.

Something in losing one parent made noticing the signs of ageing in the other terrifying. An urge to reach out and take her father's hand nearly overwhelmed Briar, but she didn't, not wanting to alarm him.

'I know this isn't an ideal time to discuss your mother's estate,' he said, and the urge dissipated.

'You're right,' Briar said coolly, grabbing one of the twins' wine glasses and taking a sip. 'It's *not* a good time.'

Her father pressed on. 'It's important you know all your options. I've a solicitor friend whose firm has a branch here in Washington. I could make some phone calls for you, help things get settled.'

Briar pinched the bridge of her nose. This part of death had truly blindsided her. In the movies, there were always dramatic scenes of wills being read while the petty siblings squabbled over inheritances. The movies never showed what happened after, when all of Susan Elwood's worldly possessions, her house and the camp that was her livelihood, were left to Briar and Briar alone.

Briar shouldn't have been surprised. It was how their family functioned: Susan as the one with the grand ideas, and Briar as the one pulling the strings, making sure everyone got what they needed. It made sense that Susan would continue the tradition in death. And Briar would do right by her siblings, even if she wanted to scream at the thought of making a single decision about her mother's estate.

She took a deep breath, staring at her hands clasped on the table, and nodded. 'Thank you, that would be helpful.'

Her father blinked, as if he hadn't expected her to agree. 'Oh, well, in that case, we really ought to get an appraiser out to the camp. A plot of that size would be a worthwhile investment for the right buyer.' He put his hand over Briar's, squeezing gently. It was maybe the most comforting he'd ever been. 'It's too much for you to take on by yourself.'

Briar nodded again, any fight seeping out of her. Her dad meant well, dealing with their mother's death in the only way he knew how: by giving financial advice. Not for the first time, Briar wondered how her parents had ever made it to the altar, let alone stayed married long enough to have four children. Money, she supposed, was the end of them. And now, her father was trying to convince her of what he could never convince her mother to do: sell the *bloody* camp.

'I'm gonna get another drink,' Briar said, only to get her father to stop looking at her.

She went to stand in line at the bar, observing others being served. Nothing sounded appealing and she thought it would reflect poorly to ask the bartender for whatever would get her drunk the quickest. Her eyes caught on a familiar mop of blond hair down the bar, and Freddie beckoned her over.

'Hiya,' Freddie said, pulling her into a tight hug. 'What are you drinking?'

She shrugged and he flagged down the bartender, ordering them each a gin and tonic.

'You ready for the summer?' she asked, taking a sip. Now that the funeral was nearly over, Briar could focus on the next disaster.

Susan's passing had left much of the camp's future up in the air. Besides an email drafted in the wee hours of the night affirming wholeheartedly that the camp would still open for the summer, Briar had done little to actually prepare. She had no idea how she would manage.

'The sous chefs have dropped out, and we're still down a few counselors… but no worries!' Briar said quickly as Freddie opened his mouth to respond. 'Cook is calling up some contacts he has.'

'Cook's contacts?' Freddie echoed. 'I don't know—'

'Everything is absolutely fine,' Briar reassured him. 'We've still got a couple weeks.'

'I know you've got it handled,' Freddie said, squeezing Briar's shoulder. 'But me and Sierra and everyone, we're here for you too.'

Freddie, Sierra and the other counselors in attendance had been coming to the camp since they were kids and Briar and Alice had been their counselors. At least Briar knew she'd have friendly faces surrounding her as camp director. She'd certainly need all the help she could get.

'We'll make it the best summer ever,' Freddie declared, clinking his glass against Briar's. 'For Susan.'

Briar's heart squeezed terribly. 'For mom.'

She spent the rest of the night with drinks materializing in front of her. At some point someone co-opted the AV system to put on one of Susan's playlists. An '80s power ballad warbled fuzzily through the speakers.

Briar found herself alone at the bar for a moment, a pleasant buzz building up in her head, and while she couldn't say it was happiness she was feeling, it was the closest thing to it she'd felt in weeks. She looked out at the sea of people who had known and loved her mother, feeling Susan's spirit acutely in the room.

And then she felt a presence behind her, and despite every instinct in her body telling her not to, she turned around.

'What do you want?' she asked, loud enough to be heard over the music, resting her body against the bar to prevent herself from swaying. Alice looked very serious, and it reminded Briar of the times they had gone to parties together in school. It had always been Alice reining her in before she got too crazy, but Briar had also always known how to get her to let loose. 'You need a drink.'

'I don't want a drink,' Alice said, crossing her arms. Briar's eyes traced the muscles of her arms, her gaze getting lost in the dip of Alice's clavicle. Her skin was dewy from the heat of the room, giving her a glow.

'Suit yourself,' Briar said, meaning to turn back to the bar. Somehow, however, she miscalculated and stumbled. Alice reached out to steady her, gripping Briar's upper arm. The touch burned and Briar shook her off. 'I'm fine.'

'You're not,' Alice said. 'Of course, you're not.'

'Right,' Briar said dumbly. Alice was looking at her with those stupid, big blue eyes again, her face full of a concern she shouldn't be allowed to have anymore. 'Of course.'

'What can I do?' Alice touched her arm again, imploring. 'How can I help?'

'Help?' Briar stared down at where Alice was touching her. She had the distinct feeling of being outside her body. 'You can't.'

'I want to.'

Briar wanted to argue, to say that if Alice had wanted to help she should've shown up a hell of a lot sooner than the day of her mother's funeral. That, in fact, there had been several opportunities Alice could've taken to fix their friendship, and she hadn't taken any of them. Briar wanted to blame her for every single thing that had gone wrong in her life since she'd left. But while staring at Alice, the words died on her lips.

'Freddie said you'll need help at camp,' Alice said. 'You need a co-director.'

'Camp.' She felt a small sense of satisfaction that the word came out flat, and not as another question. But still, she couldn't refute it, because she did need help with camp, pretty desperately. And Alice – perfect, organized, annoyingly competent Alice – could be exactly what she needed to survive the summer. 'You want to co-direct with me?'

As angry as she was at Alice, another part of her wanted to give in, to let Alice do what she had done best before she'd left, which was to fix Briar's life for her. It would be so much easier that way. And Briar was tired – of taking care of her family, of pretending like her whole world hadn't just been shattered, of taking on every responsibility her mother had left for her. It was too much. And yet no one except for Alice could see how much it was weighing on her.

'Yes.'

Briar didn't know what to say to that. Everything felt unreal about the current situation: Alice standing before her and her mother's ashes sitting in an urn in the next room over. If there was anything Briar could be sure was real, it was that Alice would leave her again.

So she had no idea why her next words came out. They certainly weren't ones she'd thought through.

'Um, okay.'

Chapter 3

Alice

Alice could only bring herself to go down to her mom's kitchen when the light streaming into her bedroom window had turned golden and her body demanded food. She hadn't had much to drink at the funeral, had barely cried, but her body felt like she'd been up sobbing all night. So much for the healthy approach of repressing tears so she didn't get dehydrated as well as aggrieved – she had a headache anyway.

The stairs still didn't have any creak to them. As a kid, when she and her mom had first moved to DC, Alice had made a game of how long she could go unnoticed walking around the early-2000s build. She wondered if that was part of why she preferred her ancient London flat: there was no hiding. The sounds provided constant proof that she was alive and present, which was apparently something her very literal brain needed.

Her mom was in the kitchen, microwaving canned soup. The choice of food suggested it was closer to lunchtime than breakfast, though with her mom, one could never know. She had always believed in food as cognitive fuel rather than something to be enjoyed.

'Hi,' Alice said, announcing her presence as she walked over to the fridge.

Her mom started, as though she'd forgotten Alice was home, when in fact she'd taken care to remind her several times of her visit. 'Good afternoon, dear. Sleep well?'

'Yeah, fine,' she said, the lie slipping out automatically. She opened the freezer and scrounged through the shelves until she found the object of her search: two heels of bread. This freezer could always be counted on for a few of them. The heels had never been up to her mom's standards. Little was, to be fair to the heels. 'How about you?'

'Well, yes, but I've been up and working for' – she checked her watch as Alice inserted the bread into the toaster – 'eight hours now.'

Alice winced, not sure if she'd meant it as a slight. She'd certainly made it clear to Alice throughout her childhood that productive people were the best kind of people, and they woke up early. The refrain had been repeated enough times that Alice had considered five hours of sleep a luxury in high school.

'How has your afternoon been?' Alice asked, chewing on her lip distractedly.

Her mom frowned. 'Making my way through a grant application.'

Alice was always thankful when the family farce ended and they could talk to each other like colleagues. Most people probably didn't speak to their parents like this. But most people didn't share the singular experience of academia with both of their parents and not much else. Alice only saw her mother when she was in London for work anyway.

She rolled her eyes sympathetically. 'The *worst*.'

The microwave beeped and her mom removed the steaming bowl. 'And how's work?'

'It's going well,' Alice said. 'I'm hoping my dissertation will be done soon, so I'll have to start job hunting to secure something by the spring.'

'Are you thinking of teaching or research?' her mom asked, sitting at the counter.

'My advisor, Jeremy, has a connection at the Royal Botanical Society and wants to recommend me for a research position. That would be an ideal option for me, since they're conducting some of the most groundbreaking work in the field.'

'That's nice,' her mom said, but she looked as though her mind was already drifting back to the troublesome grant application. 'I haven't heard of it, but if your advisor thinks it's a good fit, I'm sure he's right.'

'Yeah,' she said feebly, not feeling the same sense of accomplishment and excitement she'd felt upon Jeremy first mentioning the possibility. But then again, her parents were math professors and didn't know the significance of many of her accomplishments. That was why Oxford had been so important to Alice, why she had sacrificed her social life for it – *Oxford* was a language everyone understood. And while she didn't wield it for attention in many places, she wasn't above it when it came to her parents.

There was a long pause in which neither of them seemed to have anything to follow up with. 'Have you heard from your father recently?'

Alice blew out a measured breath. 'Yes. He sent a wedding invitation.'

Her mom's eyebrows raised slightly. 'Oh, he's marrying her? I was never sure why it took him so long.'

Alice repressed the urge to roll her eyes in a much less sympathetic way than she had before. Her mom certainly knew that refusing to sign the divorce papers for years, long after her dad had had an affair with a grad student and gotten her pregnant, was the reason he hadn't remarried sooner. When she'd moved to DC with Alice because she couldn't bear to work at the same university as him anymore, it had seemed like she'd half expected him to realize his mistake and follow them. He hadn't.

'It's probably simpler to be legally married, with the kids,' Alice said, trying for a reassuring tone.

'Yes,' her mom said distantly. 'David's always been reasonable. So, are you going?'

She recoiled at the insinuation that she might be the kind of terrible daughter who would consider spitefully skipping her own father's wedding to the woman who had destroyed their family. It wasn't the sort of question her mom would normally ask, which meant the news must have shaken her. She felt guilty for bringing it up.

'It depends,' Alice hedged. 'If my dissertation is done, the defense will conflict with the wedding.'

Her mom nodded. 'Your father understands that school always comes first,' she said, returning to her soup.

Before she lost her attention for good, Alice decided to share her news. 'I'm staying for the summer. Not here,' she said quickly, before her mom could think she was imposing, 'but at camp. I'm co-directing with Briar. The first session starts in two weeks, so I can stay here, or I can get a hotel…'

Her mom didn't look up. 'You can stay here. I'll be busy with work, but you can take care of yourself, can't you?'

'I can,' Alice said.

While she should have been proud of her independence, instead she felt a pang of longing for Susan, who would have happily welcomed her into the Elwood home and taken care of her. But Alice would never see Susan, would never be welcomed into her house, again.

—

It was only when she stepped out of Freddie's car and into the swampy air of early summer that Alice fully understood why she had offered to co-direct. She felt the pull that this land had on her so intensely, so suddenly, that it forced her to recognize that it had always been there, buried under years of bitterness. The familiar scent, a unique mixture of moss, smoke and the hydrangeas Susan had taken such care to cultivate, was overwhelming, and Alice stood there for a long moment.

She knew now that she couldn't have come back to the US without coming here, a place that somehow still felt like home to her, even if it was a fanciful thought.

Then, Briar emerged from the trees. 'What are you doing here?' she demanded, looking at Alice once more as if she were a ghost.

Freddie closed the trunk. 'Do you want me to park somewhere else, or…?' Then he seemed to notice who Briar was addressing. 'Er…' he started, glancing at Alice awkwardly.

'You hired me,' Alice said, forcing herself to look Briar in the eye. 'So I'm here.'

Briar stared defiantly back at her and Alice was reminded that Briar had won every staring contest the two of them had ever had. She looked away, and Briar pounced at the show of weakness.

'Obviously, I wasn't being serious,' Briar scoffed. 'I had a moment of insanity, but it's over now. You can leave.'

If Alice had thought about what arriving at camp was going to be like, she supposed she could have seen this coming, saved herself the trouble, and flown back to London. But, as with most things having to do with Briar, she had stubbornly refused to think about it.

'I'm just trying to help,' she said finally.

'Come on, Briar,' Freddie said, slinging his duffel over one shoulder. 'It's what Susan would've wanted.' Something flashed across Briar's face at his words, but without waiting for her response, he started through the trees on a path leading towards the cabins.

Briar opened her mouth and then closed it, narrowing her eyes at Alice. 'You can just pack up and leave for the whole summer with no warning? What about your *DPhil*?' She pronounced the word as though it was a curse. 'And don't you have a girlfriend?'

'I talked everything through with my advisor, there shouldn't be any problems.' She tucked her hair behind her ears, looking up at Briar pleadingly. She ignored the girlfriend question. Briar didn't have to know that Alice hadn't dated anyone in years. 'It's all sorted.'

Briar huffed, seeming unconvinced, but turning down the same path as Freddie. Alice followed, not expecting Briar to say anything else. But, after a moment, she continued in a jarringly upbeat tone, 'We're in pretty good shape already, there's not much to do. Really, it's thoughtful of you to volunteer, but we're doing just fine.'

'Uh huh,' Alice said as they emerged in the clearing at the center of camp, where the mess hall and the director's cabin sat on either side of a flagpole. A feeling of déjà vu struck her, as though she'd had this conversation with Briar in this exact place before. She'd only been here for a few minutes and her mind was already playing tricks on her, trying to marry the Briar in front of her with the years of memories this place held for the two of them and coming up short of any logic. Alice was always disconcerted when logic failed her.

Briar stopped in front of the director's cabin, gesturing to the door. 'Well, if you're set on staying, make yourself comfortable.'

Alice squinted at the door, confused. 'You're not staying in the director's cabin?'

Briar smiled blithely. 'No, I am. But we'll have to share.'

Alice stared at her, feeling as if she'd walked right into a trap. By the look on Briar's face, she was enjoying this.

'Look, I should have apologized at the funeral, but it didn't seem like the right time. I'm sorry, and I get that you're mad—' Alice started.

'I'm not mad,' Briar said, cocking her head in an infuriating way. 'What would I have to be mad about? We had a fight a billion years ago and, honestly, I don't even remember what it was about. It's irrelevant now.' She paused, looking Alice up and down. 'There's just the one cabin, so you can stay or you can go. It doesn't matter to me. I'm gonna go check on Sierra, so I'll see you later. Or not.' She turned on her heel and headed in the direction of the lake, leaving Alice alone.

If Briar thought she could drive Alice away with some passive aggressive comments, she was wrong. Alice knew that what she'd done had earned her a million more passive aggressive comments, or worse, but it wouldn't be enough to get her to give up on helping Briar. And now that she was here, breathing in the same humid air, remembering waking up to the sounds of birdsong, sleeping to the sounds of a cricket chorus, and everything in between, she didn't want to leave. These woods had always had an addictive quality – that was why she'd come back every summer. Before Alice had left for good, camp and Briar had been the two most constant things in her life.

Alice opened the door to the cabin, half expecting a booby trap of some kind, but it was only the dusty hallway from her memory. At the end of the hall was the camp's sole landline, where campers and counselors could call home. The door to the right led to the director's office, where Alice had spent hours mediating conflicts between campers or catching up with Susan over tea. The door to the left led to the director's bedroom, which Alice had never been in.

Opening the door, she found a cozy room with, mercifully, two beds. Alice put her bag next to the smaller one, an action which seemed to unlock a latent exhaustion in her. She collapsed on the bed, thinking she'd just rest her eyes for a moment. She hadn't slept well in her childhood home, maybe because it was where her insomnia had developed in the first place. But here at camp, after a car ride with the late afternoon sun streaming through the windows, her eyelids were heavy.

'Hey, wake up.' A voice cut through what was shaping up to be a beautiful dream about the forest floor.

'Wha…' she groaned, blinking and finding Briar looming over her. 'Where am I?'

'In my bed,' Briar said drily.

'Oh,' Alice said, squeezing her eyes closed again as she sat up. 'Sorry… I thought you'd want the bigger bed.'

'This was always my bed,' Briar said, in a tone that made Alice feel stupid.

'Oh,' she said. 'Right. The other one's Susan's?' Alice knew that Briar had spent a considerable amount of time at camp in the years since she'd left. Susan had mentioned it in her emails to Alice, always praising Briar's work ethic. Briar didn't respond, just stared down at her until she stood and moved away from the bed. It was then that Alice noticed the waning light outside. 'What time is it?'

'Eight,' Briar said. 'I just came in to grab my flashlight. I'm gonna go make sure Freddie and Sierra have everything they need before the counselors get here tomorrow.' She left before Alice could respond.

Weeks of not talking to anyone other than the well-meaning but completely oblivious Freddie, her absent-minded mother and her ex-best friend whose personal mission was to torture her was taking its toll. Alice needed to talk to someone who knew about Briar, and for that, there was only one person.

She rubbed her eyes as she made her way to the phone, dialing Tess's number into the landline.

'Hi,' Tess greeted her through a yawn. 'Have you come to your senses and booked a flight home?'

'Not yet.'

'Then what are you calling me at one in the morning for?' Tess demanded.

'Oh, just wanted to hear your sanguine tones,' Alice deadpanned. 'How I've missed them.'

'Fine, flatter me, just don't call me from a random number at this time of night again. Nearly gave me a heart attack.' She paused. 'Are you at camp, then?'

'Yes.'

'And?'

Alice sighed. 'I already want to leave. And I want to stay forever. It's complicated.'

'You *love* complicated,' Tess said, encouraging. 'You *thrive* on complicated. Those mushrooms don't classify themselves.'

'Right,' Alice said, twirling the phone wire around her finger. 'But I've avoided this particular... *brand* of complicated for a long time.'

Tess snorted. 'And how's that been? There's no denying that this drama is still holding you back, even if you're not crying about it every time you get drunk anymore.'

'That was one time!' Alice protested. 'And I was eighteen!'

'Well, since it's the only time I've seen you cry, you can't expect me to forget it.' Tess paused, clearing her throat meaningfully. 'But speaking of it holding you back, I mean, when was the last time you went on a date?'

Alice suspected Tess knew the answer to that question better than she did. 'I don't exactly see how that's related.'

'Oh,' Tess said, sounding disappointed. 'You don't? You'll get there, I suppose. You remember why we broke up, yeah?'

'Because you're so bloody annoying?' Alice tried.

'No,' Tess said, drawing the word out. 'It was because you were in love with someone else, you slag.'

'I wasn't—' Alice stopped herself, taking a deep breath. She didn't like revisiting her first semester, those early weeks of not talking to Briar. She'd been a mess. It had taken her longer than she would have liked to regain control over her emotions, and dating Tess had been integral to the process. Tess had given her an outlet to channel those messy feelings into, until she'd found out exactly what Alice was avoiding back in the States and had sympathetically dumped her. 'Honestly, I was just a dramatic teenager with no idea what I was talking about. You should forget whatever I said back then. I certainly have.'

The door creaked open behind her and she nearly jumped, not sure why the phone call suddenly felt clandestine. She glanced over her shoulder and saw Briar standing there, her flashlight temporarily blinding Alice.

'Those two are impossible,' she announced, and then seemed to notice the phone in Alice's hand. 'Sorry, I didn't mean to interrupt.' She turned into the bedroom.

'Was that Briar? Don't let me keep you.' Tess yawned again. 'It's late.'

'I'll ring off and let you sleep,' Alice said, knowing there was nothing else productive that could come from the conversation. 'Thanks for answering the phone past a reasonable hour.'

'I didn't know it was you,' Tess reminded her. 'Love you, good night.'

When Alice went back into the bedroom, Briar was laying her pajamas out. Alice dragged her duffel over to the larger bed, unzipping it and staring at the meticulously organized but random contents within.

She had flown to the US with a nightgown, a change of clothes and toiletries. She'd ended up with a strange mix of clothing for camp: some thrifted, a few picked up from the nearby mall, and some she'd found in her closet that she hadn't worn since high school.

'I didn't mean to interrupt,' Briar said, breaking the silence.

'You already said that,' Alice pointed out. She took out her nightgown, unfolded it, and then hastily re-folded it, feeling self-conscious.

'Who were you talking to?' Briar asked, just as Alice had decided that their attempt at conversation was probably over.

She looked over her shoulder. 'My friend Tess.'

Briar nodded, still staring at her sheets intently. 'Weren't you two...? I mean, um, I remember from Instagram.'

Alice hadn't expected Briar to remember their short-lived fling, especially when, for years, Alice has only thought of Tess as a friend. Their friendship had bloomed in the months after Tess had ended things, when she'd proved to be one of the most loyal people Alice had ever met. And even though she'd kept expecting Tess to realize her mistake and ditch her, she never had.

'We dated for a semester, but we were better off as friends,' Alice explained. It was strange, unfamiliar, explaining herself to Briar. A decade had passed, yet she still expected Briar to know everything about her life. 'It felt like the thing to do, you know, come out and then date the first lesbian I met.'

'Okay,' Briar said, her tone still stilted.

'What? You don't believe me?' Alice asked.

'No, I believe you,' Briar said, pushing her pajamas to the side and sitting on her bed. She looked at Alice. 'I just thought...'

'You thought what?' Alice asked, raising her eyebrows.

'I thought, you know, with this whole insistence on helping with camp thing... I just assumed you were running away from something.'

Of all the petty comments Alice had put up with from Briar so far, that was the one that hurt the most.

'Well, I'm not,' she said flatly. 'I don't have any secret motives.' She didn't know why it felt like a lie.

Briar didn't respond, grabbing her toiletries bag and pajamas off the bed and heading for the bathroom. Alice abandoned her nightgown, stuffing it to the bottom of her bag, and instead reached for a T-shirt, a relic of her time as a mathlete that read *STEMINIST* in hot pink cursive.

Alice took her turn in the bathroom after Briar, changing into the T-shirt and her middle school gym shorts before starting on her nighttime skincare routine. She massaged various oils and serums into her face, already feeling more like the competent version of herself she had left in London. If she treated camp like she did her daily to-do list, maybe she would be able to bring that version of herself back and stop caring so much what Briar thought of her. It was perfectly natural that being back in this particular place with this particular person was heightening her emotions, making her feel like a teenager again. Regression was a psychological phenomenon corroborated by years of research. Alice might be able to submit her case study of overcoming it to a publication once the summer was done. It was a comforting thought.

By the time she returned to the bedroom, she had steeled herself for eight whole hours in the same room as Briar Elwood, something that a month ago would have only occurred in a nightmare. She methodically swapped the cotton pillowcases out for the silk ones she had bought, spraying them with lavender before settling in with her book.

'Achoo.'

Alice looked over to where Briar was curled up, watching her with wide eyes. Something about it brought an acute image of their childhood sleepovers to the front of Alice's mind. She hadn't thought about Briar's typical sleeping position in years – because, of course, that was something that only an insane person would fixate on.

'Did you just fake sneeze?'

'I'm allergic to lavender. My doctor says it could be deadly,' Briar said solemnly.

'You're allergic to sesame,' Alice said. 'I'm fairly certain allergies don't develop after the age of eighteen.'

Briar scoffed. 'You don't know *everything*, Alice.'

'Actually, I basically do,' Alice argued, realizing the moment it was out of her mouth that it was exactly how she would have responded to Briar when they were kids.

Briar rolled her eyes. 'What's the deal with the whole nighttime song and dance? Trying to scare away the insomnia demons?'

Alice swallowed, surprised that Briar had remembered. But of course she did; Briar had been there for so many of Alice's sleepless nights.

'Um, yeah,' Alice admitted. 'It got worse at uni, so I doubled down. Never met a problem I couldn't create a three-step solution to fix.'

'Are you going to read that' – Briar gestured dismissively to the book Alice was holding, *Marvelous Mycology* by Herman Fjord – 'to put you to sleep?'

'It's good to have consistency, like reading the same book every night. So, essentially, yes. But not because it's boring. It's quite fascinating.'

'Sure,' Briar said, rolling over so that she was facing the wall.

'Don't pretend you think mushrooms are boring, because then I'll know you're lying to get a reaction out of me.'

'Good night, Alice,' Briar mumbled.

Chapter 4

Briar

The first morning waking up at camp was always strange. The first morning waking up at camp without her mother was unsettling. For a full minute, Briar thought she was in a dream. Surely those wood-paneled walls weren't the ones she remembered from her childhood; the deep, sleepy breaths that Briar would have recognized anywhere didn't mean that the best friend she hadn't seen in ten years was sleeping in the same room. That would be too bizarre to contemplate.

Briar hadn't expected Alice to show up the day before. It wouldn't have been the first time Alice had left her without so much as a goodbye. And yet, seeing Alice climbing out of Freddie's car, the hazy sunlight glinting off her pale shoulders, suddenly Briar was transported back to the summers of their youth. The memories took root as an ache in her chest.

Briar decided in that moment that she would have to accept Alice's presence. She could tolerate Alice being at camp, so long as she knew better than to rely on her and prepared for the moment that Alice ran away again.

She got up, stretching her arms above her head, bracing for the day ahead. Enforcing rules and delegating tasks had never been Briar's strong suit, and the new hires would be a challenge. She'd been accepting any application that had come in, and she hoped that there were a lot of smart, driven young adults out there who just happened to need last-minute plans for the summer.

After getting ready, she found Freddie and Sierra waiting outside the director's cabin.

'All I'm saying,' Sierra continued, not giving Briar a second glance, 'is that it would be really funny if we convinced people that you're my son.' Briar sighed. It was camp tradition at this point for the two of them to come up with an elaborate fake backstory for the campers. Susan had never put a stop to it, not wanting to stifle their creativity.

'It's just not practical,' Freddie argued, running a hand through his hair and looking genuinely distressed. 'I mean...' He gestured between the two of them hopelessly.

'What?' Sierra demanded, putting her hands on her hips and surveying him critically. 'You could be a light-skinned Latino boy. And who's to say your father isn't as pasty as you? Or wasn't, God rest his soul.' She crossed herself.

'There's also the fact that I'm Welsh and you're American. And that we're the same *age*,' Freddie argued.

'I'm two months older,' Sierra corrected him, flipping her purple-tipped hair over her shoulder.

'Guys,' Briar interrupted. 'Do either of you have the list of staff arriving today?'

'Right here,' Freddie said, shoving a piece of paper in her direction without looking away from Sierra. 'What if we just convince everyone that we're secretly dating?'

'Pfft,' Sierra said. 'No one will believe *that*.'

'I don't know, Fred, have you been practicing your straight voice?' Briar asked, skimming over the list.

'Of course, babe,' Freddie said, his voice becoming huskier and several octaves lower. The effect was ruined by the slant of his hips and his combination of jean short-shorts and a crop top.

Briar stared blankly at the names, knowing she needed to do something but not having any idea of where to start. Once the counselors arrived, they would need to be assigned tasks to ready the camp for the summer. Everything felt equally important, and the number of things left to do seemed impossible.

Freddie came to her side. 'I know some of them. They're all good kids. And a good contingent from the UK this year.'

One of Susan's more unconventional notions was the idea that the British education system was missing necessary outdoor education. Apparently, when Briar's parents had met at St Andrews, her father hadn't known a frog from a toad.

Upon receiving an inheritance of twenty-five acres in Virginia's north-west corner, Susan had opened the camp with her English husband in tow. Briar's dad had never fully adjusted, but her mother had been determined to raise the next generation of British schoolchildren differently. Camp Lakeside advertised itself as both a natural and cultural immersion, with half of the campers and counselors hailing from the UK and half from the US.

'Good.' Briar turned to see Alice walking out of the cabin, clipboard in hand. 'Now, let's focus. What needs to be done this week before the campers arrive?' Alice scribbled a list as she spoke.

'Cabins and communal spaces need to be cleaned, the archery range set up, program equipment accounted for and moved to the right cabins, trails cleared, and the dock checked. And I know there are some repairs that fell to the wayside over the past few months with Susan's diagnosis...'

Briar opened her mouth to interject, but Alice turned to Freddie. 'Can you go around and make a list of those for me?' He nodded. 'Anything else?'

Briar chewed at the inside of her cheeks to keep herself from butting in. Of course, Alice would be good at this. She had always been good at everything. It didn't matter that she hadn't been at camp in years. When faced with the challenge of having to organize and deploy a small army of twenty-somethings, Alice's brain was ready. Briar's, on the other hand, just drew a blank.

'Someone needs to contend with Cook,' Sierra said drily.

Alice wrote it down. 'That'll be me. Wouldn't subject anyone else to it.'

Briar crossed her arms, trying to push down whatever feeling was coiling in her stomach as she watched Alice take the lead. She couldn't decide if it was annoyance or something far worse that struck her when Alice got that familiar glint in her eyes. 'And me?'

Alice blinked at her. 'Oh! Um, you should welcome the counselors. You're good at talking to people.'

Briar found it difficult to ignore the implication that she was bad at everything else.

The counselors arrived over the next hour, with Briar directing them to the assigned cabins Alice had written down. There were familiar faces among them, since many of them had been campers when Briar had been a counselor, but others she didn't recognize at all.

After the counselors had settled in, the group gathered around the fire pit for the first-night bonfire. Briar wondered if she should address them. Susan hadn't been much of a rousing speechmaker, but she was known to say a few words at the start of the summer. She decided against it, since Alice and her clipboard hadn't told her to.

'Hi, all,' Alice called, standing on a log for added height. 'Um, I just have a few announcements before we get started.' She cleared her throat awkwardly, glancing down at her hands. 'I'm Alice, I used to work here, and I'll be co-directing this summer with Briar, who you probably all know because she hired you.'

'Yeah, no duh,' someone called from the crowd. Alice's head snapped to whoever spoke, clearly thrown at the prospect of being heckled.

Briar stepped in. 'Alice has graciously offered to help me this summer after the passing of my mother. I know she was important to a lot of you, and if you want to talk about it, you can come visit me in the director's office at any time.'

Briar waved at Alice to continue.

'Counselors drinking alcohol is only permitted when there are no campers on the premises, tonight being one of those nights. When sessions are taking place, I would ask you to please refrain. When in doubt, don't go all out.' Alice's smile froze on her face as no one laughed at what was clearly intended to be a joke. 'Finally, as most of you know, at Camp Lakeside the staff members go by nature-related nicknames.'

'Unless your mom gave you a built-in camp name from birth,' Briar said. 'You can just call me Briar.'

'And mine is Violet,' Alice continued. 'Not for the flower, but for *Cortinarius violaceus*, a violet-capped mushroom that grows in these woods. There's some interesting research suggesting that the group originated in Australasia, but this particular species diverged in very recent history, about 3.9 million years ago.' She cleared her throat. 'Anyway, what was I talking about?'

Briar took over. 'You all should spend some time thinking of a nickname for yourself if you don't already have one. And now, we'll let the assistant directors introduce themselves.'

'Hi there,' Freddie said, waving. 'I'm Freddie, but my camp name is Moss.'

'I'm Luna,' Sierra said.

'Great,' Alice said. 'Well, that's basically... everything. Briar, do you want to do the honors?'

Briar pulled a lighter out of her pocket and stuck it beneath a scrap of newspaper peeking out from under the logs. It took only a few moments for the kindling to catch, sparks popping into the night as the fire grew.

Sierra and Freddie passed around cups of cider and the fixings for s'mores and Alice made her way over to Briar, plopping herself down on the log next to her. The air was still humid, even as darkness settled in the woods; the only respite was a weak breeze.

'Not a bad first day,' Alice muttered, almost inaudible over the chatter.

Briar considered pretending she hadn't heard her, but after a long day of conceding to Alice, her petty streak won out. 'Yeah, you seem to have things sorted. At this rate, you won't even need me.'

'That's not true,' Alice said. 'You just have a lot on your plate. And I'm here if you want to talk.'

Briar accepted a cup of spiked cider from Sierra, nodding her thanks, and Alice did the same. As soon as she had moved on, Briar said, 'I have friends, you know. And siblings. A long list of people I'd talk to before I'd talk to you.'

Alice looked at her in that knowing way, and Briar felt like she was being cut open like one of her fungi. 'But would you be honest with them about how you're feeling?'

Briar opened her mouth, then closed it, her lips twitching furiously. She wanted to refute Alice, to tell her that in her absence Briar had learned to communicate when she was struggling to the people she was closest with. But it would have been a lie. Throughout their years apart, Alice remained the one person who knew all of Briar's secrets.

Sierra clapped her hands from the other side of the circle, interrupting their standoff. 'Time for icebreakers.' She looked around with a wicked smile. 'Let's do first kiss stories.'

Briar ran a hand over her face, stifling a groan.

Freddie went first, telling the story of how his had been in a production of *Twelfth Night*, with the punchline being that he'd had a crush on the twin brother of the girl playing Viola opposite him.

'For a moment there, I questioned if maybe I fancied women,' he concluded. 'I think it was the fake moustache. Very confusing.'

'Alice?' Sierra said. 'What about you?'

'Um,' Alice stalled. 'I don't know that it's appropriate… Technically, I *am* your boss.'

'Oh, piss off,' Freddie said, giggling into his cup. Briar sensed Alice's gaze on her, but she refused to meet it.

'Fine,' she said. 'I was fifteen and my chemistry lab partner asked me on a date. No boy had ever even looked in my direction before.' It was weird hearing this story again, because Briar vividly remembered her stomach dropping when Alice had gushed to her during fifth period. 'He was the school's soccer star. Every girl had a crush on him, and so did I, because heteronormativity is a hell of a drug.' That got her some appreciative chuckles. 'So we went to the movies on a Friday night. Some assholes from our class were also there and gave him a hard time for being with me. I was definitely too nerdy to be on a date with a guy like *that*.'

'No kidding,' Briar muttered into her cup. The look she received from Alice made it clear she hadn't said it quietly enough.

'And Noah,' Alice continued, 'who I had never heard utter an unkind word to anyone, politely said *fuck off* and took my hand. It was the most romantic thing that had ever happened to me, up until he dropped me off at home and kissed me at the door. I was over the moon, walking on clouds the whole next day.'

Alice told the story in exactly the same way she'd told it to Briar so many years ago. It was like it had been entered as legend in her mind, untarnished and untouched. Briar wondered if other kisses received the same treatment. She thought back to the year when Noah and Alice had started dating, trying to pinpoint which moments Alice had been faking. At the time, it had seemed so real, and it had crushed Briar.

'Bloody hell,' Freddie said, still giggling. Briar couldn't tell if his face was red from the cider or from the heat of the fire. 'Can I get his number?'

'He's engaged,' Briar said drily.

'Damn, another mediocre man bites the dust,' Sierra deadpanned, turning to Briar. 'Your turn.'

Briar's heart raced and she took a long sip of the cider to try to calm herself. Unlike seemingly everyone else, she didn't feel the least bit drunk. None of the edge of the night had been taken off, and as she glanced at Alice's profile, she wondered if any amount of alcohol could make this experience less painful. In the flickering firelight, Alice's features were striking in their delicacy.

Briar brushed her bangs out of her face, knowing she had to lie. 'It was with someone I barely knew... I was too drunk to really remember, I think I was seventeen or eighteen.'

'Boooo,' Sierra said, as Freddie gave two aggressive thumbs down and the counselors hooted with laughter. 'Everyone remembers their first kiss.'

Briar felt suffocated by Alice's eyes on her. 'Fine, I remember it a bit.' It was a night Briar hadn't stopped replaying and rewriting for ten years. She'd tell them only what was necessary. 'It was here, during pack out week. I was a little tipsy, and I told one of the other counselors that I was going to college never having kissed anyone.' She chanced a glance at the faces around the fire, trying to figure out if anyone could tell that her cheeks were burning. She didn't look at Alice. But she could picture her, all those years ago. The gleam in her eyes and the small smile playing at her lips when she had leaned in. Briar had been a mess of nerves. 'And she kissed me, just like that. It was the last thing I'd expected to happen that night. I...' Her throat closed up as she thought about Alice's lips, how they'd tasted of honey. She could still feel the softness of Alice's hair tickling her neck, the weight of her fingers against Briar's cheek. She cleared her throat.

'It was unexpected. And one thing led to another and eventually we were sharing a sleeping bag, out under the stars.' She couldn't admit out loud that none of it had felt real. Especially that Alice, the most beautiful girl she'd ever known, the one she'd been in love with for years, had wanted to kiss her. Or that kissing her had been the first time she'd ever felt alive. Briar finally glanced up, meeting Alice's gaze, her mouth dry. 'I mean, I was a horny teenager, what can I say?'

'Who was she?' Sierra asked. 'Surely thirteen-year-old me would've had eyes for this mega-babe counselor.'

Briar shrugged, looking away. 'Honestly, I have no idea who she was. I haven't seen her since that night.'

The words came out casually, and she only half-wished she'd put some bite in them. Remembering that night also meant remembering the next morning, when Alice had barely been able to look at her. She'd said they would talk, that she just needed time to sort things out, but instead, she had gotten in her car and driven away. It wasn't until Briar got back from camp that she learned Alice had flown to Scotland early, without even saying goodbye.

If she had known one night would ruin their whole friendship, Briar would have never asked for a kiss.

After one of the longest moments of silence Briar had ever experienced, Sierra spoke up again.

'Spooky,' she declared. 'Was she a ghost? I didn't know the camp ghost was a hot lady ghost. I always imagined a racist Confederate soldier.'

Briar took another sip of her drink. 'She was more like a figment of my imagination, I think.'

—

Briar left the bonfire early, needing some time away from Alice and everyone else. She called Noah.

He answered after only one ring. 'Hello?'

There was music playing in the background, and Briar could picture him in his kitchen cooking and drinking a glass of wine. It was the kind of night they often spent together.

'It's me,' Briar said, counting the panels of wood on the wall across from her. She'd called without any real reason, had just wanted to hear his voice.

'One sec, let me put you on speaker. Harper just got home.'

'Oh, how was your shift?'

The music swelled for a moment before lowering again, and then Harper's voice came through.

'I didn't get any bodily fluids on my scrubs, so I'm counting that as a win. But what about you? How was the first day?'

'Good,' Briar said automatically, though it hardly described the confusing mess of emotions she'd been feeling all day. Being back at camp was like trying to squeeze into old clothes; she was wearing a different version of herself around, one that was younger, one that longed for things that Briar had given up on years ago.

And then there was her mother, metaphorically haunting every corner of the woods.

'Yeah?' Noah asked, clearly not believing her.

'I mean, not bad?' Briar tried. It was technically true – despite having to relive one of the best and subsequently worst moments of her life, the day itself had been fine. 'It sucked the correct amount and nothing actively went wrong.'

'All you can hope for,' Harper said.

'Do you need help?' Noah cut in. 'I've got a few weeks free before I need to start prepping for school. I could take the bus up.'

'No,' Briar said, almost too quickly, anxiety constricting her chest at the thought of Noah and

Harper disrupting their lives for her. The image of them in their apartment in DC, happy and in love, was practically the only thing keeping her going. She didn't want to ruin it for them with her feelings. If she had to be miserable, then she could be miserable alone. And if her misery was contagious, well, she already had the perfect target.

As if on cue, Harper asked, 'How are things with Alice?'

Briar didn't know how to respond. She could tell them about finding Alice in her bed the day before, the STEMINIST shirt or Alice taking charge of everything. She could say that Alice being there was bringing everything up again, stuff she thought she'd buried along with their friendship. She could tell them how pretty Alice had looked in the firelight.

'Alice is fine,' Briar said. 'How are you guys?'

There was a pause, but without being able to see their faces, Briar couldn't discern what it meant. 'Good.'

'Good?' Briar asked, voice rising an octave.

Harper sighed. 'Don't ever plan a wedding.'

'It's not that bad,' Noah said immediately.

Briar had heard this all before. It seemed like every few weeks Noah and Harper had some tense, almost-argument about the wedding. Briar had suggested elopement many times.

'Are you guys fighting?' She tried to keep her voice light, but the thought of anything else going wrong was almost too much to bear. She just wanted everyone to be okay for a little bit, for her to not have to worry. She was so tired of worrying.

'No,' they both said in unison.

Briar tried for a laugh but landed on something closer to a cough. 'Okay, because you're not allowed to. I can't take it.'

'Alright,' Harper deadpanned. 'We'll be happy. For you.'

'That's all I ask for,' Briar said. 'I miss you guys.'

'We miss you too,' Noah said. 'But you'll see us before you know it. You're still coming back for the Fourth, right?'

Briar smiled, thinking of the one weekend of the summer when she would have no responsibilities except to have fun. 'Of course. I wouldn't miss my own party.'

Chapter 5

Alice

The next day, while the counselors began their assigned opening duties, Alice busied herself doing anything she could think of to avoid Briar. After a few hours of manual labor, she found herself – as she often had throughout her years as a counselor – in front of the art cabin.

It was a hobby she had dropped, tapering off slowly in university and then abandoning it entirely as her graduate program had filled up her whole life. She didn't have time for hobbies or for anything non-mushroom-related, aside from a weekly dinner with Tess which was entered into her calendar as: *DO NOT WORK LATE – dinner w/ tess*.

She was seized with the sudden desire to paint something, even though it wasn't on her ever-growing list of tasks for the week. And in an act of rebellion that surprised her, Alice went into the cabin and grabbed supplies.

It had been years since she'd held a brush, but she'd always had a steady hand, and she marveled at how easy it felt to paint the side of the cabin, stroke by stroke.

And as she painted, she thought about the morning after she'd kissed Briar, the decision she'd regretted for the past decade. She had gone over the morning after again and again in her head, trying to think of some way she could have fixed things, but even in her imagination, it was hopeless.

She'd woken up pressed against Briar, not knowing exactly when they'd fallen asleep. It had seemed normal, natural, like waking up from any of the countless sleepovers they'd had. But it had all come back when Briar had stirred in her arms, and Alice hadn't been able to look at her, hadn't even been able to return her sleepy *good morning*.

She'd only meant to give Briar a peck, the sort of kiss that would be a funny story when they were older. Nothing about the kiss had been what Alice had expected. And as she had studied her best friend one final time, she'd felt every speck of dirt on her body acutely. She had known then that things would never be the same. So she had promised Briar they would talk later before getting in her car and driving straight to Noah's house.

It was the first time Alice had mustered up the courage to disappoint Noah, by telling him she couldn't be with him anymore. The revelation that the kiss had actually mattered made what she'd done impossible to ignore. It was the same thing that had torn her family apart, the thing that she had never forgiven her father for. She hadn't seen Noah or Briar since that day.

She knew at some point Briar must have told Noah what happened, that the two of them had probably bonded over her betrayal and cowardice. Alice was sure that she and Noah both hated her, and that they were right to.

Watching Briar grow closer with Noah, then Harper, via sporadic social media updates had been torture for Alice. It had felt like life in the US had continued on without her, like she'd never been a necessary part of it, and she had no one but herself to blame. And of all their high school friends, of course Briar would become closest with Alice's ex and the girl who had never had a nice word to say about her.

'What's this?' Freddie's voice rang out from behind her.

'A mural,' Alice said, not taking her eyes off the paint.

'We've not had a mural before,' he said, coming up beside her.

'I was thinking the campers could paint between the lines throughout the summer and, by the end, it will be all filled in,' Alice said, chancing a glance sideways at him, nervous to see if he liked the idea. Camp was so steeped in tradition that straying felt sacrilege. 'What do you think?'

'I like it.' He shook his head, looking bemused. 'I forgot you were such a great artist. What's the inspiration, then? Is this in Susan's honor?'

She blew a strand of hair out of her face. 'It's more of an apology to Briar, since she won't listen to anything I say. She can ignore me, but she can't ignore this.'

Freddie was silent for a moment and Alice's face grew warm as she assumed he was putting the pieces together – the half-completed outline of a campsite under the stars, Briar's story from the night before, and the fight between them he'd heard about. She wasn't embarrassed that she had kissed Briar that night, but she also didn't want to explain to someone who'd always looked up to her how badly she'd fucked things up by doing it.

But Freddie just said, 'Briar can ignore a lot.'

'Yeah?' Alice asked, slowly adding a moon to the sky in front of her. 'I didn't realize how much the two of you had kept up over the years. I thought *I* was your camp big sister.'

'Well, you never asked. And I figured it was a sore subject for you, so I didn't bring it up.'

Alice sighed. 'It's not a sore subject. I never meant to give you the idea that Briar had done wrong by me. She didn't, and I'm not mad at her.'

'But she's mad at you?' Freddie asked.

'She says she's not. She says the fight was so long ago she doesn't even remember what it was about.' She stopped herself from absent-mindedly filling in the moon. 'She's always been good at hiding her emotions, I guess. She just never hid them from me.'

'Then you were lucky,' Freddie said. 'She never told me how she was, even when Susan got sick the first time. It was summer when she was diagnosed, so we were all around. Everyone was upset, but Briar wouldn't talk about it. When she didn't go back to college for her senior year, we knew things were bad.'

Alice looked at him sharply. 'Susan said that Briar dropped out because she decided she didn't want to be a teacher anymore.'

Freddie raised his eyebrows. 'I think she might have even believed it. That's how tough Briar is to crack. She convinced her own mother that she'd dropped out of school because she wanted to, coincidentally at the same time Susan needed a caregiver.'

'Oh,' Alice said, mulling over Freddie's recollection of events. Of course she remembered the initial diagnosis six years ago, but Susan had written to her about it with her usual pragmatic attitude:

> Dear, I've had some bad news from the doctors, but they've cleared me to finish out the end of camp before starting treatment. If

all goes according to plan, I should be back on my feet by next May, which is the most important thing.

There had been no mention of Briar in the initial email, but when Alice had asked after her, Susan had written back:

> She seems to be feeling directionless lately. She's dissatisfied with her teaching program and doesn't feel that the material matches up with her pedagogical approach. I understand her concerns, but have still encouraged her to finish out the program. She's always wanted to be an English teacher, and I know she'll be a brilliant one if she can just push through.

If it had seemed strange that Susan hadn't mentioned Briar's reaction to her diagnosis, Alice had written it off as something Susan considered too private to share. She wondered now whether the window she'd had into Briar's life – the updates of her achievements and happiness that had led to Alice convincing herself that Briar was better off without her – was Susan's way of protecting her from the truth.

She shook that thought off quickly. It was clear, even with everything Briar had been through, that she was resilient enough to weather any storm without Alice. She'd already bonded with the new cohort of counselors, earning their respect before Alice could say two words to anyone. If anything, Alice felt like her presence in Briar's time of need was only making things worse.

'I thought about reaching out to Briar when Susan was first diagnosed,' she admitted to Freddie. 'But I figured she had a good support system, since she was living with Noah and Harper.'

Alice had eventually dismissed the impulse as selfish, wanting to soothe her own anxieties over Susan's condition rather than make things easier for the whole family. She had decided that Susan needed a peaceful environment to recover, and she didn't want to disturb that.

Freddie didn't bat an eye at Alice's awkwardness when talking about Noah and Harper. 'None of us realized how bad it was. Susan made it sound like she'd essentially come down with a bad flu. And there were no other updates, except that she was cleared to come back to camp, and, after a couple of years, that she was in remission.' He looked over at her, a pained expression on his face. 'I found out the cancer was back a week before she passed, and Briar had only known for a few days at that point. I'll never understand why Susan didn't tell us earlier.'

Alice was struck dumb by his words, by the realization that she had known Susan's prognosis weeks before she'd told Briar. It didn't seem possible.

'I understand it,' Alice said, trying to hide her surprise. 'If there was nothing to be done by the time she found out, why prolong others' suffering on her behalf? Susan would've found that unseemly. She would hate for us to cry over her.'

'Fuck that.'

Alice snorted. 'I still can't believe she's gone. I mean, I *actually* can't believe it. Does it feel real to you?'

Alice wasn't practiced in mourning, at least not anymore. Mourning was inefficient, a waste of precious time she could use to be productive and fix the situation. There was little Alice couldn't fix, and little she wanted so badly that it didn't even matter if it shattered into pieces in front of her. Everything she surrounded herself with, from her flat to her social calendar to her sex life, was workable, good enough for her needs, but not irreplaceable. Susan was the exception. The empty feeling inside her since her death reminded Alice acutely of why avoiding caring was the better option.

'Denial is one of the stages of grief,' Freddie said, and Alice worried for a split second that he was going to pull out a pamphlet. But then he continued, jokingly, 'And I hear artistic expression is another.'

Alice looked back at the landscape she had painted. To her eyes, it was angular and frantic, an explanation hastily formed which had never been asked for in the first place. 'You know, I think you might be onto something with that one.'

—

Alice finally paid Cook a visit at the end of the day. As a university friend of Susan's who'd been working at the camp since its inception, his camp preparation routine was a well-oiled machine that he didn't allow to be disturbed.

However, there were certain things that – while predictable – Alice was required to put a stop to now that she was an authority figure. When she didn't find him in the kitchen, she climbed the stairs that led to his room and knocked on the door.

'Who is it?' came a deep Scottish brogue from inside.

'It's Alice.' She paused. 'Alice Hughes.'

The door swung open. 'Alice Hughes?' Cook echoed, sticking his head out and peering at her. 'Can't be. Alice doesn't come 'round these parts anymore. She renounced our friendship years back. Called me an old coot and said she wanted nothing to do with me.'

'I've missed you too,' Alice said drily, not able to or wanting to articulate how strange it was to have Cook, an ever-present figure from her childhood, in front of her again. His hair was fully grey now, another reminder of the years she'd left behind. She wondered if it would have felt any different to see Susan in person before she'd died, because they'd kept in such close contact. And she was immediately seized by a familiar guilt – she should've flown home as soon as she knew Susan was dying. She should have flown home years ago, when Susan had first been diagnosed. If she hadn't let her shame stop her, maybe things would feel different now.

'Well, come in,' he said, gesturing for her to step inside. 'Let me get a look at ye in the light.'

She'd never been invited in before; it wasn't the sort of place campers or counselors were welcome. The whole place was smaller than her room in London. But there was a record player quietly spinning The Grateful Dead's *American Beauty* and a few knickknacks – a family crest, an intricately-designed bong – that marked it as lived in. With her new access to the camp financial records, Alice knew that in addition to room and board, Cook made a decent salary. What he did with the money, she had no idea. Well, she maybe had *some* idea.

'Cozy,' she said, eyeing the bong.

He narrowed his eyes at her. 'Well, yer a smart-ass just like Alice was. But yer missing the Goldilocks.' He waved a hand toward his own hair.

She shrugged. 'I've accepted my very boring brown hair.'

'Ach, don't say that,' he scolded. 'You've never been boring, always been extraordinary. Extraordinarily annoying, that is. Breaking into my kitchen with Briar at all hours, as I recall. I'd wake up and half me ingredients would be missing.'

Alice stifled a laugh. Camp was the only place she'd ever let herself break the rules. It was something she'd convinced herself was dangerous when she was eighteen and had broken the biggest rule of them all. But being back here, it felt like that was what childhood was meant to be: no academic pressure, no filling all hours of the day with meaningless resume-stuffing extracurriculars, and no perfect-girlfriend act.

'You'd rather I'd have starved?' she asked, folding her arms.

He scoffed. 'As though I weren't feeding ye well. I just hope ye haven't taught the new counselors yer old tricks,' he said gruffly. 'I assume as I've been told yer now *camp director* that there'll be no more funny business.'

He inflected her title with a warranted dose of skepticism. He had often referred to Susan as simply *the camp director* when he was in a mood with her, and the invocation made Alice acutely aware that Susan was gone. She swallowed.

'Co-director,' she corrected him. 'Me and Briar.'

'Well, of course,' he said, as though anything else were inconceivable. 'Could never separate the two of ye, could we? Even when ye were assigned different cabins for the summer, ye'd find a way 'round it.'

A laugh escaped her. 'I forgot about that,' she admitted.

When they were fourteen, Susan had decided the formidable Alice-Briar alliance was preventing them from properly socializing. She'd explained that it would be good for them to meet new peers, to prevent stagnation and co-dependency. Alice had paid another camper in smuggled Silly Bandz to switch bunks with her in the middle of the night, night after night, until Susan had given up on the idea.

'What have you come to tell me?' Cook asked, but he sounded like he already knew.

Alice shifted her weight uncomfortably. 'I've heard mentions of, um, certain odors emitting from this vicinity.'

'A snake, that Sierra is,' Cook griped. 'She just wants to direct the attention away from whatever she's getting up to.'

'Yes, well, as camp director, it's now my responsibility to remind you that when the campers arrive in a week, you will have to partake in any substance use outside of the grounds. And, of course, outside of any working hours.'

'Hmph,' Cook said. 'Yer as bad as Susan.'

She felt oddly proud at the thought. 'Thanks, I think.'

'It wasn't a compliment,' he clarified.

'Well, she *was* your best friend.'

'Aye,' he said softly. 'That she was.'

—

As soon as Alice set eyes on the unmown clearing where the archery range should have been, she knew it was one project she wouldn't be able to do on her own. So she sent Sierra for backup while she opened up the dusty shed housing the bows, arrows, and targets along with an ancient lawnmower.

'Sierra said you needed help,' a voice said from behind her, and Alice turned to find Briar there. 'I was kinda hoping you'd been mauled by a bear.'

'No mauling. Just need help setting up,' Alice said, turning back to the shed. She pulled out the lawn mower and pointedly pushed it in Briar's direction. Somewhere, under all the grass, were lines of bricks that made up the lanes. 'I thought she'd send Freddie.'

'Well, you've got me instead,' Briar said, eyeing the mower dubiously.

Alice shrugged. 'You could clean the spiders off the targets if you'd prefer.'

'Mowing it is!' Briar said, like Alice had known she would.

'While I have you, maybe we should talk about the start of the session,' Alice called out as she began to roll one of the targets to its proper spot and Briar started the mower.

'Right now?' Briar yelled over the motor.

'Yes,' Alice replied. 'While you're mowing and can't run away from me.'

Briar turned, making a face. 'Running away? Isn't that your thing?'

'Sorry,' Alice said, 'I was trying to make a joke. You know I'm no good at those.'

'What's there to talk about?' Briar asked, biting her lip in concentration as she pushed the mower.

'Well, I was thinking we should come up with a system,' Alice said. 'So we'll know where everyone is at all times.'

Briar laughed. 'My mom always said it was better to have half a system.'

Alice frowned. 'How can you have just half of a system?'

'You've gotta be ready for the unexpected,' Briar said simply. 'These kids, they're gonna do whatever they want. We have to be able to roll with the punches.'

That was a sobering thought for Alice, who'd never been one to roll with anything. 'Okay, half a system. Got it. Let me think.'

She set herself to work as she thought. In the summer heat, it didn't take long before they were drenched in sweat. Alice stared when Briar stopped to pull off her T-shirt, hanging it on the mower's handle and leaving her in just shorts and a sports bra. She thought she caught Briar glancing back at her to see if she'd been looking, but she wasn't sure if her mind was playing tricks on her. There had been a few times she'd thought Briar was looking at her this week, but when she'd checked, Briar had always been engrossed in something else. It was making Alice feel crazy.

It had been such a long time since she'd been self-conscious like this, but it was familiar to her. In high school, she had marveled at Briar's easy confidence. She had moved through the world so effortlessly, and Alice felt like a try-hard in comparison.

It had taken her a long time to realize that her constant observation of Briar hadn't been jealousy, but attraction. She had thought she'd wanted Briar's approval, when really, she'd just wanted Briar to look at her.

'You're going to get sunburned,' Alice called after her. Briar waved a dismissive hand, not turning around.

It took Briar almost an hour to finish mowing the green, but by the end of it, the clearing looked infinitely better. As Briar wheeled the lawn mower back towards the shed with a satisfied smile, Alice was still struggling with the last target.

Briar came up next to her, adding her own weight, and the two of them pushed the target into place.

Alice cleared her throat, backing away and keeping her gaze off Briar's barely clothed torso. 'If we have half a system, do we just have to know where half of everyone is half the time?'

'Something like that, yeah.' Maybe it was just the endorphins from the manual labor, but Briar looked like she was hiding a smile, and Alice seized the opportunity.

'Do you want to give it a go?'

'God, no,' Briar said, immediately shrinking away from the bow Alice offered. 'I'm terrible.'

'You're decent,' Alice said supportively. 'Just not as good as me.'

Briar scowled, but took the bait, grabbing the bow and quiver. She lined up her shot, and Alice admired the determination in her eyes as she sized up the target. Alice's eyes caught on the sliver of tongue that brushed over Briar's lower lip as she drew back the string, way too hard.

'Woah,' Alice said, reaching out and stopping just before she grazed Briar's elbow. Instead, she shifted closer, stepping in behind Briar and kicking her front foot forward a little. 'Good, now relax your elbow.'

Alice wasn't touching her, but she was acutely aware of how little clothing Briar was wearing, how close they'd become. Briar sucked in a breath, and Alice felt like she was about to vibrate out of her skin as she placed a hand on Briar's hip, shifting her weight to her back foot. 'Look at the target.'

Alice watched Briar squeeze her eyes shut then blink them open again, her gaze focused across the field at the target. She didn't move her hand from Briar, even though the heat of her skin was burning her. It should have been too much in the sweltering summer, but Alice's mind was playing the sorts of tricks that made the radiating warmth between them pleasant. She couldn't help herself, moving impossibly closer, her mouth just below Briar's ear.

'Now let go.'

Briar's arrow hit the third ring of the target. Not a bullseye, but it was the best shot Alice had ever seen her make. Alice stepped away, lightheaded, and brought a hand up to cover her eyes and shield her reddening cheeks. She didn't know what she had been thinking, getting so close to Briar. Nothing good could come of that.

'Not bad.'

Briar looked down. 'Shut up.' She held out the bow to Alice. 'Come on, I know you want to show off.'

Alice grabbed the bow. Even though she hadn't done this in years, her muscles remembered the basics. Her fingers notched back the arrow, shoulders and hips squaring, and she looked straight at the target, bringing the butt of the arrow to the corner of her lips. She breathed deeply, and released.

The arrow sunk into the yellow of the bullseye. Alice felt a thrill at the sight.

She turned back to see Briar grinning. 'You always were good at that.'

Alice shrugged, resting the bow on the ground. 'That's what happens when you develop a thing for Legolas at an impressionable age.'

Briar laughed. 'That should've been my first clue you were a lesbian.'

Alice smiled, hoping that Briar joking with her meant that she was at least a little forgiven.

'I think there were a lot of clues, actually,' Alice tried to joke back.

Briar's face shuttered, and Alice realized she must be thinking of that night again. There was an awkward pause where she didn't know what to say. The easy air between them had suddenly turned cold. Alice opened her mouth to say something, but Briar beat her to it.

'Well, I think we're good here. I'm gonna go check on Cook.' She turned on the spot and disappeared down the path leading back to camp, leaving Alice standing in the middle of the field, holding the bow and wondering how she could possibly fix this mess.

Chapter 6

Briar

'Alice?' Briar whispered, leaning over to peer at her. It was pitch black in the cabin, but she could just make out the soft lines of Alice's face, still slack with sleep. 'Psst. Alice!'

No response. Briar gritted her teeth as she reached out to touch Alice's shoulder. She shook her firmly, snatching her hand back when Alice groaned and shifted positions.

'It's time to wake up,' Briar said, as she heard the beginnings of murmurs from counselors outside.

'Still dark,' Alice muttered, turning away from Briar and pulling the sheets up over her head.

With possibly too much relish, Briar grabbed the duvet and yanked it off the bed. Alice whipped around, sitting straight up. Even without being able to see her face, Briar knew Alice was sporting one of her seething glares, and she grinned in response.

'What's going on?' Alice said, sounding much more awake.

'Night hike,' Briar said in an almost sing-song tone. 'Get dressed.'

She walked out of the room, flicking the lights on behind her.

Briar hadn't reminded her about the hike. After all, she figured that Alice, being so organized, would remember something like that. She found a twisted satisfaction in watching her scramble through getting ready and then nearly miss the caravan of cars headed to a nearby trail.

Alice hated the annual sunrise hike, and had usually found a reason to avoid going, anything from faking sick to letting the air out of her tires one year. There was nothing more terrifying to Alice than having to climb a mountain in the dark, which was perfect for Briar's ongoing campaign of psychological warfare.

It only took fifteen minutes on the trail before a quiet string of curses rose from behind her.

Briar snickered. 'Alright back there?'

They were in a single file line, with Sierra leading the group. Most of the counselors had headlamps strapped to their foreheads that glowed red, bright enough to see the ground, but not bright enough to disturb any of the wildlife.

'Yes,' Alice said, her voice wobbling. Briar had made sure Alice didn't get a headlamp. All the more fun to hear her stumble. 'I'm just *so* glad we were able to go through with this illegal endeavor.'

Hiking at night wasn't strictly allowed in the state park, but it was a common enough occurrence that the park rangers had taken to leaving the park gate unchained.

'Anyone know a good ghost story?' One of the younger counselors called from further up the line. Briar smiled – she couldn't have planned anything more perfect to spook Alice.

'Sierra does,' came Freddie's voice. He was bringing up the rear, making sure everyone stayed together.

'You guys want to hear about some *brujeria*?' Sierra's voice echoed against the boulders.

Alice groaned pitifully and Briar's smile widened.

They passed the next hour or two with counselors swapping stories they'd heard around the campfire. Many of them Briar already knew, but there were a few spooky additions. It had been years since she'd been a counselor, and she'd forgotten the sense of camaraderie and fun that came with the job. In her counselor days she would've been the one coming up with the entertainment for the hike. It had always been her thing, keeping morale alive.

Now, she felt ancient, disconnected from the carefree girl she'd once been. Being back here, it was like she was haunted by the younger version of herself. The one that hadn't lost her best friend to another continent, the one who hadn't had a dying mother to take care of, the one that still had a future to plan for. She envied them, like she envied everyone who made their way through the world trusting that everything would be fine without constantly thinking of the worst-case scenario.

'Fuck.' Alice crashed into her, her foot catching on Briar's heel and nearly taking her shoe off. 'Sorry.'

Briar hissed as pain shot up her leg. 'It's fine.'

Alice's hand shot out, and Briar could sense it hovering above her shoulder before it disappeared.

It took another half hour before someone suggested singing, which was met with groans and followed by a half-hearted rendition of 'Country Roads'. Briar listened for Alice's slightly off-key voice but could only hear heavy breathing from behind her.

Light crept back into the world. The earth slipped into wakefulness, starting with one bird call, and then another, until the sky was full of song. Everything was tinged blue, like a lens had been put over the world, giving it a magical appearance.

Briar would often be the first one awake at camp, stealing precious moments of peace in the early morning light before the chaos of the day caught up with her. It was a trait she'd shared with her mother.

They finally reached the rock scramble that signaled the final stretch before the peak – and the trickiest part of the trail. Two boulders met, creating a small crack for hikers to wedge into and climb. There were footholds to balance on, but reaching the overhang required relying on upper body strength. It was a difficult feat for anyone of below average height.

Briar always found this part unpleasant. As the shortest of the group, she had never managed to ascend it by herself. Alice moved ahead of her, scrambling up with no issues. Briar held in a huff of annoyance.

Alice turned around, her arms outstretched. She did it seemingly without a second thought, and Briar remembered how Alice was always the one to help her up this particular spot. She swallowed, unsure if she was more upset about forgetting the small detail or that she had to relive the memory now. The realization that she'd never resented Alice's help when it came to things like this hit her the hardest. It was something she would never let herself have with her friends now.

She got into position, the balls of her feet perched in the footholds, her whole body straining upwards. She ignored Alice's outstretched hand, using the momentum from her legs to jump for the overhang. Her fingertips grazed the edge, but not enough for her to find purchase. As she fell back, Alice's hands caught her forearms, holding her midair. Briar's head snapped towards her, taking in the look of concentrated effort as Alice struggled to hold her. Briar found another foothold and pushed off it, feeling Alice guide her arm until her elbow wedged itself in the next divot, and she could lift herself up the rest of the way. It didn't escape her notice how Alice's hands never left her body.

Briar shook her off and stood, trying to erase the feeling of Alice's skin, slick with sweat, against her own. She pushed ahead of Alice again, not meeting her eyes, the places where she had touched burning under her clothes.

They reached the peak just as the sun was coming out over the horizon. Briar watched silently as sunlight crept across the valley below, cutting through the trees. As she took in the vast stillness of the world below her, an overwhelming sense of loss crept in.

These were the woods her mom had loved, the ones she had uprooted her life for. There was no way for Briar to be here without seeing her mom everywhere, seeing the years of memories she'd made with her family.

Her eyes pricked and she squeezed them shut, trying to stop the tears from falling. Grief had the ugly habit of showing up at the most inopportune moments.

'Alright,' Freddie called, shucking off his backpack. 'Who wants coffee?'

Briar brushed a hand over her face, happy for the distraction, as Freddie and Sierra passed around metal cups and thermoses for people to serve themselves.

The rock face they sat on was cold without the sun beating down on it. Briar shivered, gripping her cup of coffee gratefully for warmth. The group chatted around her, but she couldn't focus on any of the words, her eyes drawn to the woods below. She tried not to think about her mother, but not thinking about her was impossible.

'Here.'

Alice leaned over her, a down jacket in her hands. 'I brought an extra, just in case.' Briar stared at the jacket, annoyed. No matter how many years had passed, Alice would always be the kind of person to pack an extra layer *just in case*, and she'd always be the person sitting out in the cold. She couldn't take the jacket and admit weakness, that much was obvious. Another shiver racked her body and Alice rolled her eyes. 'Don't worry, this won't make us friends or anything.'

'Fine.' Briar pushed her arms through the sleeves of jacket, feeling immediately warmer. 'Thanks.'

'You're welcome.' The smugness in her voice was almost enough to make Briar give it back, but Alice walked off before she could.

Briar eyed her as she sat with Freddie. The orange light of the sunrise caught on the strands of Alice's hair, giving its color an auburn tint. Her skin was golden and her eyes sparkled. She looked just as beautiful as Briar remembered, maybe even more so. Because this version wasn't a vague memory from high school, or a flattened image on her phone screen. This Alice was real, and right in front of her. And Briar hated her for it.

Chapter 7

Briar

'Hello?' Laurel's voice came through weak and tinny. 'Bri? Can you hear us?'

'Yes! Can you hear me?' Briar shouted into the phone.

'There's no need to scream,' Hazel admonished. 'Anyway, we just got in. Dad took us to Edinburgh for the weekend.'

'Did he?' Briar asked, her eyes narrowing. 'Don't you have take-home exams to finish?'

The University of Southern California had given Laurel and Hazel an extension to finish their coursework, but it didn't stop Briar from worrying. She knew firsthand how hard getting back into the rhythm of school could be once disrupted. They were so close to finishing their final semester and Briar was determined that they'd get their diplomas.

Laurel groaned in the background and said, barely distinguishable, 'We've got until the end of summer. Tell her to lay off.'

'Lay off,' Hazel repeated, and Briar rolled her eyes.

'Are you at least having fun?' Briar kept any anxiety out of her voice. It was silly to not trust her siblings with their father, but Briar knew how he could be, engaging for a week or two, then disinterested the next. Having spent most of her adolescence making up for his absence in the twins' lives, Briar wasn't sure they understood how easily he could let them down.

'Yeah!' Instant relief coursed through her at the excitement in the twin's synchronous answer. 'We went to Gran's last week, then to the Lakes.'

She wanted to be happy, to trust that they were having a good time, but the constant travel their father seemed to be pushing concerned her. It could've been intended as a distraction from their grief or, more likely, it was just another symptom of his inability to provide stability for his children. The twins would have to face reality at some point, and Briar would be the one to see them through it.

'You would have loved it,' Laurel cut in. 'So many dead poets for you to swoon over. Could've found some more words to immortalize on your body.'

Briar smiled. 'If anything caught your fancy, send it my way. I could always use another tattoo.'

She glanced down at her forearm, the collection of images there scattered with some of her favorite quotes from her college literature classes. There would be a new one soon, whenever she figured out what words or illustration could capture the way she'd changed over the past few months. Sometimes she felt like her tattoos were an anthology of every time she'd thought she'd reached her final form, only to be thrown another curveball.

'For your street cred,' Hazel said sagely.

'To add to the hot bartender mystique,' Laurel agreed.

'Oh, fuck off,' Briar said good-naturedly. 'How's Dad?' She didn't know why her heart clenched at the question, especially after just having doubted him, but as her only living parent, his well-being was suddenly much more salient to her.

'He's good, the same,' Laurel said.

'Maybe a bit more melancholy,' Hazel added. 'But the love of his life died, so I think we can give him a pass.'

Briar ignored that comment, neither encouraging nor dissuading the twins' fanciful notion that their parents were secretly soulmates who had just been too short-sighted to stay together. They were still in diapers when their parents had split; they didn't remember the pointless arguments or the endless litany of passive aggressive comments as vividly as Briar did.

'Is he there?' she asked, twiddling the cord of the landline around her fingers. She didn't want to talk to him, but they had business to discuss. There was a long pause that made Briar's heart pound. 'What's happened?'

'Oh my god, nothing!' Hazel said. There was a loud clapping sound that Briar suspected was one of the twins hitting the other, but from across the ocean she wasn't sure who to scold. 'He's not here.'

'You can't sell the camp!' Laurel's voice cut across her sister's, and Briar blinked. She had been trying to think of a way to bring it up to the twins, but it seemed that, as with many things, her father had made that decision for her.

'Dad told us,' Hazel explained.

Briar nodded her head slowly before remembering they couldn't see her. 'An appraiser came out, but I'm still waiting to hear back.' There was silence on the other end of the line. 'I'm sorry I didn't say anything before.'

'Bri, you can't sell,' Hazel said, sounding much younger. Briar was suddenly struck by the memory of the twins, then only seventeen, sitting in the hospital waiting room when their mother had first gotten sick, looking to her for answers. 'It's mom's camp. It's our home.'

'Nothing's been decided yet.' She heard voices and glanced out the open doorway. Freddie, Sierra and Alice were attaching the camp flag to the flagpole, the forest green and light blue fabric fluttering in the wind. Briar remembered when her mother had sewn the flag. A 6-year-old Briar had helped her cut out the two pine trees that sat in the middle. '*I* haven't decided yet.'

'Okay,' Laurel said. 'But will you tell us before you do anything?'

'Of course!' The words came out louder and more emphatic than she'd intended, but it made them laugh, which in turn made her smile.

'We love you,' they said in unison.

'I love you, too.'

Briar hung up and stood there for a few minutes watching the group by the flagpole. Alice laughed at something Sierra said, her whole face lighting up. She tugged on the rope, hoisting the flag higher and higher. Sierra and Freddie watched, shielding their eyes from the sun with their hands. Alice tied off the rope and stepped back, admiring her work. Freddie slung his arms around them, a picture-perfect image of camp camaraderie.

Briar sighed, turning back to the landline and punching in a new number.

'Briar,' her brother greeted her.

'RJ.' Briar matched his business-like tone.

He sighed. 'I told you to call me John.'

'I'm sorry. River it is.' She could almost hear his eyes roll through the phone.

'What do you want?' There was a faint clacking sound in the background, meaning he was at work. He always was. It couldn't be good for him, especially when he'd hardly taken any time off for bereavement. Every time she spoke to him, he sounded exhausted, and she had no idea how to convince him he needed a break and a trained professional to talk to about his grief.

'Did dad tell you about selling the camp?' she asked.

Despite their differences, she had always appreciated her brother's preference for bluntness. He'd stopped letting her baby him when they were teenagers, and while she never forgot that she was the eldest, RJ had become a confidant and co-conspirator against the rest of their family. It was a relief not needing to manage him to the same degree she did the twins.

'Do you have an offer already? I thought it would take at least another month.'

Briar blinked. 'No, no offers yet.'

RJ hummed. 'Well, don't get discouraged. You've got all summer.'

'You *want* me to sell it?'

RJ had never loved camp as much as her or the twins, but he'd still come every summer until college. It was as much his home as theirs.

'Of course.' The typing stopped. 'What would you do with a camp? What would any of us do with it? I'm in New York. The twins are in California. You're the closest, but it's still two hours from DC. It's better to sell it and then split the profits. I mean, if you're willing to share.'

'Obviously we'd split the money,' Briar huffed, hearing the hint of wryness in his tone.

'It would be a good thing. I mean, that money could be a down payment on a condo, or I could invest it for Hazel and Laurel and give it to them when they're twenty-five. You could go back to school…' he trailed off meaningfully.

Briar nodded along, knowing he was making very good, very smart points. But she ignored his comment about college. Any thoughts of her own future were on hold until she was confident her siblings were settled.

'Right.' She couldn't stop herself from adding, 'But it's mom's camp…'

'And she's not here to run it.' He paused, and Briar heard him inhale an unsteady breath. She prepared to say something comforting, to remind him that she was there for him during this difficult time, but he cut off anything she might have said, his tone steely. 'That was crass, but whatever, it's true. She's not here anymore. You can't keep it just because you miss her.'

Briar swallowed around the lump in her throat, every fiber of her being wanting to scream, *Why not?* 'I know.'

They sat in silence for a few moments, before RJ finally said, 'You have all summer, just try to enjoy it and worry about this later. I've got to go. Work.'

'Right.' Briar leaned against the wall, the weight of her body suddenly too heavy to hold up.

'Be well.'

'You too.'

He hung up, and Briar slid down until she was sitting on the floor, the dial tone ringing in her ear. She had forgotten to ask him about his therapist search, again.

She sometimes wished she had RJ's logical approach to life; it seemed much simpler than being bogged down by constant feelings. On paper, selling the camp was the right thing to do for her family. If it were up to simple practicality, like her father and brother seemed to think, it would be an easy choice. But being in the same cabin that her mother had spent the last twenty years making a home, seeing shades of her in every acre of woods, it felt impossible to say goodbye.

She didn't know how long she sat like that, only that it was Alice who eventually found her. She was covered head to toe in dirt, with a cobweb stuck in her ponytail, but, despite the mess, she was grinning wildly.

'You alright?' she asked, wiping her hands on her T-shirt and leaving two dark trails in their wake.

'I could ask you the same thing,' Briar grumbled, annoyed that Alice seemed to be having a better time than her despite her attempts at sabotage. Alice looked down at herself and shrugged.

'Oh, I was cleaning out the boathouse,' she said, her face lighting up again. 'There was an interesting variety of shelf mushrooms growing off one of the bows – *Laetiporus sulphureus* – my first time seeing it in the wild! It was an incredible specimen; the color was so rich…' She visibly collected herself. 'Anyway, I was just coming in to grab my notebook and sketch it.'

Briar stared at her. It was confusing that this woman who had felt so elusive for so many years, whose life Briar only knew about through social media, could be so similar to the girl she had once loved. This Alice didn't *feel* different, and it would be so simple for Briar to let herself slip back into the comfort of their old dynamic. Being friends might even be easier this time around, since Briar knew better than to fall for her again.

But then came her common sense, telling her that no matter how nice it would be to let Alice fix her life, she'd still leave it in ruins.

'God, you're a nerd.'

Alice shrugged again and walked into their bedroom. Briar pulled herself off the floor, not wanting to still be there when Alice returned.

—

Briar managed to avoid Alice for the rest of the day, volunteering to help Sierra sort through art supplies in the art cabin. She spent nearly an hour testing out every single marker, writing *fuck* or *shit* or *goddammit* over and over again in vibrant colors. It was juvenile, but it made her feel better. Sierra said it reminded her of a modern art piece she'd seen in a San Francisco gallery and asked to keep it when Briar was finished.

'So,' Sierra started, after they had sat in silence for quite some time, 'how's it going?'

'Oh, you know,' Briar said, tracing over a particularly fancy *F*. 'Not great.'

Sierra nodded. 'Yeah.'

Briar stopped writing. 'I just don't get what Alice is doing here, you know?'

'Oh.' Sierra blinked at her. 'Okay, sure, let's talk about *that.*'

'This girl shows up after a decade of silence. Like, not even a word when my mom got cancer, and now all of a sudden she's here. We're sharing a bedroom. And it's so *weird,* like living with an alien who's wearing my best friend's face.'

Sierra shrugged. 'At least she's helping, right?'

A small, childish part of Briar wanted to refute her. 'Yeah, she is,' she sighed instead, putting down her pen and scrubbing a hand across her face. 'I'm no good at this.'

'At what?' Sierra asked, cocking her head.

Briar chewed on the inside of her cheek, not wanting to talk about it. But she had been the one to bring it up in the first place.

'Being camp director. I hate logistics and have no attention to detail, and that's all this job is. And my mom made it look so easy. Alice makes it look so easy,' she said.

It was hard for Briar to admit that Alice was better than her, especially at something that her mom had expected her to be able to handle on her own. Briar had spent years feeling like she was disappointing her mom when she didn't go back to college, and she wished this one thing would just come as naturally to her as it seemed to for Alice.

'Your mom did this for twenty years,' Sierra reminded her. 'Cut yourself some slack.'

Briar pursed her lips, not willing to concede. But she didn't want to think about her mother and how she wasn't measuring up to her expectations. She'd rather focus on the problems she could control.

'And now, Alice is a lesbian,' Briar said, deftly changing the subject.

Sierra gave her a look that made her flush. 'I think she's been a lesbian for a while.'

'Right, yeah, but now she's a lesbian *here*.'

Briar thought back to the night before, when she'd walked in as Alice was getting out of the shower, padding around their bedroom in nothing but a towel. Briar had never turned around so fast in her life. The smell of lavender and Alice's shampoo had lulled her to sleep that night, the image of Alice's wet, bare shoulders burned into her retinas.

'You never struck me as a homophobe,' Sierra joked.

Briar wasn't doing a good job of explaining what she meant, that the Alice from high school – the one with the tennis skirts, perfect hair, jock boyfriend – had been completely untouchable in her eyes. She'd spent years in love with a girl she could never have and, suddenly, that girl was sleeping in her room. And she still couldn't have her, but for completely different reasons.

Briar sighed. 'I don't know. Ignore me. I'm just being crazy.'

Sierra leaned in close, resting her hands on Briar's knees and looking at her intently. 'You're not being crazy. Ever.'

Briar found the eye contact unnerving but made an effort not to squirm away. 'Okay.'

'Grief is weird. When my dad died, I did a lot of weird shit,' Sierra said. 'Like cyberstalking a pop star and convincing myself she'd been replaced by a lookalike clone kind of weird shit. This summer you get a pass, okay?'

Briar nodded, staring down at her hands. 'Thanks.'

Sierra leaned back. 'And I'm here if you need to talk or whatever.'

'Yeah, I'll let you know if I have any more crises about my ex-best friend's sexuality.'

Sierra laughed. 'But seriously, how does Alice being here make you feel?'

'Like I'm in high school again,' she answered, but that wasn't quite right. It felt more like Briar was stuck in a dream where she found out that an outstanding credit was preventing her from graduating and she was being forced to repeat every class over again.

'Hmm,' Sierra hummed. 'What are you going to do about it?'

Briar shrugged. 'Keep torturing her until she eventually leaves.'

That surprised a laugh out of Sierra. 'That's one way to deal with it.'

—

That night, the counselors decided to go swimming to celebrate the opening of a newly spider-and mushroom-free boathouse. Cook had finally gotten the PA system working so they could blast music out over the dark water of the lake, while Freddie and a few of the counselors had strung up lights over the dock and small beach.

Briar ignored the rest of the counselors and waded into the water. Even with the extra light, the dark water gave her pause. Briar had never loved the lake, no matter how much her mother had encouraged her, preferring the clarity and cleanliness of a pool over slime-covered rocks. But the water was refreshingly cold against her aching body.

She enjoyed the relative peace, listening to the group talk and laugh together. It was comforting to listen to other people's happiness even if she felt far removed from it. It was as if happiness was reminding her that it was still there, waiting for her whenever she was ready to feel it again.

'Um, Briar?'

Briar knew who it was without turning around. 'Yes, Alice?'

'I was hoping we could talk?' She swam out past where Briar was standing, then turned back to her. Her hair looked black in the moonlight, her eyes catching the light dancing off the water. Her pale pink bralette was practically transparent when wet. Briar swallowed, realizing Alice must have forgotten to pack a bathing suit. Her eyes involuntarily traced a droplet of water down Alice's neck. Alice coughed and Briar's eyes shot back to her face.

'I don't think so.'

Alice pouted. She'd always been able to convince Briar with that look.

'I just wanted to go through the final to-dos before the campers get here,' Alice said. She tilted her head into the water and ran a hand through her hair to slick it back. Briar was distracted from responding by the faded tattoo hiding just behind Alice's left ear. It was her first glimpse of the tattoo she'd sketched for Alice; Briar had assumed she'd gotten it removed.

'Hmm,' she said. Alice cast dark eyes up at her, patiently waiting for Briar's response. 'Fine.'

Alice stood so they were eye to eye. Briar was very aware that they were both almost naked under the line of the water.

'The upper cabins need to be cleaned and the greenhouse needs tending to. Cook said the fridge is acting up so I'm going to call the repairman tomorrow. A camper's parents have already called the office twice to talk through her list of medications and allergies, so I'll follow up with them tomorrow. Freddie said we need more towels, so I'll be sending a group to the nearest Walmart for provisions. It couldn't hurt to also stock up on sunscreen and bug spray. Also, Sierra mentioned putting tampons and pads in all the bathrooms for any individuals that need them. You don't have an issue with that, right?'

Briar's eyes had squeezed shut long before Alice finished her list, an ache already forming above her left eyebrow. There was still so much to do; she couldn't fathom how Alice kept it all straight in her head. She opened them to Alice's expectant face, and whatever calm she'd found within herself dissipated.

'Don't you ever relax?'

Alice blinked at her. 'Um, no, obviously.' A ghost of a smile played at her lips and Briar almost returned it before catching herself.

'That all sounds fine,' Briar said, not caring enough about their feud to refuse help that she knew she needed.

'And then, I think we should really come up with some sort of sys—'

Briar didn't let her finish. 'Any system will be shot in two days, trust me.'

Alice frowned. 'But it would still be good to prepare somehow.'

'Okay,' Briar said. 'How about you handle anything logistical, and I can handle mediation between campers? You always hated that part.'

She had said it without thinking, instinctively, but the look Alice gave her made her realize she'd messed up. The offer was veering into friendly territory, and they weren't friends.

'That would be really nice,' Alice said, laying a hand on Briar's arm. 'Thank you.'

Briar looked down at where Alice was touching her, suddenly feeling much warmer. 'I'm gonna head in.'

Alice nodded, looking a little sad. 'Yeah, sure, of course. Good night.'

'Good night,' Briar said, wading back to the shore. She pulled on her shorts and slung her T-shirt over her shoulder.

She turned back and watched Alice swim over to where Sierra and Freddie were, feeling lost. Had she and Alice just had a civilized conversation? That wasn't right.

Briar didn't want to give up her anger towards Alice. She needed it, needed to feel it every day, because if she wasn't angry at Alice then that left her open to other emotions, uglier ones, sadder ones, ones she wasn't ready to feel about Alice, about her mother, about herself. Briar frowned, looking away from the water, and her eyes settled on the pile of Alice's clothes lying on the beach nearby.

She didn't let herself think as she tucked them against her chest and headed down the path towards the director's cabin.

She felt giddy, smiling as she brushed her teeth and washed her face. She took her time getting ready for bed, hoping to catch Alice coming in. Finally, she got in bed with a book, reading idly with her ears perked for footsteps.

It was another hour before she heard stirrings from outside. She quickly clicked off her lamp, pretending to be asleep. Loud stomps sounded from the steps, the front door snapping open and banging closed. Suddenly, the bedroom was flooded with light.

'Oh, fuck off,' Alice said. 'I know you're awake.'

Briar opened her eyes and laughed.

Alice stood in the doorway, wearing an old pair of waders she'd probably fished out of the boathouse. The army green rubber ended around her belly button, with straps over her shoulders that looked ridiculous paired with her lacy bra.

'Are you happy now?' Alice asked, crossing her arms. The rubber squeaked as she moved, which threw Briar into another fit of giggles. 'All of the counselors saw me leave like this, just so you know. So there goes their respect for me.'

'You mean if they had any to begin with,' Briar said between giggles, wiping her eyes.

'It is so on, Elwood,' Alice said menacingly, though her words lost some of their effect as she tried to pull her leg out of the wader and made a horrible squelching noise. Briar hadn't laughed so hard in weeks.

—

Briar wasn't sure how it happened, but they miraculously seemed somewhat prepared for the campers' arrival. She tried to soak up the final day without them, enjoying sitting in the mess hall with the counselors, eating an uninterrupted meal.

Briar's gaze fell on Alice, as it so often did. She knew that none of the previous week's success – the readying of the cabins and land, the training and coordination of the staff, and even Cook acting more attentive than he had in years – could have happened without Alice. Though she wouldn't admit it to anyone but herself, she had needed help and Alice had delivered. But that only made it hurt more that Alice hadn't come home sooner, before her life had completely spiraled out of control.

After dinner, they made bingo cards for disasters that would likely occur by the end of the summer. It was another activity Susan had made a tradition, so that the summer was fun for campers and counselors alike. Among the conversation and laughter, it was like Briar could feel her mom there with them, like at any moment she would walk in from one of the trails and come back to her. When Briar thought of her mother, it was always like that, brimming with life and flushed from a day of hiking.

She felt tears prick at her eyes. Since her mom's diagnosis, she'd learned that if the tears were coming, she should let them. So, she stood, inadvertently catching Cook's eye as she headed for the door. He nodded in understanding, and Briar made her escape.

The walk back to the director's cabin was quiet, a lone owl hooting in the night, harmonizing with the crickets. Pulling the screen door open, Briar was overwhelmed by the smell of old books, pine and something musky she'd always associated with her mother. Tears blurred her vision as she stumbled to the bathroom, turning on the shower and shucking off her clothes.

She let the warm water wash over her as she sobbed, tears trickling down her face and body before slipping down the drain. She cried until the water went cold, and then she climbed out of the shower and brushed her teeth.

Changing into her old ratty Fleetwood Mac T-shirt and a pair of boxers, she hoped another try at *The Brothers Karamazov* would put her to sleep. She flicked off the overhead light, leaving a soft glow from her bedside lamp. She pulled back her duvet and top sheet, grabbed her book and climbed into bed, only for her feet to stop short, shoving her knees painfully into her face.

Briar rubbed at her bruised lip, raising the blankets to look. A surprised laugh bubbled out of her.

Someone had shorted her sheets, remaking the bed with the top sheet reversed and folded over so that there was nowhere for Briar's legs to go. It was a ridiculous prank, juvenile in the best way, and only one person could have done it. As she got up to fix her bed, a torn corner of paper peeked out from under her pillow.

It only had one word on it, written in Alice's perfectly rounded script: *Gotcha.*

Chapter 8

Alice

Things fell apart as soon as the campers arrived.

Briar had taken on most of the camper mediations, as promised, but she'd been conveniently pulled away by mysterious phone calls during others. Alice was trying to be accommodating, but mediations had always been hard for her. She froze when facing a simple argument. Even friendly debates amongst their high school friend group would often make her leave the room.

She didn't understand how these campers found the energy to argue so consistently over nothing, and she frequently wanted to shout that they should wait until they were adults with *real* problems. Which she, of course, refrained from doing, both because she was an adult who was responsible for their well-being and because she was a little scared of them.

When Alice entered the bedroom late on the third day of the session, she was wondering whether she could keep going at this rate. Meanwhile, Briar was the picture of coziness, snuggled in bed with a book.

'Hey,' Briar said, and Alice immediately wanted to forget whatever sort of tentative truce the two of them had constructed. She knew that tone, and she knew that it meant more bad news for her.

'What is it?' she asked, trying not to sound overly antagonistic. It was hard for her to believe that Briar didn't find any pleasure in watching her squirm.

'There's a kid waiting for you in the office,' Briar said, gazing innocently up at her from behind the book.

'And you couldn't deal with them yourself?' Alice asked, already turning back to the door in defeat.

'He's homesick for England,' Briar said. 'I thought you'd be better suited to talk to him about it.'

She supposed, in a way, Briar was right. Maybe Alice was homesick, if that's what you called being sick with longing for the simple life she'd left behind in London. A small, sunless bedroom, a basement desk at a lab and a best friend who she'd never had a catastrophic falling out with all sounded ideal at the moment. If not thrilling, her life in London was at least manageable. The highs and lows of the past few weeks were both foreign and unsustainable.

'Okay,' Alice said, and waited until she was in the hallway to let out her sigh. She opened the door to the office with trepidation. A kid who couldn't have been more than eight sat in a chair across from the desk, a stuffed rabbit tucked under his arm, anxiously nibbling on the collar of his shirt. He didn't look up when Alice came in.

'Hi,' she said. 'I'm Violet. Nice to meet you.'

'Hullo, Violet,' the kid said, still staring straight ahead.

She settled into the chair behind the desk. 'What's your name?'

'Robin.'

'That's a nice name,' she said, hoping a few compliments might be enough to fix his problems. Briar would have been able to cheer him up immediately, but Alice had no idea how to go about it.

'Yes,' he said, his eyes meeting hers. 'My mum named me after the bird. It's her favorite.'

She nodded. 'A great choice. And what's your favorite bird?'

He scrunched up his face. 'I don't like birds. They're scary.'

'Oh,' Alice said. No wonder he wanted to leave – the constant birdsong was one of Alice's favorite things about camp. She'd forgotten after years in the city how comforting waking to the sounds of nature was. 'Why?' she couldn't help but ask.

'The feet,' he said, as though that explained anything.

'Right…' Alice said slowly. 'Well, Briar told me you're homesick? Do you want to talk about it?'

'I'm not homesick.'

'Oh?' Alice asked. Maybe Briar had misunderstood and she could just talk to Robin about something not bird-related for a few minutes then send him on his way.

'I'm *going* home, so that's probably what she meant,' he explained.

Alice breathed out. 'I live in England too, did you know that?' He shook his head. 'So I understand how it's difficult to go from being there to being here.' What she couldn't tell the eight-year-old was how impossible she was personally finding the transition.

'I hate it here,' he said.

'Is there anything in particular that's bothering you?' Alice asked. 'Maybe I can help you make some adjustments to make camp more fun.'

Robin shook his head, his voice pitching up. 'I don't like the woods. I don't like the other boys. I don't like the birds. I don't like—'

'Alright,' Alice said, holding up a hand before he worked himself into hysterics. 'Let's take on one thing at a time. The woods and the birds I'm afraid I can't change for you, but what about the other boys? What's wrong with them?'

'They aren't very nice to me. I think they want me to leave so that one of their friends can take my place in the bunk.'

'I'm sure that's not true,' Alice said. 'It's your first year at camp, right?' He nodded. 'It always takes a little while to make friends. I came to camp for the first time when I was around your age, and it was so big and scary. The first week, I felt like I didn't have any friends. But do you want to know what happened?'

'I guess,' he said dubiously.

'I met my best mate that summer. She gave me a friendship bracelet at the final campfire and we promised we'd be friends forever.'

Alice still remembered that moment so clearly, the fire transforming Briar's hair into the same gold as sunshine, her rosy cheeks and shy smile. It had been the best moment of Alice's life, the first time since her parents' divorce that she'd felt like maybe everything would be fine.

'That's nice. You're not wearing any friendship bracelets, though,' he noted.

'Well... it's back at my flat.' She knew exactly where it was, in a box of trinkets under her bed she never touched but also never threw away. 'I didn't want to lose it at camp,' she lied.

Robin looked suspicious. 'But she still knows you're mates, even though you're not wearing the bracelet?'

'Yes,' Alice said, through gritted teeth. She didn't know how she'd managed to mess this conversation up to the point that an eight-year-old was interrogating her about her failing social life. 'So just give it a few more days, yeah? Are there any boys here who are nice?'

'Only my brother, Timmy,' Robin said glumly. 'But he has to be nice to me.'

Alice nodded. She'd always wished she'd had a sibling, someone built in to share the burden of life with her, someone to help her to understand her parents better. It was one of the many reasons she'd envied Briar growing up.

'Use that to your advantage, okay? Spend some time with him when you're feeling excluded by the other boys. And we'll meet at the end of the week to see how it's going. Can you do that for me?'

Robin frowned.

'If you do it, I'll call your mom, okay?' Alice said, putting out her pinkie finger. 'And we'll see what she says about you coming home.'

'Really?' Robin's eyes lit up, and he linked his pinkie with hers.

She rifled through the desk drawer and found her stash of Cadbury Dairy Milk. 'In the meantime, here's a sweet treat to remind you of home.'

Robin looked at her like she'd performed a magic trick. 'Thanks, Violet.'

It was the first time all week that Alice felt like she'd done something right. This was the part she loved, helping kids find a home at camp, the way that Susan had helped her all those years ago. Camp had always been an escape for her, the place she felt safe and the place she found community. If she could make it that for Robin, the hell of the past few days would have been worth it.

She stood. 'Briar will take you to your bunk, okay? I'll go get her.'

She went into the bedroom. 'Can you bring Robin back?' she asked. 'I can't look at him anymore, he's too sad.'

'Fine,' Briar said, getting up and following Alice into the hallway, where Robin was waiting.

'See you tomorrow, Robin,' Alice promised.

'What's this?' Robin asked, reaching up to place a deliberate finger on Briar's forearm tattoo.

'Oh,' Briar said, her cheeks turning pink and giving Alice a petty sense of satisfaction. 'It's a tattoo. Do you know what a tattoo is? It's like a drawing, but perm—'

'I know what a tattoo is,' Robin interrupted. 'What's it meant to be?'

Briar seemed to be deliberately not looking at Alice. 'It's a briar, like my name.'

'A *sensitive* briar,' Alice corrected, referring to the flower's proper name. 'Like she is.'

Briar shot her an inscrutable look, then said, 'It's important to remember that tattoos are permanent and you shouldn't make that decision lightly. Don't get something inked on your skin unless you're certain it's what you want forever.'

And then, without looking at Alice again, she herded Robin outside.

—

Alice groaned as she scrolled through the myriad of emails she'd received since the start of the session. It was inevitable that she would have neglected her real life in favor of camp, but she also knew she needed to be more attentive to Jeremy in case something important came up. He'd sent her a few job postings and she shot back a quick response: *I don't have the required years of experience or desired publication credits for these roles.*

Jeremy was nothing if not overly ambitious on Alice's behalf, believing in her more than anyone other than Susan ever had. But he didn't seem to understand that Alice wasn't *ready* for this next step, not yet. It wasn't something she felt like she could be honest with him about – it was something she'd only ever admitted to Susan.

Next, she opened an email from her father, which contained the link to a newly published article about moss classification and the note:

> A colleague in biology sent this to me – thought it might interest. Could you confirm you received the wedding invitation?
>
> Cordially,
>
> David

Alice put her head in her hands, massaging her temples. Quickly assessing that there was no way she would be able to respond in her current state, she moved on. Her dad was sure to send her another academic article within the next month anyway. Then there was an email from her flatmate in London.

> Alice—
>
> I've been texting you but my messages are not delivering, so I looked up your email on

the Oxford server. Apologies for any intrusion. Are you alive? Landlord has not said anything, so I assume you've paid rent?

Your plants are suffering in your absence. Please advise on their care and, if possible, when you will be returning.

—AHR

He had attached several pictures of her plants in various states of withering, which Alice flipped through, growing increasingly sure that she had made a terrible mistake. The fact that her flatmate, who she'd never had a proper conversation with and who frequently disappeared for weeks at a time, was concerned enough to reach out to her was a sign that this whole scheme had been the maddest decision of her life.

As if mocking her, the landline started ringing. Alice closed out of her email, trudging into the hall.

'Alice Hughes, camp director, speaking.'

'Hello, this is Cynthia Smith. I got your voicemail about my son, Robin?'

Alice closed her eyes. 'Thanks for returning my call. I was just calling to let you know that Robin is feeling homesick at the moment. He's quite upset—'

'I'm sorry,' Robin's mom interrupted, 'but don't campers get homesick all the time? There are other English children there, too. Surely you've handled this sort of situation before.'

Alice studied the grooves of the wood-paneled wall in front of her, trying to think of reassuring words for a mother who had placed her child in Alice's incapable hands. 'Well, yes, of course the staff at Camp Lakeside have dealt with this before...' she started vaguely.

'He'll get over it soon enough,' Cynthia said. 'His older brother, Timothy, went through the same thing when he first got to camp. But he did fine, and so will Robin. Frankly, I'm surprised that you're giving me a call about this. Susan wouldn't have bothered.'

Alice blinked back what felt suspiciously like tears. She hadn't let herself cry at camp yet and she wasn't planning on starting any time soon, no matter what happened.

'No, she wouldn't have.' It occurred to her that she should have asked Briar to make this call. As Susan's daughter, she seemed to have more authority with the parents, and was more liked in general. But Briar was mysteriously missing, leaving Alice to deal with the stuff she was worst at, again.

'Look,' Robin's mom said, in what was maybe meant to be a comforting tone, but just came off condescending, 'honestly, you seem a little overly anxious. Kids will be kids.'

'Right,' Alice said dully, not feeling better at all. 'I'll take that under advisement.'

'Great!' Robin's mom said cheerily, and hung up.

Alice sat there, staring at the wall for a few minutes, dread that she couldn't shake off settling heavily on her chest. She couldn't face Robin, now that she knew for sure that there was no way for her to help him.

The door creaked open and shut behind her.

'I need a hand with—' Briar broke off when Alice didn't turn to look at her. 'Is something wrong?'

Alice wiped away an escaped tear, glancing over her shoulder at Briar. 'Everything's fine.'

Briar squinted at her. 'You have that classic sad Alice posture,' she said, gesturing in a way which clarified nothing. 'Easy to spot from miles away. It's how you'd look when you got a B on a test.'

'That's ridiculous,' Alice said, scowling. 'I never got Bs on tests.'

'It's the angle of the shoulder hunch,' Briar explained, and then seemed to realize at the same time as Alice that she was digging herself into a hole.

Alice decided to ignore her, not wanting to examine Briar's memorization of her posture any further. 'I just spoke to Robin's mom. She says to give him some more time and he'll adjust.'

Briar nodded slowly, as though Alice was stupid. 'Yeah, obviously. Jeez, I didn't say to send the kid home. I just said to talk to him.'

'I *did* talk to him. Which you refused to do, thank you very much,' Alice said, cross. The night before she'd felt confident that she had a handle on things with Robin, but after talking to his mom she wasn't so sure. 'He hates it here and he wants to leave. I don't think it's my job to stop him.'

'Of course it's your job to stop him,' Briar said. 'We can't just send campers home if they miss their families. We'd have no camp to run.'

'He feels like no one wants him here. And I just talked to his mom and she didn't even seem to *care*.'

Alice knew she was getting too emotional. She'd normally never let something affect her this much, but Robin's mom's callousness nagged at her. Her responsibilities as a mother didn't even register, as though she could offload them onto the camp and wipe her hands of it. It felt far too familiar to Alice.

Recognition clicked behind Briar's eyes. 'Oh.'

'Oh, *what*?' Alice stood, crossing her arms defensively.

'I think you're not in a place where you can see this situation objectively,' Briar offered, almost gently, which only made it worse. Her pity stung. 'Maybe leave it for now, okay? I'll check in with him this afternoon, see if maybe the birds aren't so scary anymore.'

'Okay,' Alice agreed, because she didn't want to do it anyway. Robin had been Briar's problem originally and she'd tried to pawn him off on Alice.

'But something else has come up,' Briar said.

'What is it?' Alice asked, suspicious.

'The drama counselors are both projectile vomiting behind the boathouse.'

'You want me to tell them off for drinking?' Alice guessed. 'God, where are they even finding the time to get drunk? I *wish* I could get drunk right now.'

Briar raised her eyebrows. 'I'm pretty sure they've got the flu or something.'

'Oh,' Alice said. 'So what?'

'I need you to cover drama class,' Briar said quickly. 'With me. Please.'

Alice shook her head. 'No, no, *no*. Isn't there anyone else? Sierra?'

'Sierra is the only certified lifeguard who hasn't come down with this bug. She has to stay stationed by the lake.'

'I'm a—' Alice stopped herself short, sighing. Her lifeguard certification would have expired years ago. 'Okay, fine. Pray for the children who are about to be subjected to this.'

'Already have!' Briar called over her shoulder as she walked back out the door.

Chapter 9

Alice

The rain came the next day. And it didn't stop, no matter how many reverse rain dances the kids performed. As Alice headed out to deliver more ponchos to the campers braving a short hike with Sierra, the phone rang. For a moment, she considered leaving it, since it was almost certainly a parent she didn't want to talk to, but it was part of the job.

'Hello, this is Alice speaking.'

'Alice!' a voice boomed from the other end. 'It's Tom. How are you?'

Alice frantically ran through the list of British campers' parents in her head before realizing she was talking to Briar's dad.

'Oh, Mr. Elwood,' she said, wondering how she had ended up having to speak to the man twice in the span of a month. 'I'm on my way out at the moment, but I'll let Briar know you called.'

'She's been avoiding my calls,' he said jovially. 'Maybe you could deliver a message for me?'

'Um, I guess?' Alice said distractedly, thinking about the kids in the rain. 'I don't have a pen and paper or anything…'

'No matter. Just let her know the appraisal came back, so she'll have to call the estate agent for next steps. Then she can cut me out as the middleman, since she clearly doesn't want me involved anyway.'

'I think I can remember that. Appraisal back, call the estate agent— Wait,' she said, comprehension finally setting in, 'is Briar selling Susan's house? Is that why she keeps disappearing?'

'No, no,' Tom said, 'she's selling the land.'

Alice frowned. 'Well, you can't exactly sell the land without selling the house, can you?'

'The camp, dear,' Tom said.

'The… camp?' Alice echoed blankly.

And suddenly everything made sense. Briar's cagey responses when Alice had asked her where she'd gone to, her insistence on just pushing through for the summer, and why Briar was even here in the first place. She was making moves to sell the camp.

Alice felt stupid for not realizing sooner. Logically, something would have to happen to the camp now that Susan was gone. It shouldn't have been surprising, yet Alice was blindsided by hurt. Camp had always been the part of her life where her emotions came to the surface, and that was happening acutely now.

Tom was still prattling on about something, so Alice interrupted him. 'Sorry, I've got to go. I'll give Briar your message.'

She stomped out to meet Sierra and the campers at the flagpole.

'Thank god,' Sierra said, taking the rain ponchos from Alice and distributing them to the campers. 'Kids, are you ready to see some worms?' The campers cheered and Alice found herself jealous of their ability to enjoy themselves despite everything.

'I'm coming too,' she said to Sierra, because the last thing she wanted was to be alone with her thoughts. That had always been the best thing about camp – everywhere you went, there was a friend. Even if some of them stabbed you in the back.

They trudged down the trail, Sierra and Alice taking the lead. As Sierra had promised, there were many worms for the campers' viewing pleasure and not much else.

'What's wrong?' Sierra muttered, seeing Alice glare at a particularly gross-looking worm. 'You love worms. They're composters!'

'Decomposers,' Alice corrected. 'And of course I love the worms. I'm just in a foul mood.'

'Couldn't tell,' Sierra deadpanned, earning herself a glare even more scathing than the worm's. 'Is it something other than...' She trailed off, gesturing around them.

'Briar...' Alice closed her eyes for a second and almost tripped over a rock. Right. She was not on the sidewalk in London; she had to pay attention to where she was walking. 'Briar is planning on selling the camp.'

She had expected a dramatic reaction, a gasp or a string of curses, but Sierra just said, 'Oh. Yeah.'

'You *knew*?' Alice asked, feeling even more betrayed.

'No, I didn't know,' Sierra said. 'But it was obvious, right? At least to me. Susan's not here anymore to run things, and Briar doesn't want to. She could hire someone to take over, sure, but would it be worth it? Would it be the same camp, without Susan?'

Alice tucked her wet hair behind her ears irritably. 'But what about the campers who come every year? Susan died, so they just have nowhere to call home anymore?'

Sierra looked at her pityingly. 'That's how death works. People lose things. Their lives change, and nothing is ever the same. Did you think we could all just go on like Susan was still here? She's not.'

It was the first time Alice had heard Sierra sound genuinely emotional since Susan's death, and it made her want to cry or scream into her pillow about how unfair everything was.

'We can't just give up,' she insisted, not willing to let go of her anger. If she did, she was sure something far worse would surface. 'This isn't what Susan would have wanted.'

'What she wants doesn't matter anymore,' Sierra said simply.

'That's not true!' Alice said, her voice pitching up. She paused to collect herself. 'This is her legacy, her life's work. I hope when I die no one decides to burn my research because cataloguing it all is too difficult. This camp is Susan's mark on the world.'

Sierra didn't seem to have anything to say to that. 'It's crazy how well Briar still knows you,' she said instead.

Alice almost stopped in her tracks. 'What?'

'I just never would have pegged you as someone to get so emotional over this. Over anything, really. But no wonder she didn't tell you. She must've known you'd flip out.'

Alice took three deep breaths, willing her steely resolve to rise to the surface again. 'Please don't tell anyone about this,' she said. 'I don't want Briar to know that I know.'

Instead of taking her anger out on Sierra, who didn't deserve it, she made a hasty excuse that she'd forgotten something back at camp and abandoned the hike. She felt like one of the worms: soft, exposed, and in danger of being crushed.

Alice wanted to talk to Briar about it, like two mature adults. She did. But every time she saw Briar in the following few days, one or both of them was in a terrible mood. And what Alice didn't want was a confrontation. If she'd wanted to fight with Briar, she'd have stuck around ten years ago.

Alice was hiding in the office, going over the next day's activities with Sierra and Freddie, when there was a sudden bang from the bedroom.

'That didn't sound good,' Sierra said. Alice crumpled onto the desk.

'It can't be too bad,' she said, pulling herself back up and forcing cheer into her voice for the sake of her employees. 'Surely it's something we can fix?'

When they went into the bedroom, the AC unit that Alice had half-expected to have smoke rising from it looked harmless. She pressed a furiously blinking button, and the unit stuttered to life again. Ice cold air washed over her face and Alice smiled.

'See, that's—' Alice started, but was interrupted by another terrible clanking noise. Harsh air shot out, covering her with dust. She coughed out a mouthful, turning back to Freddie and Sierra.

They wore twin looks of disgust.

'Er, maybe Cook can help?' Freddie tried. 'I'll fetch him, shall I?'

'Typical man,' Sierra said, watching him rush out the door. Alice stood there, blinking and holding her arms out, trying not to get dust everywhere. The urge to scream nearly overwhelmed her. 'Let me get you a towel.'

Alice was able to wipe most of the mess from her clothes and the floor. Her hair, however, was a different matter.

'Shit,' she heard Briar call over the rushing water of her second shower, 'I thought Sierra was just messing with me. The AC is seriously out?'

Alice stepped out, wrapping a towel around herself and padding into the bedroom. 'Yes. I had a go at fixing it. Let's just say I have a newfound appreciation for circuitry.'

Briar snickered. 'Of course you thought you could fix it.'

'I was willing to try,' Alice said crossly, grabbing her old, puff-paint-laden camp shirt out of her bag. Maybe it would serve as a signal to Briar of where her priorities should be. 'I wasn't just going to give up,' she continued, while Briar stared at the shirt.

'Are you actually going to wear that?' Briar said disbelievingly. 'It's ripped.'

'I'm going to wear it,' Alice said, with as much dignity as she could muster while fishing a pair of Soffe shorts out of her bag, 'because I *love* camp.'

She thought she heard Briar mutter, 'The lady doth protest too much,' as she headed to the bathroom.

'I'm having an amazing time,' she continued loudly. The shirt did, in fact, gape at the armpit so significantly that it was a bit indecent, but there was no way she was admitting defeat at this point. She marched out into the bedroom, her head held high.

'You are?' Briar asked, raising her eyebrows as she spotted the armpit tear and then glancing away. It was the first time Alice had fully caught Briar noticing her body, and she flushed. She remembered suddenly that this was the shirt she'd been wearing when they'd kissed, when

Briar's hands had traced up her sides to where the hole was, had made it even bigger in her eagerness to get closer. 'Could've fooled me. After we taught theater together, I could have sworn you asked Sierra about the criteria for joining witness protection.'

'And then I went on a walk to see the worms, and I remembered what's so sacred about this place.'

Thinking about the walk immediately soured Alice's mood even further, reminding her how thoroughly she and Briar were at odds over the place she loved the most.

'God.' Briar rolled her eyes before collapsing onto her bed dramatically. Her legs were on full display, and it was impossible for Alice to not look. 'Not the fucking worms. Not again, Alice. I won't be subjected to another lecture on decomposition.'

'It's a very important biological process!' Alice insisted, perching on the edge of her bed and refusing to relax. Even though she was annoyed, she couldn't stop herself from staring while she knew Briar couldn't see her. Her eyes traced up Briar's calves, taking in the smooth tanned skin of her thighs. Her shirt had ridden up, and Alice could see the soft plane of her stomach, the dip of her belly button, and just the barest strip of lace from Briar's underwear. She had the strangest urge to touch Briar and see if her skin was still as smooth as it had been the last time.

Maybe she had been fooling herself by thinking that her attraction to Briar had disappeared with time. But attraction, she reasoned, was fine – she knew where she stood with Briar, and she would never allow herself to feel anything truly dangerous for the girl who was selling her favorite place in the world. She'd become adept at avoiding developing feelings towards women she was attracted to; she could practically boast a DPhil in that subject too. Briar had been the one person she'd ever allowed herself to have feelings for, and she remembered how that had ended.

'You are the only person in the world who will go to bat for the worms.' Briar sighed, putting her hands behind her head. Alice could have been imagining it, but Briar almost sounded... wistful? Maybe she'd been approaching this incorrectly. Briar had never caved to a bully, but she did have a sentimental side Alice could exploit.

'You'd help me, though,' she tried, prodding Briar more than she had so far in this disaster of a week. 'When I went out in the rain to move them off the trails so no one would step on them.'

Briar nodded, still looking at the ceiling. 'Of course I'd help you. There was no saying no to you when you had an idea. You could've rallied anyone, with that glint in your eyes.' She paused. 'You were annoying as hell,' she clarified, her voice soft.

'Oh really?' Alice asked, trying not to feel flattered when she knew Briar hadn't meant it as a compliment. 'Was I annoying when I won our team the 2012 Capture the Flag game by shooting an arrow with the flag attached over the boundary?'

'No, that wasn't annoying,' Briar said, still not looking at her. 'But it *was* reckless. You could've hurt someone.'

'I have perfect aim,' Alice reminded her.

'There's nothing scarier than a teenage girl with an encyclopedic knowledge of poisonous fungi and perfect aim.'

Now she knew she should definitely be offended. 'I never wanted to hurt anyone.'

'Could've fooled me,' Briar said under her breath, and then continued, louder, 'You were always so perfectly controlled at school that it was hard for most people, even Noah, to figure out what you really wanted. And then we would come to camp and everyone here would see the side of you that I saw all the time. The side that was a little bit dangerous. The side that was allowed to *want*.'

Alice clung to those words, the closest thing she had to an admission of nostalgia from Briar so far. She settled back into her pillows, getting comfortable.

'It was easier to be myself here,' she admitted. 'If I messed up, I could bounce back from it. Susan never reacted the way my mom would've. I liked the me I was here better than the me I was anywhere else.' She didn't add that she liked who she had been around Briar all the time, because it was too painful to admit. Even more painful was that Briar was the person who made her brave, by accepting her as the person she really was, not the one she tried to present herself as. 'Didn't you feel that way too?'

'It wasn't as simple for me as it was for you,' Briar said. 'Your parents were miles away, and my mom was right next door.'

'Yeah, but Susan was never disappointed in you.'

Briar didn't say anything for a long moment and Alice worried she'd messed up and they were no longer in the place of easy nostalgia that would remind Briar how important the camp was to both of them. She knew with certainty she had messed up when Briar spoke, her voice wavering.

'She was a good mom.' Briar's voice cracked on the word. 'But I wouldn't say I never disappointed her.'

Alice thought about what Freddie had said, about Briar telling her mom she didn't want to be a teacher anymore. Telling Susan she had dropped out of college couldn't have been easy for Briar. Knowing that Briar had done it because she thought it was her responsibility made Alice's chest ache, and she forgot her anger.

'You're making her proud with how well you're doing this summer,' Alice said.

She meant it. While Briar had been self-conscious about how she'd done in school, Susan had never batted an eye at her missing deadlines as long as she'd put in her best effort. And now Briar wasn't only putting in her best effort. In Alice's eyes, she was the person the campers trusted most with their problems, the person who problem-solved with the counselors when things went wrong. It was a shame she couldn't see that and only saw the ways in which she was letting Susan down.

Briar didn't respond, and Alice heard sheets rustling as she turned over. 'Fuck, it's hot in here,' she said finally. Alice knew that it signaled the end of their conversation, and the beginning of the first sleepless night of many.

–

Alice stumbled out of bed the next morning, feeling like her eyes had barely closed through the whole sweaty night, only to find that she had slept through breakfast. Briar hadn't woken her up, which seemed like a bad omen for the day. Whatever goodwill she'd garnered must have dissipated overnight. No matter how many steps forward she took in rebuilding their friendship, it seemed like Briar took three steps back.

When Alice walked out of the director's cabin, Freddie was standing there with Robin, wearing a stern expression.

'What's wrong?' Alice asked, hoping the words came out as though she wasn't about to fall over from exhaustion.

'Robin had an altercation,' Freddie said. Alice admired his stoicism, a trait she'd once possessed, but these children and Briar had leached from her all within a week's time. 'I thought the two of you could have a chat.'

'Let's go talk in my office, shall we?' she said to Robin, taking his arm and guiding him toward the director's office. Over her shoulder, she mouthed, *Where's Briar?* in Freddie's direction and received only a helpless shrug in return. Great. Briar had disappeared again, doubtless to meet the estate agent and finalize the details of selling the land. Alice had failed to get through to her about how much the camp had meant to them. And now Briar wasn't here to help Robin, who Alice felt wildly out of her depth with.

'Okay.' Alice deposited Robin in a chair and settled behind the desk. He gazed up at her, pitiful as ever, not looking remotely capable of a fight. 'What happened?' she asked, as gently as she could.

'One of the boys tried to take away my stuffy,' Robin said, and tears started falling from his eyes immediately. 'Am I in trouble, Violet?'

Alice kneaded her forehead. 'What did you do to the boy who tried to take away your stuffy?'

'I pushed him,' Robin said. 'I didn't mean for him to fall over, I just wanted him to get away from me.'

Alice, in a not-strictly-professional capacity, was somewhat impressed by the child in front of her. Robin had confronted a total stranger, had stood up for himself in a way Alice had never managed to. Even with Briar, the person she knew best in the world – and even for a cause as noble as keeping Susan's camp – the most Alice could land were a few passive aggressive comments.

'I'm sorry that he made you feel unsafe. But you shouldn't touch another camper even if you're feeling big emotions. You're still discovering how strong you are, and I know you don't want to hurt anyone.'

Robin nodded. 'Are you sending me home now?'

'No,' Alice said. 'But can you promise to not do that again?'

She was surprised to see Robin's eyes fill with tears again. 'I just want to go home!' he cried. 'Nobody wants me to be here. *I* don't want to be here.'

Alice's throat tightened. She couldn't say she didn't know exactly how Robin felt. It was clear the help she'd meant to give to Briar, the apology that she still owed her, was only making things worse. She wasn't a competent co-director, she wouldn't be able to convince Briar to keep the camp, and she was beginning to think that she was the last person on earth who could help Briar through her grief. Having been Briar's best friend ten years ago didn't mean she was anything to her now, that was clear.

'Um,' she said, trying to pull herself together. 'I'm going to step out for a moment to talk to Freddie, okay? Can you stay here?'

Robin nodded, and Alice went into the hall with the full intent of finding Freddie and talking to him. Instead, her feet led her into the bedroom, where Briar was now infuriatingly not missing anymore.

'What's wrong?' Briar asked immediately, and Alice knew she must have looked truly terrible based on her reaction.

'It's Robin again,' she said, sighing. 'Where did you go during breakfast?'

'My mom's,' Briar said, and Alice was annoyed because she had no idea how to tell if Briar was lying anymore. 'The cable company thinks me saying she's died is some sort of ploy to get on a cheaper plan, so I had to make some calls and request another copy of her death certificate.'

'You could've woken me up before you left,' Alice said.

'I thought you would've been happy to get the extra sleep.'

Alice huffed. 'Yeah, it did me a lot of good when the first thing I encountered this morning was Freddie telling me that Robin had gotten into a fight at breakfast.'

'A fight?' Briar asked. 'I didn't think he had it in him.'

'That's not the point.' Alice squeezed her eyes shut, unable to look at Briar. 'He says no one wants him here. And honestly? I understand the feeling.'

And then she whirled around and went to go find Freddie.

Chapter 10

Briar

It was raining, again. The sky was an angry grey, spewing the kind of rain that fell in all directions, soaking anyone who ventured out into its downpour. The forecast for the next few days didn't leave much hope for the end of the session, and the campers were once again playing board games in the mess hall. Briar sighed for what felt like the hundredth time that morning, catching Freddie's eye as he strolled by.

'Up for another round of bingo?' she asked, and he shuddered.

'Absolutely not,' he said. 'That should only be used as a last resort.'

Briar nodded. 'Then what? We can't keep them inside all day without an activity.'

Freddie shrugged. 'Musical chairs?'

'We played that two days ago.'

'Dodgeball?'

'Did it.'

'Bowling?'

'With what pins?'

'Movie?'

'It's a VHS system and we only have *Chitty Chitty Bang Bang*. It'll give them nightmares.'

'Quiet reading time?' Briar glared at him, and Freddie threw his arms up. 'It's never rained this much in one session. I'm tapped out.'

Briar groaned, letting her head fall onto the table in front of her. Once upon a time, she'd been the fun counselor, the one coming up with games and entertaining the campers with wild stories. She had connected with her kids, known all their favorite colors, what animals they liked, made friendship bracelets for them. As a co-director, she didn't even get that. She was either stuck in the office with Alice breathing down her neck or disciplining rowdy kids. Or, even worse, she was at her mom's house, going through the painstaking process of fixing it up.

She wasn't sure she felt the same pull she once had to this place. It would always be her mother's camp, and maybe that was the problem. Briar hated that she kept failing her. It was what she'd been feeling every day of the session. Failure after failure. She wasn't sure she could take any more.

As she scanned the room hoping for a miracle activity to appear, her eyes caught on Robin and Timothy in the corner working on a puzzle. Briar watched as Timothy helped his younger brother find the right pieces, presenting options for Robin to try until they found the piece that fit. Each time it worked, Robin's eyes would light up, a satisfied smile appearing on his face. It made Briar miss the twins.

She knew she owed them a call, but she was avoiding her dad. She didn't want to think about selling the camp yet, but she also knew she had to. It was what was right for her family, and this session had certainly proved that she couldn't run it on her own. Even with Alice's help, it had gone completely to shit.

'Er, Briar?'

She turned to see Cook looking even more haggard than usual.

'What's up?'

'Ye'd better come look,' Cook said.

She followed him back to the kitchen, where he gestured to a wall with a finality that suggested it perfectly explained his mood. Briar looked at it, and then back at him, not understanding.

Cook sighed. 'There's a hole.'

'What?' Briar said, inspecting the wall more closely and finding a small hole near the baseboard, hidden by shadow. 'Jesus, where does this go?'

'To the crawl space,' Cook said, drawing in a deep breath, 'where the racoons are living.'

'Raccoons?' Briar tried to keep the panic out of her voice. Like spiders, small mammals with creepy little fingers were a definite phobia.

Cook nodded grimly, opening the pantry door. 'They got into me buns. Hotdogs and hamburgers, even the brioche.'

Briar suppressed the childish impulse to laugh as she surveyed the damage. There were fluffy crumbs and half-eaten buns scattered all over. Just one more thing to add to the never-ending list of problems.

'Hmm,' she said unhelpfully. 'I guess we're not grilling tonight.'

Cook leveled her with a look that would've terrified her younger self.

'I'll just go out for more bread,' she said quickly.

'And some caulk,' Cook said. Briar blinked at him. 'For the hole.'

'Right,' Briar said, tamping down a hysterical giggle. 'That too. Be back in a jiffy.'

Nearly two hours later, Briar pulled back into the parking lot, her trunk filled with every bread roll available within county lines and one tube of caulk. She hopped out of the car, loading her arms in an attempt to carry everything in one trip.

'Where were you?' Alice materialized beside her, grabbing the remaining grocery bags and closing the trunk. Briar looked at the bags and then back at Alice.

'Give you one guess.'

'You didn't tell anyone you were leaving,' Alice said, and Briar noticed that she looked frantic, her hair disheveled and eyes wild. 'We went looking.'

'I told Cook,' Briar said, starting down the path to the mess hall.

She could practically hear Alice roll her eyes. 'Someone reliable.'

'Did you need something?' Briar asked, attempting to wedge her foot into the gap of the open kitchen door. 'I'm busy.'

'Yes, actually,' Alice said, grabbing the handle and yanking the door open. 'Cabin 5 has lice.'

'Gross.' The modicum of peace Briar had found away from camp slipped away. 'Keep them quarantined and get a nurse.'

'We don't have a nurse,' Alice said, dropping her bags on the counter and crossing her arms. 'As the only one with more than basic first aid training, you're our nurse, i.e., you should've been here.'

She let it slide that Alice had just said the phrase *i.e.* out loud in regular conversation. The look on her face told Briar that Alice would snap if she was outright mocked.

'I was busy,' Briar said again, through gritted teeth. 'Just back off, yeah?'

'Fine.' Alice's mouth pulled into a frown, the way it always would in school when she had wanted to argue with the teacher but had known it wasn't worth it.

'Good.' Briar pushed a bag towards her. 'Give this to Freddie on your way out, would you? I found an old video store in town, got them on clearance.'

Alice grabbed the bag on her way out of the room. Briar unloaded the groceries, shoving packages of rolls onto shelves haphazardly.

'Watch it,' Cook called out from behind her. Briar hadn't even noticed him; all her focus had been on Alice. 'Gentle with the buns.'

Briar was too irritated to smile. 'What do I do with this caulk?'

'Here, let me.' Cook took the tube from her and crouched by the hole. 'It'd be better if we had a new wood plank, but this'll hold until we get the wee buggers out of our hairs.'

'Are you talking about the kids or the racoons?' Briar joked, the familiar lilt of Cook's accent soothing her. She bent down next to him, watching as he expertly filled in the gap.

She remembered when she was younger, still too young to be a camper, and her mom would leave her in the kitchen with Cook for the day. She remembered watching his hands as he'd cut up vegetables.

It was the same now, only his hands were older, more worn, and when they moved there was a slight tremor.

She knew she needed to tell him about selling the camp. This was his home as much as hers, maybe even more so. But telling him seemed impossible. The whole domain he and her mother had built together was going to be gone, just like Susan. Maybe Cook could sense that she was on the brink of a breakdown, because he started talking again.

'Ye know, yer mum's first summer was pretty shite too. There was these nasty little bugs, cicadas, fecking everywhere. We had to put up nets over beds, in the doorways. I considered dressing in a fecking beekeeper getup to keep them out me mouth.'

Briar laughed, remembering her mom telling her the same story. In her version, she had woken up to tiny bug legs in her bed for months, which Briar believed was the cause of her own aversion to anything of the creepy-crawly variety.

'The worst, though, was at the end of the summer, all them cicadas had procreated themselves to death, and their corpses were everywhere. Ye couldnae step outside without crunching them.' Cook shuddered at the memory and Briar grinned, leaning into him and resting her head on his shoulder.

'Thank you,' she said. He patted her shoulder.

'Dinnae mention it. Got a reputation to uphold,' Cook said, winking. Then he grew serious. 'I had been meaning to talk to ye.'

Briar braced for the worst, her good mood dissipating instantly. 'What's up?'

'Well, as ye've probably noticed, I'm getting on in years,' he said, gesturing to his wrinkled face. 'I'd been telling yer mum I was too old to keep up with these kids. But the stubborn woman wouldnae let me retire.' He paused, misty-eyed. 'I think this will be my last summer. I've got a fair bit saved up and am planning to live out me dreams of sitting on a porch and smoking to my heart's content.'

'I'm gonna miss you,' she said, even as she was overcome with relief. Selling the camp wouldn't mean kicking Cook out of his home. So she didn't need to tell him – not yet.

'You cannae get rid of me that easily,' Cook said. 'I'll expect ye to visit.'

Chapter 11

Briar

Briar heard a knock and turned to see Freddie standing in the door frame, a look of trepidation on his face.

'Yes?' she asked. 'What's gone wrong?' She tried to keep her tone light, but she was pretty sure if there was anything else, she'd throw her hands up and cancel the rest of the summer. After spending the past two days fielding calls from concerned parents of Cabin 5 campers – during which none of them offered to collect their lice-ridden child – Briar was at the end of her rope.

'Er,' Freddie started, 'could we sit?'

Briar nodded to the seat in front of her. 'What's up? You're making me nervous.'

'So, thing is,' Freddie said, looking at his hands, 'I've gotten some bad news.'

She suddenly became aware of her heart beating through her whole body, like she now did whenever anyone said anything even vaguely ominous. It was like she was expecting to hear her mother had died all over again, her body constantly pitching her back into that feeling of the floor falling out from under her.

'The job I was meant to start in September says they can't sponsor my work visa anymore,' he explained.

'Oh,' Briar said, feeling guilty at the relief rushing through her system. 'That sucks.'

'Yeah,' he said, his mouth a tight line. 'Anyway, I was wondering if you could maybe hire me in the fall and sponsor me? I could do admin stuff, whatever you need.'

She blinked, wracking her brain for something to say. Hiring Freddie should've been easy, and she wanted to help him. He was one of the best counselors they'd ever had. This was just another item on the *don't sell your mom's legacy to the highest bidder, you idiot* list that she'd been keeping a running tally of.

'Susan had emailed me about it being a possibility when I was still waiting to hear back,' Freddie continued, anxiously running a hand through his hair. 'Obviously, I understand if that's not possible anymore.' He fidgeted, looking more unsure of himself than Briar had ever seen him.

'Um, can I get back to you?' Briar asked, already running through her very short list of options, fleetingly wondering if she could call in a favor and get Freddie a job at the bar. 'I just haven't quite figured out the fall yet.'

Freddie nodded again. 'Of course. Just thought it couldn't hurt to ask. And moving back to England wouldn't be the worst thing. I'd know Alice, at least.'

'I don't know, sounds pretty dire to me.' Freddie cracked a smile at that, and Briar reached over the desk to squeeze his hand. 'I'll do whatever I can.'

'Thanks,' he said. 'Well, I better get back out there. I'm playing hide and seek with Cabin 11.'

After he left, Briar sighed, leaning down to open the desk's bottom drawer and pulling out her mom's laptop. When Briar had first arrived, she'd taken one look at the device and had promptly shoved it out of sight. Now, Briar was assaulted by a series of windows opening, the laptop regurgitating everything her mom had been doing the last time she'd logged on.

Luckily, one of the tabs was her email. There were nearly three hundred unread emails. Briar couldn't read them; instead, she typed Freddie's name in the search bar, hoping to find the email her mom had sent him and that it would somehow give her a convenient solution.

Instead, the first email to pop up was from Alice, dated nearly a year before. The subject line read *Just checking in…* Briar's eyes caught on the message preview: *How was your holiday? I saw Freddie while he was in town. I hope he passed along the shortbread…*

Briar clicked on it, intending to scroll to the beginning of the thread just to satisfy her curiosity. She kept scrolling, stunned. There were hundreds of emails between her mother and Alice, spanning years. The words passed in front of Briar's eyes, but her brain didn't retain any of it. It was a protection mechanism, probably, since the last thing Briar needed right now was to know for certain that Alice had always cared more about her mom than her. She finally hit the bottom of the page and saw that the thread had started in the fall of freshman year. Not even a full month after Alice had stopped speaking to Briar.

Briar's throat seemed to have fallen through to her stomach, and she couldn't breathe. Her mother had stayed in contact with her ex–best friend the entire time. Nearly a decade of correspondence, and Susan had never once mentioned she'd heard from Alice. As it turned out, Alice hadn't abandoned her entire life back home; she had just abandoned Briar.

She scrolled back to the top, intending to exit the page, but her eyes caught on a recent message.

Alice, my darling girl,

My cancer is back. There, I told someone…
It's inoperable, unfortunately, and the prognosis is fairly bleak. Do keep this to yourself, dear. I'm still sitting with it.

All my love

Susan

It was dated a month before she had died.

Tears blurred her vision, and Briar slammed the laptop closed. She stood, feeling like there was too much blood rushing through her veins, and frantically paced. Every moment from this summer where it had felt like she and Alice had been almost rebuilding something like a friendship suddenly shattered. How could her mother have told Alice that she was dying *first*?

She did the only thing she could think of. She called Noah.

'Hey.'

'Hi.'

'What's wrong?' Noah asked, his tone shifting immediately. Briar could picture him leaning forward, brows furrowed. She didn't know how to explain to him the complete betrayal the emails represented. Honestly, she wasn't sure who she felt more betrayed by: the friend who'd disappeared from her life or the mother who simply hadn't thought to mention it at any point in the last ten years.

'Oh, you know,' Briar said vaguely, waving a hand in front of her even though she knew he couldn't see. She couldn't tell him about the emails even if she'd been able to make sense of it; telling him would mean admitting more about her relationship with Alice than she ever had before. 'Everything's shit. How are you?'

He ignored her question. 'Is it Alice?'

'Always.' Briar sighed. She felt foolish for letting herself soften towards Alice, as if they could ever be friends again, as if they hadn't crossed too many lines to go back to what they'd had.

'Well, I bet you'd call a week ago, but Harper had more faith in your ability to coexist. I owe her dinner now. Thanks for that.'

Briar choked out a laugh, her throat still feeling like something was stuck in it.

Noah hummed on the other side of the line. 'Anything I can help with?'

Briar mentally ran through the long list of things that had gone wrong in the last week and a half. 'Our AC is out?'

Noah's laugh was warm and tender, making Briar's chest ache. His side of the line sounded so pleasant: air-conditioned, lice-free, and, most importantly, far away from Alice.

'I don't think I can do this,' Briar said numbly. 'Alice being here. I mean, she's *actually* helping, and that's so much worse. Like if she'd shown up sooner, my mom wouldn't have died.' She squeezed her eyes shut. 'No, I don't believe that. But maybe my life wouldn't be such a mess right now? Does that make any sense?' Her breath was shaky and weak. 'I just don't think I can forgive her.'

'I know,' Noah said, and there was a brief pause that Briar knew meant he was gearing up to say more. He always seemed to understand her when it came to Alice, and it made sense, because they had both been heartbroken over her at one point. Even if Noah had never known the full story. 'It *is* okay to forgive her, though, if you want to. She was your friend first. If you're doing this out of some kind of loyalty—'

'I'm not,' Briar said, before he'd even finished his sentence. 'Alice and I...' She sighed, still at a loss for how to tell him what was going on. She would never be able to explain her feelings about Alice, especially to Noah. 'It's got nothing to do with you.'

'Cool,' Noah said. 'Just wanted to make sure you knew.'

Briar didn't know what else to say. She stayed like that, the landline receiver pressed to her cheek, cool against her overheated skin. She listened to Noah's breath, comforted by knowing he was there.

'Look...' Noah said, 'I'm not gonna pretend to understand why she never reached out to you after everything went down, but I do know what you were like after she left.' Briar scrunched her eyes shut against the onslaught of memories. Memories of sleepless nights that fall semester, of constantly checking her phone for messages, of drafting her own – paragraph after paragraph of apologies, explanations, appeals – of the deafening silence from across an ocean. 'I wasn't in great shape either, I know.' Noah sighed. 'I guess, just... be careful?'

Briar nodded, feeling like that advice had already come too late.

'I gotta go,' Briar said.

'Okay.'

She hung up, pausing for a moment before racing out the door and into the woods, trying to outrun her thoughts.

Chapter 12

Briar

The next time Briar saw Alice, she was brushing her teeth. Alice's face appeared next to hers in the mirror like a bad horror movie and Briar blinked, not convinced that it wasn't a continuation of the nightmare she'd woken from that morning.

'Whassup?' The words came out garbled around her toothbrush.

'There's an issue down at the lake,' Alice said. She was already dressed and teeming with too much energy.

'Of course,' Briar grumbled, then spat.

When she followed Alice outside, she was immediately assaulted by the harsh morning sunlight. Lines of sleepy children blindly followed their counselors to the bathrooms for showers. Breakfast wouldn't be ready for another hour at least. The day hadn't even started yet – she couldn't fathom what could have gone wrong already. She made a vague gesture for Alice to lead the way.

The problem became very apparent when they got to the lake.

'Well, that's not supposed to be there,' Briar said, staring at the speedboat drifting in the middle of the water and then at Freddie, who looked like he'd just been for a swim.

'Cabin 10 thought it would be a fun prank to untie it last night,' Freddie said. 'Don't worry, I've already dealt with them. They'll be cleaning the bathrooms today, listening to my *'90s Pop Princess* playlist. I can't think of anything more unpleasant for a group of thirteen-year-old boys. I'm off to supervise, good luck.' He saluted them, then took off down the path.

Briar grimly took stock of the situation. Because it was the only motorized boat on the grounds, they would have to row out to get it.

Her anxiety spiked with every jerk and wobble of the canoe as she and Alice slowly made their way towards the middle of the lake. When their discordant strokes led to a particularly bad rocking, Briar grabbed the side to keep from falling out.

'We have to pull together,' Alice said, looking over her shoulder at Briar, her frustration evident. 'Otherwise, we're just wasting energy.'

'I'm trying,' Briar said, huffing out a breath. She waited for Alice to dip her oar into the water before following suit, pulling hard. The boat teetered the other way. They were now zigzagging wildly, no closer to the speedboat.

'You did that on purpose,' Alice accused.

'No, I didn't.'

'Look,' Alice said, 'I'm not in the mood.'

Briar snorted. 'Oh, well, if you're not in the mood, then that's that.'

'What's that supposed to mean?' Alice bit out. She'd sped up, leaving Briar to match her pace, their paddles flying. The canoe rocked horribly, and Briar felt her stomach flip. This was exactly how they'd operated in school, with Alice dictating everything and expecting

Briar to follow her lead. It was how their friendship had ended the first time.

Briar gritted her teeth. 'I think you know.'

Alice whipped back around. 'No, actually, I don't. Why don't you enlighten me? Because from my perspective, this whole summer you've been punishing me. And I've just been taking it because—'

'Because *what*?' Briar asked, eyes narrowing.

Alice took a deep breath as if to calm herself. 'Because I deserve it, obviously. And I know you're going through a lot with Su—'

'Don't talk about my mother,' Briar snapped. All her pent-up frustration from the past few weeks rose up. It didn't matter that Alice was being helpful now, all Briar could focus on were the times that she hadn't been there. The years where Briar had needed to figure it all by herself. 'Why are you even here? Out of guilt? If I absolve you, will you leave me alone?'

'I can't,' Alice hissed. 'Not if you're going to sell the camp.'

Briar stopped rowing. 'What?'

Alice turned fully, her expression furious. 'Your dad said—'

'Oh, you're moving in on Tom now too?' Briar cut in.

Alice glared. 'I know about the appraisal. How could you not tell anyone? Don't you know how many people rely on this place? This is people's home. You can't just get rid of it.'

Briar had the awful impulse to laugh. 'Actually, I can. It was in my mother's will. I can do whatever I want.' She didn't need to justify her actions to Alice. She knew the implications of selling the camp, and Alice had surrendered any say over her life a long time ago. Alice opened her mouth, but Briar didn't want to hear another word.

'Ten years, and you didn't have the decency to reach out *once*?' It wasn't what she had meant to say; it wasn't where she wanted this conversation to go. She didn't want to hear whatever explanation Alice could come up with for what she had done to Briar – nothing she could say would make it hurt any less.

'Oh, we're talking about this now?' Alice's voice dripped with sarcasm. 'I thought we were still pretending you didn't care.'

Briar ignored her. This was the conversation she'd played out in her head a million times but never thought she'd get the chance to have. And it was all going wrong. She was too angry; she couldn't play it off like her life hadn't been miserable without Alice. The words came out like vomit.

'You completely ignore me, but not my mom? I don't know why I'm even surprised. I'm nothing compared to your precious Susan. Ten years of emails, huh? Did you finally get the parental validation you craved?'

There was a moment where it looked like Briar had stunned Alice into silence, before she spoke again, her voice low and angry. 'You were fine without me. You got Noah and all our friends, even fucking Harper. And I had nothing. I was completely alone. You have no idea how hard it is to see yourself replaced. You just carried on like I never existed.'

'Noah and I bonded over the messes we were after *you* left,' Briar said. 'And I'm sorry if my feelings are too much for you to handle, but' – her voice cracked – 'my mom got sick and you didn't even come home. I needed you and you weren't there. But you know who was? Harper.

So don't tell me I replaced you. You left. Was I supposed to wait for you to come back?'

'You didn't reach out either!'

'Reach out?!' Briar stood up, shouting now. 'You kissed me and then fucked off to Scotland!'

She had only a split second to remember that they were in a canoe before she lost her balance and plunged straight into the frigid water.

–

In the end, they left Sierra and Freddie to bring the boat back.

There was something humiliating about having to swim the overturned canoe back to shore, dump all the water out of it, and then trudge together, completely soaked, to the director's cabin. Briar felt like she had the morning after they'd kissed, the same nervous energy choking down anything she could have said to make it better. But now she knew she didn't have anything to apologize for.

The cabin door slammed shut behind them, and the only sound in the still air was the faint pitter-patter of water dripping onto the hardwood floor. The sound was driving Briar crazy – or maybe the lack of sound, the apology she desperately needed not materializing from Alice's lips – so she shucked off her shirt without thinking. It landed with a *thwack*. Alice followed suit, long arms stretching to pull her tank top over her head. Briar blinked at her, feeling like things were moving in slow motion, reminding her of a movie or a dream. Maybe even a dream she had dreamed before.

'I—' Alice looked at Briar helplessly, then seemed to gain some resolve. 'I didn't think you still cared. About what happened.'

Briar turned, sure her face would give her away. 'I don't.'

Alice tutted behind her. 'Then why bring it up?'

'Because I was mad,' Briar bit out, digging her nails into the flesh of her palm. The pain grounded her as she turned back to Alice. 'My mom told you she was dying before she told me.'

'Oh,' Alice said. She looked like she did when solving a particularly difficult math problem. 'But why bring up the kiss?'

'Jesus, it's not like I'm hung up over one lousy kiss. Sometimes I just say things. They don't have to mean anything.'

She willed Alice to believe her. She'd said a lot of things out on the lake that she hadn't meant to, not because they weren't important, but because they were. Alice watched her carefully, and Briar felt like she could see right through her.

'Like the parental validation thing?' Alice asked, crossing her arms, which only drew Briar's gaze to her chest. 'Because that was uncalled for. And not true. My mom and dad have always been my biggest supporters.'

'Sure,' Briar said. Having met Alice's mom and read her dad's emails, Briar knew that wasn't the case.

'And those were my private emails.' Alice's voice was becoming more heated. 'They weren't for you to read.'

'*That* was clear.'

'And whatever you read,' Alice continued doggedly, 'probably wasn't even true. I was really emotional when I was younger.'

'I disagree. Emotions were never your thing, even when we were younger,' Briar said archly. 'What are emotions to heavy doses of logic and denial?'

'I wasn't in denial,' Alice argued.

'Oh yeah?' Briar said. When Alice uncrossed her arms, Briar took in her light blue bralette for the first time. It looked like the one she'd worn the night they'd kissed. She remembered running her fingers along the lace of the cups, touching Alice there, and her cheeks burned. 'You wanna try that again, but more convincing this time?'

Alice took a step forward, a coy smile playing at her lips. This was the Alice that Briar had been missing all summer, the one that only came out at camp, playful and a little dangerous. Her eyes traced a droplet as it ran down Alice's cheek, along her throat, and then disappeared between her breasts. 'I was *never* in denial.'

Briar took half a step back, her thighs hitting the low dresser behind her. She had nowhere else to go; Alice had cornered her. 'So you're not running away this time?' Briar asked, barely above a whisper.

Alice's hands came to rest on the dresser on either side of Briar's hips. She was so close Briar could feel the heat radiating off her. When Briar tried to breathe in, the lace of Alice's bra dragged against her chest, drawing a gasp from her instead.

'I'm not,' Alice said, the words a burst of air against Briar's already hot face. It was hot in the room. It was so always so fucking hot when they were together. She met Alice's stare, mesmerized by the blue of her eyes, and leaned in.

There was a loud knock on the front door, and they sprang apart.

'Briar?' came a familiar voice. 'You there?'

'Noah?' Briar called back. Her brain was short-circuiting, the split second when her lips had grazed Alice's repeating over and over. Had they even touched, or had she just imagined it?

'Noah?!' Alice echoed in a panicked whisper.

Briar ignored her, pulling a shirt on and stumbling out of the cabin to see Noah standing on the porch, a large box at his feet and a sheepish expression on his face.

'Why are you here?' she asked, hovering in front of the door to discourage Noah from going inside and finding his ex-girlfriend half-naked in Briar's bedroom. '*How* are you here?'

'You said your AC was out.' He kicked the box towards her. 'So I hopped on a bus and Sierra picked me up from town.'

Briar stared down at the AC unit before leaping into his arms. As Noah squeezed her against him, Briar pushed away every feeling that didn't have to do with her best friend showing up and saving the day.

'Why are you all wet?' Noah asked.

Briar ignored him. 'Thank you.'

'Oh hey, Alice,' he said over her shoulder, and Briar released him.

'Hi, Noah,' Alice said, shifting awkwardly. Her face was flushed, but whether from embarrassment or annoyance, Briar wasn't sure. 'I'm needed in the mess hall. I think you guys can handle the installation alone.'

'Oh yeah,' Noah cut in, when Briar didn't respond. 'We've got it.'

Alice nodded, heading towards the mess hall, and Briar watched her go.

'Wow,' Noah said, disbelief evident in his voice.

'What?' Briar said, too quickly, nervous that her emotions were playing out on her face.

'Just a fairly icy atmosphere here,' he joked. 'You sure you even need this thing?'

Briar's wildly beating heart seemed to only now be calming, the flush of her skin returning to normal. 'Oh, trust me, it gets hot.'

Chapter 13

Alice

If Alice had thought that speaking in front of Briar and Noah at a funeral had been bad, it was nothing compared to sitting in Briar's car as they crawled through Fourth of July weekend traffic into DC. The holiday marked the break between sessions. Initially, Alice's plan had been to ruminate on what had happened between her and Briar for the entirety of the long weekend, maybe checking in on how Sierra and Freddie were handling the British campers staying over until the second session as a convenient excuse for staying at camp. But Noah had insisted that she get a lift back to DC with him and Briar for a real break, and Alice had never been able to say no to him. Some things, it turned out, hadn't changed since high school.

The road trip was different, though, like a twisted version of how it had been. Before, Alice would have been in the front seat playing sad indie music that Briar begrudgingly tolerated and Noah would've been stretching from the backseat to hold her hand on the console, a comfortable third wheel to her and Briar's friendship.

Now Alice was in the backseat, feeling like the most awkward third wheel of all time. As hard as watching their friendship from afar had been, seeing it up close was torture – being met so starkly with the realization that the life she once lived had gone on without her.

Briar had always insisted she didn't understand what Alice saw in Noah, so Alice hadn't expected their tentative alliance to survive without her as the connecting thread. But she'd supposed, and Briar had confirmed, that Alice's leaving had brought them together. She wondered how Noah had reacted when Briar had told him everything, about how unfaithful Alice had been to him. About how she'd been disloyal to them both, abandoning her friendship with Briar over a kiss that had meant nothing to Briar anyway.

The car ride could have been worse. Harper could've been there too, dealing out her trademark backhanded remarks along with everything else. And, to his credit, Noah was making a valiant attempt to pretend that everything was perfectly normal, asking Briar and Alice questions in turn and accepting their stilted answers as if they were having a normal conversation. Alice assumed he was doing it for Briar's benefit, sensing the tension in the car.

'Are you looking forward to the party?' Noah asked Briar, the third in a series of questions which had only earned him grunts or sighs in response so far.

This time, Briar just shot him a warning look that Alice assumed was meant to communicate *Not in front of Alice, she's not invited*. Alice became more confused about where they stood with each other every minute. The fight on the lake had been bad, but it was the conversation after that had left Alice reeling. She'd been cataloguing Briar's every move in the subsequent night and morning, and she'd been unable to draw any conclusive determinations.

If the brush of their lips had had any effect on Briar, Alice certainly couldn't tell.

For Alice, almost kissing Briar had reminded her of exactly why she hadn't come back. She couldn't stop thinking about it, playing it over and over in her head.

'I'm looking forward to the break between sessions,' Briar said, when it became clear that Noah was still waiting for an answer. 'Surrounded by non-sticky adults, AC that works and no raccoons.'

'That's good,' Noah said, turning to Alice. 'Are you excited to see your mom?'

'Um, yeah,' Alice said, cringing slightly as Briar's eyes met hers in the rearview mirror. Alice had always preferred for Noah to not understand her relationship with her parents, wanting him to see a version of her that both deserved and received unconditional love. 'I got an email a couple days ago from my advisor. He's read through my latest chapter and he thinks I'm nearly there. He's always saying I'm nearly there, though. I still feel like it needs tons of work.'

She omitted the part of the email where Jeremy had suggested that she should stop focusing on making what he referred to as 'minute edits' to the dissertation and instead start thinking about what she wanted to do after graduation.

'As long as you have professional success to share with her, it'll be a great visit,' Briar said lightly, as though it were a joke. Alice didn't know how to take it, so she decided to ignore it.

'How are your parents doing?' Alice asked Noah. She was genuinely curious, too. Noah's parents had always been kind to her, and she missed the warmth they had brought to her life.

'Good!' Noah said. 'They're excited for the wedding. My mom has been super helpful with planning, which Harper is grateful for. Juggling her nursing schedule and wedding planning is hard, and I'm useless with that kind of stuff.'

He told his ex-girlfriend about his wedding with an ease that would have astounded most people. One of the things Alice had loved most about Noah was his ability to defuse any awkward situation with genuine good humor. Alice had needed him for that in high school, when she'd never once been able to say the right thing in a conversation with her peers.

'He tries, though,' Briar said, her eyes not moving from the bumper of the car in front of them.

Noah nodded. 'I've become an Excel pro to keep us organized.'

'A useful skill set for a music teacher,' Briar teased, almost smiling now. The easy intimacy between the two of them, the way he quickly cheered Briar up, made Alice ache with regret.

'Every woman in STEM needs a failing artist boyfriend,' Noah said, grinning.

'Fiancé,' Briar corrected. 'You've been engaged for nearly a year, you'd think you'd have gotten used to it by now.'

'How is Harper?' Alice asked, because hearing about Noah and Harper's relationship seemed somehow less painful than witnessing the clear love between him and Briar.

They exchanged a look that Alice couldn't read, reminding her again that she no longer spoke their language. She felt like a sidelined actor, watching the scenes of her previous life play out before her and knowing that it wasn't the original script, but a warped imitation.

'She's good,' Noah said, a touch too cheerful this time.

'She's different now than she was in high school,' Briar said quickly.

It struck Alice right in the chest. She'd seen the birthday posts on Instagram, the declarations of *best friends forever*, and the pictures of the apartment they'd decorated together. It still made her feel hollow.

'What does that mean?' Noah asked, frowning. 'Harper was cool in high school. We were friends with her.'

'Oh, dude…' Briar said. 'You know she and Alice hated each other, right?'

Alice opened her mouth to protest, then closed it, not sure how to pull off a convincing lie.

'No,' Noah said, looking between the two of them, scandalized, 'that's not true.'

'It's true,' Briar confirmed. 'Tell him, Alice.'

'Harper and I were just… very different people back then,' Alice said diplomatically, not sure why Briar was doing this, 'but it was a long time ago. We're all different now.' She couldn't resist adding, 'I mean, I hardly recognized Briar when I saw her again.'

She was surprised to see Briar's expression flicker with hurt. 'You're one to talk. You've changed way more than I have. I mean, you've dropped the Barbie aesthetic—'

'That's a dramatic way to frame me not dyeing my hair anymore—' Alice started.

'And you weren't such a pushover,' Briar barreled on. 'I mean, you've spent the last session letting campers and parents walk all over you.'

'They're intimidating,' Alice retorted.

'And you once argued with the school principal – and won.' Briar caught her eye in the rearview mirror. 'Over a grading error.'

'Well…' Alice flushed; she'd forgotten about that. It had been eighth grade, and Briar had missed getting an A in Geometry over a rounding technicality. When their math teacher hadn't seen reason, Alice had been forced to go over his head.

'You didn't scare so easily back then,' Briar said quietly.

Alice had no idea what to say to that, the idea that she'd ever, at any point in her life, been fearless, or that she now lacked that apparently quintessential part of herself. She'd grant Briar that she used to be better with the kids than the past few weeks had shown, but anyone would have atrophied social skills with children after years of talking to mostly academics. She'd found herself treating them like particularly immature botany students as a compromise, which clearly hadn't been working.

Briar watched her in the rearview mirror, the same intensity in her gaze as the day before. And for the first time since getting in the car, Alice didn't look away. If Briar wanted brave Alice back, well, she could have her.

Still, Briar's face didn't betray any emotion. At least when she had been antagonizing her, Alice had known exactly where they stood. Now, she had no idea what was going on in Briar's head, and there was nothing Alice hated more than the feeling of not knowing something she should be able to work out.

'Hey, kids and parents can be tough!' Noah said, glancing between them in his first display of awkwardness. 'Believe me, us teachers know all about that.'

For the first time since they'd gotten in the car, it felt like Noah was the third wheel again. And Alice didn't know what to make of that.

–

'Mom?' Alice said, poking her head through the door to the study. Her mom had been out when she'd arrived the day before, and Alice hadn't had the chance to share her good news from Jeremy. She also was starting to feel very lonely in the house, which was strange since she spent almost all of her time in London alone without any issues. 'I was wondering if you wanted to go for a walk or something. Stretch our legs?'

Her mom turned from her hunched position over the keyboard. 'Oh, Alice,' she said, seeming faintly surprised even though Alice had told her she'd be back between sessions. 'You decided to come back from that camp of yours?'

'Just for the weekend,' Alice re-explained patiently.

'Very nice,' her mom replied, and Alice had the feeling that she hadn't registered the question about taking a walk. She didn't try again, knowing her mom didn't share her love of nature – it had been a pitch made out of desperation. 'And how are you?'

'Good,' Alice said, swallowing hard. She sometimes wondered what it would be like to have a mother who offered comfort, someone to commiserate with rather than hide her feelings from. But hypotheticals like that were hardly useful thought exercises.

'Glad to hear it,' her mom said.

'I actually wanted to talk to you about…' – Alice searched for some connection, something they could discuss – 'the wedding,' she finished, not knowing why she'd said that of all things.

'The wedding,' her mother echoed. 'Whose wedding?'

'Dad's,' Alice said quickly. 'I mean, I've decided I'm not going, and I wanted you to know.'

She wasn't entirely certain she had decided that until the words were out of her mouth, but they sounded true enough. It wasn't as though she was itching to come back to the US in the near future; it had worked out about as poorly as possible this time around. And, most importantly, they communicated to her mom what was important: Alice took her side in the divorce.

This show of loyalty, unfortunately, seemed to go entirely over her mother's head. 'That's nice,' she said. 'Because of your dissertation?'

'Um… yes,' Alice said. 'It sounds like Jeremy thinks it will be ready by spring. No need for another year of revisions.'

'Delighted to hear it,' her mom said. 'I'll come out for the graduation ceremony.'

She didn't ask what Alice was thinking about doing next, which was relieving but also confusing. Surely, she wanted to know what Alice's plans were with her degree, and whether she would be staying in London or moving somewhere else.

'Thanks,' Alice said, forcing a smile. 'It would be lovely to have you there.'

She wished she could talk about Briar, about Susan, about the things that had driven her away from this place, or even about something as simple as how terrible the last session had been. But her mom wouldn't understand any of it – she would have never cast aside her research over sentimental stuff like old friendship the way Alice had. She'd advise her to go back to London, if she asked.

And maybe, it struck her, that was the only reasonable thing to do.

Without saying anything else, because she knew her mom considered their conversation finished, she went to the backyard.

Her bare feet sank into the soft, long grass and she felt instant relief. This was one way in which home was unequivocally better than London. She had once spent all her time in this yard, grass-stained, staring at the clouds chasing each other through the sky. Living in the city, it was so easy to forget the life behind what she was studying. She dug her hand into the cool blades of grass.

Her phone buzzed with an Instagram DM.

noahpinion

hey! party's in an hour, come through!! :)

She found herself calling Tess.

'Hiya! Got service again?' Tess asked, and Alice closed her eyes, treasuring the sound of her voice. She hadn't managed to call Tess in a week, because her only free time seemed to be between midnight and two a.m., and she felt like she'd be keeping Briar up if she was on the phone. Instead, she would stare at the wall and compose emails to Susan in her head.

Dear Susan, I tried to make things better and only made them worse.

Dear Susan, I'm hurting Briar all over again, just by existing.

'I'm at my mom's for the weekend,' Alice explained. 'The second session starts on Monday and I rode up with

Noah and Briar because they have a Fourth of July party between sessions.'

There was a pause, then, 'And how's it going?'

Tears fell down her cheeks. Before Susan had died, Alice couldn't remember the last time she'd cried. Things didn't usually affect her much. It had taken her childhood ghosts rising back up to make her start feeling again.

'I'm coming back to London,' she admitted. She had hoped that saying it out loud would make it any easier. It didn't.

'Why?' Tess asked, thankfully without any hint that she'd noticed Alice crying.

'I can't do it,' Alice said. 'I'm a disaster. I don't know why I thought loving camp was enough to be a camp director. I'm letting the kids down,' she said, thinking of Robin in the director's office. 'And… I miss Susan.' Her voice broke on the word.

'Well, babe, of course you miss her,' Tess soothed. 'But I think you'd miss her just as much if you were here, wouldn't you?'

'No,' Alice said, more forcefully than she'd intended. 'You don't understand, everything here reminds me of her. I can't stop thinking about her, and how I'm failing her.' The tears were streaming now.

'Coming home isn't going to fix that,' Tess said reasonably. 'Maybe you'd think about her less if you were here, but thinking about her isn't a bad thing. You're grieving, of course you're thinking about her.' There was a long pause. 'And if you don't want to come home a failure, then you only have one option, and that's to turn things around. I know you can do it. You're the most brilliant person I've ever met. If anyone can do this, it's you.'

Alice sat up, wiping at her eyes. 'God, what have I done to deserve you?'

'I believe you made the great sacrifice of buying me a drink at a seedy bar when we were eighteen and haven't managed to shake me since.'

She choked out a laugh. 'Can't believe you were bought for six quid. Ought to raise your rates.'

'I have,' Tess said drily. 'But I was both skint and dazzled by your eyes.'

'I love you and your faith in me,' Alice said seriously. 'But I really don't think there's a point in sticking around. Briar is planning on selling the camp at the end of the summer.'

'So give everyone one last great summer to remember the camp by.' When Alice didn't respond, Tess kept going, her tone soft. 'Anyway, you're leaving, so it's not like it makes much of a difference to you if it's sold or not.'

'Right,' she said, because of course Tess would think that, even though it felt like the most catastrophic loss in the world to Alice. There was only so much about who she was when she was here that she could ever expect Tess to understand.

'And Briar?'

'Umm…' Alice stalled, trying to think of anything other than Briar's lips brushing hers. She was beginning to accept that it might be the only thing she'd think about for the rest of her life.

'Ah,' Tess said, in a knowing tone.

'What?'

'Something happened,' Tess said, and Alice considered rescinding her just-uttered declaration of love. 'That's why you're trying to leave, isn't it?'

Alice groaned, putting her head between her knees. 'No, nothing happened.' Tess didn't respond, waiting for her to say more. 'Like I'd do something as incredibly idiotic as come back home and try to make amends with my ex-best friend who I kissed and then ran away from, only to kiss her and run away from her all over again.'

She hadn't thought about it that way until it had come out of her mouth, and it made going back to London seem like the cowardly option.

'You kissed her?!' Tess exclaimed.

'Well, that's a slight exaggeration,' Alice said.

She thought back to Briar's breath on her cheeks, her hazel eyes flashing. The first time they had kissed, Alice hadn't been able to look at Briar without her whole life realigning before her eyes. Briar had made her thoughts too dangerous, and that was what Alice had been running from the whole time. Looking at Briar had made anything seem possible, when Alice knew it wasn't. She was worried the same thing was happening again now.

'How slight?' Tess asked.

Their lips had touched, hadn't they? She could remember the feeling of it, just barely, but maybe that was her overactive imagination after years of picturing their lips touching again. In her mind, she and Briar had already kissed a thousand times.

'It was over before it started,' she said. 'Noah interrupted us.'

'Noah was there?!' Tess nearly screeched. 'The most interesting thing to happen to either of us in years and you didn't call me immediately? Tell me everything, now, and maybe I'll find it in my heart to forgive you.'

'It wasn't like that. He didn't know anything happened, he just knocked on the door and we were, um, startled.'

An alarming thought occurred to Alice. 'Unless Briar's told him already, which I guess she probably has— Shit. There goes Noah not completely hating me.'

'Alice, focus,' Tess chided. 'We don't have time for boys right now. You just kissed the girl you've been in love with for ten years. Have you talked to Briar about what this means?'

'I'm not in love with her,' Alice said, burying her face in her hands. 'I know you're still stuck on that, but can we please move on? I was infatuated with her once. I'm not anymore. And am I really supposed to talk to her about what it means that I've kissed her twice now when she wasn't asking for or expecting it? Sounds like an exercise in humiliation.'

'After all that, you think the best option is to leave?' Tess asked, incredulous. 'Is it really about the kiss, or is it something else?'

'Of course it's not just the kiss. It's the way she looks at me like she hates me, or worse, doesn't know who I am. I thought I'd feel less alone in losing Susan if I was with her, but I feel more alone than ever. And I'm worried she feels the same.'

'I'll never forgive you if you leave without talking to her,' Tess said, and Alice snorted. 'I'm not having a laugh, I'm serious. No one to tell you to get your shit together like your best mate. And you need to get your shit together in a big way. I'm not going to let you do what you did last time and take another ten years to recover from it. If you're going to leave, you at least need to tell Briar to her face what you're doing and why.'

'That sounds horrible,' Alice mumbled.

'Sometimes the right thing *is* horrible,' Tess said cheerily. 'It's called being an adult.'

She groaned. 'Why are you always right?'

'So,' Tess continued, not letting her off easily, 'when are you going to talk to her, then?'

'Her party's in an hour, so I guess I'll call her tomorrow morning before she drives back to camp.'

'How do you know when the party starts?' Tess asked, suspicious.

'Noah invited me' – she sucked in a breath before Tess could interrupt – '*not* because anyone actually wants me there, but because he's physically incapable of not being a ray of fucking sunshine.'

Tess gasped, much to Alice's chagrin. 'Oh, you've *got* to go to the party.'

'I'm not going—'

'You will *not* deny me this drama. You're going to the party and you're going to drink some beer and make merry or whatever it is you Yanks do, and then you're going to grow up and have an honest conversation with Briar, because she deserves that.'

'Well, the last part, sure…' Alice said dubiously.

'Oh, I'm sorry, do you have other plans? To putter around the house and feel sorry for yourself?'

Alice thought of another night with nothing to do in her silent, uncreaky house with her silent, uncaring mother and shivered in the nearly hundred-degree humidity.

'Okay, I'll go.'

Chapter 14

Alice

Alice couldn't remember the last time she'd been to a party, or, at least, the type of party that splayed out before her as she entered Briar's house. Her flat could fit five friends before it started to feel claustrophobic – that was, if she had five friends – and there were at least fifty people already crammed into the narrow living room.

A hand tugged on her arm, and she turned to find Rafa, one of Noah's friends, beaming at her.

'Alice!' he cried, wrapping his arms around her and thankfully managing not to slosh his beer all over her in the process. 'Oh my god, I thought it was you, but then I thought maybe I was tripping. No one told me you'd be here!'

'Hey, Rafa,' Alice said, desperately wishing she'd taken a shot for courage before coming in. She felt shaky and unpracticed at small talk.

Maybe noticing her expression, he herded her towards the kitchen, pointing to the fridge. 'Beer's in there. Liquor's on the counter.'

'Beer's fine,' she said, grabbing an IPA and taking several large gulps before turning back to him. He was still wearing a huge smile that made her feel like he was expecting her to launch into a circus routine. She refrained from asking *What do you want from me?* which she decided would be a weird and maybe even hostile question.

'So, how have you been?' he asked.

'Oh, good.' She leaned against the kitchen counter and winced at the stickiness.

Rafa raised his eyebrows at her expression. 'These things always have a college feel to them,' he explained. 'Or *uni* to you, I guess.' He chuckled. 'Keeps us young. I promise Briar can be classy when she tries.'

Alice looked around, noting the touches that she'd missed as she'd been taking in the abundance of bodies and booze. There were plants perched on the windowsills, a collection of colorful cake plates sitting on top of the kitchen cabinets, and several quirky lamps within eyesight.

'It's a nice place,' she admitted.

'Much nicer than my dump in New York, anyway,' Rafa said. 'I have about 500 square feet to share with my roommate, and only one of us has a bedroom window.'

'Is it you?' Alice asked politely, taking a few more sips of beer in quick succession.

'Nah, I make him pay more for the room with the window. I'm usually sleeping when it's light out, so it works out for me.' He grinned. 'And how's London?'

'Very little sunlight, even with a window in my bedroom and being awake during the day,' Alice said. 'What do you do again?'

Rafa put his hand to his chest in mock offense. 'And here I thought you were a part of my fan club! I'm wounded.'

'Sorry,' Alice mumbled.

'Just joking,' he said hastily, and she remembered that this was the sort of banter they'd have had back in high school. There was a whole school year where she and

Rafa had had a running joke that they were enemies, but Alice had never been fully confident it was a joke on his end. He'd been Noah's friend, after all, and she'd taken up Noah's free time and then broken his heart for good measure.

'Are you still DJing?' she ventured, thinking back to his social media posts during college – a series of photos of him on a dark stage with captions pleading for people to come to his shows.

'See, you *do* know!' he said, clapping her on the shoulder. 'I've actually been booking stuff recently, which is pretty sweet.'

'Hey, man!' Noah's voice came from behind Alice. She turned to see him with Harper and her fleeting hopes of not being completely awkward evaporated.

'Hey, Alice,' Harper said, looping an arm around Noah's waist. 'Cute top.'

Her tone was innocent enough, but Alice recognized the comment immediately as one she would have made in high school when Alice was dressed incorrectly for the occasion. She glanced down at her slightly too-small white frilly top, dotted with embroidered cherries. It was the closest thing in her high school wardrobe to red, white, and blue, but it was garish upon second review.

'They changed the forecast,' Noah said to Rafa, oblivious to the slight. 'It's not supposed to rain anymore, so fireworks are on.'

Harper's eyes widened. 'You didn't.'

'You're looking at someone who illegally transported fireworks across state lines, baby,' Rafa confirmed, pointing two thumbs at his chest and looking far too pleased with himself.

'Come on,' Alice blurted out, 'you guys are really trusting the weather report?'

'Whether it rains or not, it's still illegal.' Harper nodded as though agreeing with Alice.

'But most importantly, you're listening to meteorologists,' Alice said.

'Oh my god,' Rafa said, choking on a laugh. 'I forgot about your beef with meteorologists. This is my favorite Alice-ism.'

'It's not *beef*,' Alice corrected. 'It's logic. The whole point of science is to make sense of the world that we live in, so why do I feel more confused every time I open the weather app?'

'Oh, right,' Noah said, snapping his fingers before pointing at Alice as though he'd pulled a trivia answer from the back of his head. 'You think meteorology is pseudoscience.'

'Of course it is,' she scoffed. 'Would you trust someone who lied to you every day, knowing they would be caught out immediately?'

'No,' Harper said.

'Exactly,' Alice said, waving her now-empty beer bottle in agreement. Her limbs felt loose with alcohol. IPAs always snuck up on her. 'Why? Because it doesn't just make them unreliable, it also makes them *stupid*.'

'Oh, are we talking about meteorologists?' Briar asked, sliding into the circle and grabbing the solo cup out of Harper's hand to take a sip. 'It's impressive that you can turn any conversation into your tight-five on meteorology, Alice.' She gave no sign that she was either surprised or annoyed to find Alice in her home.

'I brought it up,' Noah said, like the loyal ex-boyfriend he was.

'Man, I've missed you,' Rafa said, straightening and wiping a single tear of laughter from his eye as he looked at Alice. He turned back to the fridge and handed her another beer, cheers-ing demonstratively before they each took large gulps.

A warmth spread through Alice at being in on the joke. It felt unreal to be standing in a circle of her high school friends, as though she still belonged here. As though she'd never even left. She wondered what that life would be like, if that alternate Alice was happy here. It would certainly look very different from London, where Alice rarely left her flat except to take the train to Oxford.

'Rafa,' Briar said, 'help me with the grill?'

'On it.' He hugged Alice from the side. 'Catch up later?'

'Mmkay,' she said into his shoulder before he departed along with Briar. 'That was weird,' Alice said, blinking at Noah in confusion. 'I never thought he liked me very much.'

'What?' Noah said, his brows pulling together. 'Of course Rafa liked you.'

'Just a theory,' Harper said, her tone dry, 'but have you ever considered that you're not good at telling when people like you?'

Alice had nothing to say to that. She didn't want to voice what she'd suspected for years: that nobody except Briar had talked to her at school before she'd started dating Noah, so it followed that they'd all only liked her for his sake.

Harper didn't seem to notice Alice's silence. 'I see Valentina mixing margs outside, I'm gonna grab one.'

She kissed Noah on the cheek and went out the back door, greeted by hollers from a girl Alice assumed was Valentina.

Noah shook his head ruefully, then looked back at Alice. 'So, how are you doing? How's camp?'

Alice shifted uncomfortably. 'You don't have to talk to me. You can hang out with your friends.'

'I *want* to talk to you,' Noah said, as though he were explaining something obvious. 'It's been a while.'

Alice narrowed her eyes at him suspiciously, the beer making her a little too honest. 'I don't get it. How can you be so nice to me after what I did to you?'

'Neither of us was perfect,' Noah said, like it was that simple. Alice was gripped with the desire to shake him by the shoulders, just to get him to finally be annoyed at her – which was how she knew she was definitely the less perfect of the two of them.

'Maybe, but you were a hell of a lot closer,' she said, taking another sip of beer. 'Shit, I'm doing this all wrong, aren't I?'

Noah grinned, she assumed in reaction to her tipsy cursing. 'What are you doing wrong?'

Alice took a deep breath, with only the alcohol fueling her next words. 'I meant to apologize as soon as I had a moment alone with you. Because I'm so sorry for how things ended. So, so, fucking sorry. So—' She hiccupped.

'Fucking sorry?' Noah guessed, raising his eyebrows. 'Yeah, I got that.'

Alice ran her hand over her face. 'I'm trying to explain.'

'You're doing great,' Noah said. 'You're sorry. That part's covered. Can I say my piece?'

Alice squinted at him, trying to figure out his angle, and then nodded.

'Look, I spent a lot of time thinking about what I could have done differently, so that you didn't feel like you could never face me again. I mean, am I that scary?' He paused, but Alice just stared at him, confused, and he finally shrugged. 'It was a long time ago. We were just kids. And I'm getting married to the love of my life, so I think it all worked out.'

'What *you* could have done differently?' Alice echoed, stuck on that phrase. 'You must know there wasn't anything you could have done. It was my fault.'

Noah tsked. 'When you told me before graduation that you didn't want to try long distance, I should have just accepted that. I shouldn't have drawn it out, pretending things were fine while you were at camp. Then I wouldn't have been blindsided by you showing up to my house and telling me things were really over between us.'

'Even if we'd ended things before camp, I don't know that it would have made a difference,' Alice said honestly. 'I don't know that I would have been able to come back, either way.'

Because it wasn't the kiss itself that had upended Alice's life, but how it had brought everything into focus. When she'd seen Noah for the last time, after spending the entire car ride to his house thinking about Briar's body clinging to hers, she'd realized she'd been unfaithful to him for far longer than she'd been aware of. Every inside joke and teasing touch with Briar had taken on an entirely new meaning. She'd been openly flirting with her best friend in front of him, and she hadn't even noticed herself doing it.

It had made her wonder if cheating was her destiny the whole time, if history was bound to repeat itself. Alice knew the power of inheritance better than most.

'I'm sorry you felt that way,' Noah said, his eyes soft.

'I guess I just couldn't deal with the shame of it. And it just kept growing every year I was gone.'

'You felt that ashamed?' Noah asked.

'Yes,' she said. Surely Noah understood her enough to know that Alice's worst fear was ending up like her dad. But, then again, she had never let him see that side of her. She had never let him know she was afraid of anything at all.

Noah's expression grew wistful. 'I thought you'd eventually come back, we'd talk, and we could be friends again. You were the person I told everything to.' He paused, glancing meaningfully at where Briar stood on the porch. 'I know I wasn't that for you, but I was something, wasn't I?'

'Of course you were,' Alice said softly.

He nodded as though he'd truly been waiting for confirmation, which made her ache with regret. 'But you're here now,' he said finally. 'So, friends?' He extended his hand towards her for a shake.

'Oh.' Alice was taken aback. 'Of course. But, um, you should know that I'm leaving.'

His hand fell to his side again. 'What?' he asked, sounding genuinely disappointed.

She winced. 'I came today to tell Briar that I'm going back to London.' She tried for a smile. 'Turns out she's better off without me after all. Figures.'

Noah eyed Briar through the window again, and Alice turned her head for what she hoped was a semi-subtle assessment. Rafa was laughing through the cloud of smoke emitting from the grill, but Briar's eyes were wide as she stared into the leaping flames.

'Is there any part of you,' Noah said, looking through the window, 'that still considers Briar your best friend?'

Alice finished her beer in one large gulp, wishing it were something stronger. 'Is that relevant?'

'I think you're still hers.'

'Oh,' Alice said stupidly.

'And you're the only one she let help with camp. Harper and I offered, she turned us down, and that was that. But you didn't take no for an answer… and she let you.' He looked at her, his eyes searching. 'Don't you think that means something?'

'Well, yes,' Alice said. 'That I'm a presumptuous, high-handed, self-righteous—'

'If she didn't want your help, she wouldn't have let you help,' he said, spreading his hands out in front of himself as though to ward off her attack.

'I didn't give her much choice.'

He nodded. 'Why did you offer?'

'Guilt,' Alice said simply. 'That I didn't come back sooner, when Susan got sick the first time. I wanted to apologize for never talking to her about what happened that last summer and running away from her instead.'

'Running away from *her*?' Noah cocked his head at her. 'What do you mean?'

She had missed something crucial in their conversation. Finally, Noah's words, every confusing comment, slid into place in her brain, where the alcohol had previously not allowed them to align.

'Shit,' she said.

'What?'

'What do you think happened that summer, Noah?' she asked, almost not wanting to hear the answer.

'I don't know,' Noah said, frowning at her. 'You figured out you were a lesbian, I assume?'

Alice leaned back against the fridge, lightheaded. She tried to think things through linearly, but her brain wasn't cooperating.

If Noah didn't know about the kiss, it meant that Briar never told him. Which meant that Alice had some questions for Briar. Questions she needed answered now.

—

Alice spent the rest of the party trying to get Briar alone, but it seemed that whenever she spotted her in the mass of bodies, Briar would disappear again. Alice had all but given up, nursing her fourth beer by the back door, when Rafa found her.

'There you are! We're playing beer pong. Briar needs a partner, you in?'

Alice nodded eagerly and hopped off the counter, stumbling but recovering quickly. 'Lead the way.'

In the dining room, a crowd surrounded a worn, ornate table. Briar was racking up a set of cups, while Harper poured beer into the opposing set.

'You said you were getting Noah,' Briar said, her lips pouting in a way Alice found incredibly distracting.

Rafa shrugged. 'I found Alice first, and I know how competitive she is.' He punched her on the arm and winked. 'Figured this way you may have a chance to beat the champs!' He pounded his chest.

Alice rolled her eyes but made her way to Briar's side of the table. If nothing else, she'd be able to corner Briar after the game and ask her the questions that had been swirling in her mind for hours now. They kept coming, tempting her with the possibility of realigning what had happened in the years Alice was gone, the years she had been certain no one wanted her to come home.

If Briar had never told Noah, then a part of Briar, however deeply buried, still was loyal to Alice. Still protected her, even from her own actions. Which meant that Briar hadn't been able to replace Alice as easily as she'd feared, the same way Alice had never been able to replace the person Briar had been to her.

'Winner goes first,' Harper said, bouncing a ping-pong ball on the table and forcing Alice to focus on the scene in front of her.

She easily sunk it into the center cup. The crowd whistled and cheered as Alice drank. The beer was warm and watery, but it went down easily.

Gasping in her next breath, she wiped the foam from her mouth and nodded at Briar, who brought the ball up to aim, her brows furrowed in concentration, her lips wet and open. In that moment, Alice was sure she'd never seen anyone more beautiful, and her eyes stayed on Briar even as the ball sank into a cup.

She pulled her gaze away as Rafa's next shot bounced off the rim of a cup.

'Better luck next time,' Alice chirped, aiming for a cup on the end.

'Yes!' she exclaimed when the ball sunk. She raised her hand towards Briar, who eyed it for a moment, as though suspicious of Alice's good mood, before high fiving her.

Rafa glared at them as he drank. 'I forgot what you two were like as a team.'

They continued until both sides were down to two cups. Alice had hit her sweet spot of being just drunk enough that muscle memory took over.

'Nice one,' Briar said, beaming as Alice sank another shot. Alice would play beer pong for an eternity if it meant that Briar would keep looking at her like that.

Harper passed the cup to Noah, who'd joined the crowd mid-game, for him to drink.

'Cheater,' Alice cried, slamming a hand on the table. She misjudged the force of her blow and stumbled slightly. Briar's hands grasped her arms, steadying her. Alice wished she didn't notice how warm they were, and how her skin still burned even after Briar had withdrawn.

It was Rafa's turn to throw, and by the looks of it he wasn't faring any better than Alice. He squinted, clearly trying to regain his depth perception. Still, the ball landed firmly in the center of one of the cups.

'Let's goooo!' Rafa cried, flexing his muscles for the crowd.

'We've got this,' Briar whispered. As she drank, Alice noticed a droplet escape from the side of the cup and down Briar's chin. She pulled her eyes away from Briar's throat after she'd finally finished what seemed like an endless chug, wordlessly gesturing for her to throw.

'You got this.'

Briar grinned at her, not looking away as she threw the ball. Alice was so caught up in her gaze, she almost didn't notice the uproar around them. Briar's ball had sunk. They'd won.

Briar whooped, slinging her arms around Alice's waist and jumping in celebration. She tucked her face into Alice's shoulder and Alice was hit with a floral scent that she knew immediately was the same perfume Briar had used in high school: honeysuckle and bergamot.

In the last decade, Alice had been so caught up in the aftermath of their kiss, had overanalyzed every mistake she'd made the morning after, that she had never considered anything beyond her initial assumption that it had just been practice for Briar. That the kiss would have been the same with Alice or anyone else. But maybe Briar not telling Noah meant that the kiss hadn't meant nothing to her, like she had said. Maybe it had meant something to Briar the same way it had meant something to Alice.

The roar of the party hit Alice all at once, and she grabbed Briar's arm, feeling dizzy. Briar turned to her, confusion in her eyes.

'Can we talk?' Alice asked.

Chapter 15

Briar

Alice was looking at her, eyes glassy, and Briar suddenly felt too exposed in the swarm of people huddled in her living room. She slid a hand into Alice's and wondered if hands could remember each other, as their fingers found their preferred positions through memory alone.

She tugged Alice through the crowd and up the stairs, leading her down the hall towards her bedroom, the roar of the party cutting out as Briar closed the door behind them. A salt lamp, nestled among the trinket dishes on her dresser, cast the room in a soft pink light.

She'd cleaned up a bit, on the off chance the party made it to the second floor, but she still felt self-conscious having Alice in her room. Most of the furniture had come from her childhood bedroom, taken from the house she'd grown up in when her mom had moved closer to camp. Distantly, she recognized her bed was the same one she and Alice had slept in during countless sleepovers.

Alice watched her, a dazed look on her face that Briar knew meant she'd had one too many drinks.

'Do you want to lie down?' Briar asked. In high school, the roles had been reversed. Briar had always been the one letting loose, with Alice taking care of her. But the urge to make sure Alice was okay was something Briar felt instinctively.

Alice shook her head, but sat on the bed. 'I talked to Noah.'

Briar nodded, though she was confused by this topic of conversation. Noah wasn't a subject they'd broached in their few weeks together and Briar had taken him as one of the things, among many, that would remain unspoken between them.

'And?' she said, when it looked like Alice wouldn't say more. Alice sighed, letting her head fall into her hands. For a moment, Briar was worried she might be crying, but when she raised her head again her eyes were dry, and maybe a bit clearer.

'He didn't know about us,' she said, gaze boring into Briar. She had the vague sense that something between them was shifting, but didn't know how. 'You didn't tell him about us.'

The way she said it was more a question than a statement, and Briar nodded again. 'Of course not.'

As she said it, she wondered if it would have been obvious to anyone else. She couldn't explain why she had never told Noah about the kiss; it wasn't as if there hadn't been moments she had considered it. But what had started as simple self-preservation had become a secret too sacred and twisted to share with anyone else. That night had only ever been between her and Alice.

'Why not?' Alice asked.

That was Alice, needing the empirical evidence of every situation, needing to know the catalyzing event and the resulting reactions. It was something Briar admired about her, but that also left her feeling like she'd never fully measure up. Briar couldn't contain her feelings to strict labels. She often didn't know the reasons why she did anything, and certainly not well enough to explain them to anyone else.

Alice was looking at her intently, like whatever Briar said next was vitally important. It was a kind of pressure that Briar couldn't handle, not surrounded by her mother's old furniture, not with her entire future still only outlined in pencil.

'What was I supposed to say? That you gave me my first kiss and it was so bad you had to flee the country?' Briar joked. Alice visibly deflated, her whole body slumping.

'That's not why,' she mumbled into her hands. Her hair fell in a curtain around her, hiding her expression. It looked lighter in the pink glow of the lamp, reminding Briar of its color in high school. Briar had obsessed over her hair, convinced there was power in its sheen. Alice had worn it like a weapon, or, now Briar realized, maybe more like a shield. 'It was a good kiss.'

Briar grinned despite herself, some part of her still needing to hear that from Alice, though it was a small consolation for nearly a decade of heartache. Without thinking, she crossed the room to sit beside her.

'I've gotten better.'

Alice scoffed, leaning to the side. Her warm skin brushed Briar's, and the pressure was back in her lungs, making it hard to breathe. She thought about the last time they'd been this close, in the cabin, with Alice's lips just a hairbreadth away. If she was being honest with herself, she hadn't stopped thinking about it, and now it was consuming her.

Briar's hand moved without conscious thought, coming to rest on Alice's thigh just below the hem of her shorts, her thumb rubbing at the frayed edge there. Alice inhaled sharply, her head turning, bringing her face much closer to Briar's.

'If this is your best move, I'm not so sure,' she teased, and Briar flushed. Maybe it was being away from camp, maybe it was being in her own room, but having Alice there with her was like something out of a dream.

'I could prove it to you.' It came out as a whisper.

'We did get interrupted last time,' Alice said, her hand skimming up Briar's arm. 'One kiss couldn't hurt.'

It was an echo of what she'd said years ago, and Briar fell for it just the same. She had the same rush in her ears, the same frenetic energy in her veins singing that *this was it*, this was happening, finally, finally, finally. She leaned in.

Her lips pressed against Alice's slowly but firmly. She breathed in the smell of beer and something vaguely sweet that she recognized as Alice's skin. And then Alice's hand tangled into her hair, cupping the back of her skull and pulling her closer. She nipped at Briar's lower lip, moaning softly.

She'd forgotten that this was how Alice kissed, fast and wild. For all the control Alice exercised in her life, there was nothing of it in the press of her lips. She kissed so desperately that Briar struggled to breathe.

They pulled away and stared at each other for a moment, then Alice was back in her arms, pushing her down on the duvet and sliding on top of her. Briar's hands went to the dips of Alice's hips, rucking up her top and reveling in the smooth skin underneath.

'It was never about you,' Alice whispered against the skin behind Briar's ear, dropping a kiss there then mouthing down her throat. Briar's mind was racing, her brain shorting out at the draw of Alice's tongue across her collarbone. She'd forgotten everything that wasn't this exact moment.

'What?' Her voice cracked, her whole body shaking with the effort to keep from getting lost in the feeling of Alice's body against her own. Her fingers tucked under Alice's shirt, stroking up her spine, grazing along the lace edge of her bralette.

Alice sat up. Locking eyes with Briar, she reached for the hem of her top and pulled it off along with her bra. Briar's mouth went dry. This was much further than the fumbled groping they had done as teenagers. She stared at Alice's naked chest, her brain trying to take in every single detail. Alice grabbed Briar's hands and moved them to cup her breasts.

'Me leaving,' Alice said, pulling Briar up for a kiss. Together, they managed to wrestle Briar's tank and bra off. 'I cheated on Noah. That was why.' She ducked her head, kissing down Briar's chest and then mouthing at her nipple. She looked up at Briar through hooded eyes, a smile playing at her lips, and Briar's mind went blank.

'No more talking,' she said, falling back onto the bed and pulling Alice with her. Briar kissed her cheeks, her jaw, her throat, everywhere she could reach, the smooth slide of skin against skin overwhelming her. Alice's hands were back in her hair, pulling at the roots, the sharp pain pounding through to her core, and then she was lost to the feeling.

—

The incessant beeps of a garbage truck in the nearby alley woke Briar up early the next morning. She opened her eyes, glancing out the window to see the barest of pink streaks in the sky. The city was still asleep, and so was the girl beside her.

Alice's arm was slung over Briar's waist, her fingers wedged into the crook of skin where thigh met hip. They were pressed tight together on Briar's twin bed, sticky from the heat between their bodies. Briar kicked off the blanket covering her legs, careful not to disturb Alice.

She tried to go back to sleep, but the magnitude of what had happened the night before couldn't be ignored. Flashes of it swirled in her mind as she absentmindedly flexed her muscles, taking stock of where she was sore.

She groped for her phone, finding it tucked between the mattress and the wall. She had a few messages, mainly from her roommates working out the cleaning tasks for the morning. She had three from Noah asking her where she'd gone, another telling her that he and Harper were leaving and, finally, one more asking for proof of life. She hearted his final text and sent off a quick reply saying she'd fallen asleep.

Despite the amount of alcohol that had been in her system the night before, she felt a lightness that reminded her of happiness. Alice mumbled something, her breath hot against Briar's neck, and then turned over.

It was miraculous, Alice in her bed. Alice back in her life. If anyone had asked her what her summer would've looked like two months ago, she'd have been so wrong it was almost funny. Ex best friend in her bed after nearly a decade, working at camp again of all places, mom dead.

Her heart clenched in the now-familiar way it did when her thoughts accidentally stumbled into her mother. The beginning of a headache grew behind her eyes. Of course, the afterglow couldn't last forever.

She got up, tiptoeing across the hall to the bathroom. As she brushed her teeth, her mind was no longer blissfully quiet, but instead descending into a discomforting fuzziness. She stared at her reflection, at the mascara melting into the bags under her eyes. She spat.

Briar carefully crept downstairs, avoiding the floorboards she knew creaked. In the kitchen, she filled two large glasses with water and then rummaged in a drawer for a bottle of painkillers. She grabbed a carton of strawberries before heading back upstairs.

Alice hadn't stirred yet, so Briar gently set a glass and two pills on the bedside table. She nibbled on the strawberries, something about the night before nagging at her. As she scrubbed through the party and its aftermath, she searched for clues unfiltered by the haze of lust and instead with the clarity that only came from sobriety.

They'd been talking about Noah. Because for some reason, they couldn't talk about their friendship without it relating back to Alice and Noah. Alice had said it, the fallout from that night had been about Noah, and not about Briar at all. *It was never about you.*

A chill crept over Briar, but she refused to pull the blankets back over herself no matter how much she wanted to. Getting back into bed with Alice felt dangerous now, everything that had happened the night before suddenly tainted by this new memory.

Briar had spent the greater part of the last decade going over their kiss in excruciating detail. It was the thing she thought about when sleep evaded her, examining what had happened from every possible angle. Thinking through everything she could've done differently to change the outcome, to stop Alice from leaving.

It had never occurred to her that the implosion of her friendship with Alice might have had nothing to do with her at all. To Briar, what had happened that night had been about the two of them, about Alice being unsure of her sexuality, about Briar being too forward, or them being too close friends to do something as stupid as kiss.

But if Alice had only left because she couldn't face cheating on Noah, then Briar hadn't factored into the decision at all. She was the catalyst but not the cause; she could've been anyone and Alice would have left all the same.

She bolted off the bed, barely making it to the toilet before vomiting. She stayed like that for a while, head propped against the porcelain lip, enjoying the coolness against her skin. Last night Alice had asked for one kiss, and Briar had given her everything instead. She had let Alice have as much as she wanted. All for a girl she hated, a girl who would leave her again, a girl who had never, ever wanted her back.

Finally, she pulled herself off the floor.

When she re-entered her room, Alice was blinking, bleary-eyed, at her. She grabbed the water Briar had brought her, gulping it down immediately and breaking off with a gasp. Neither of them spoke.

Briar's ears were ringing, louder and louder, warning her that this was going to be exactly like last time. That Alice was going to leave again.

'Are you coming back to bed?' Alice asked.

'Not yet,' Briar said. Alice sat up more fully, seeming to sense Briar's mood.

'We should talk,' Alice said, her voice pitching up as if it were a question. She hugged her knees to her chest, a motion that reminded Briar of her younger self.

'Yeah,' Briar said, sitting in the armchair in the corner. She stared at Alice, willing her to say something that would get rid of the dread in Briar's stomach. Whatever happened next, it had to come from Alice.

'Obviously, last night was irresponsible of us – of me.' Alice pulled at a loose thread of the sheet. 'I'm sorry. It won't happen again.'

Briar wanted to laugh, if only to drown out the voice in her head saying *I told you so*. She no longer had it in herself to be mad. Instead, she was numb. It was her own fault, because she *knew* Alice, and expecting anything more from her was pointless. Whatever she'd been hoping for Alice to say, she knew now she would never hear.

And honestly, Alice was doing her a favor. Briar had always wished she'd behaved differently all those years ago, that maybe if she hadn't worn her heart on her sleeve, she wouldn't have gotten hurt. Well, here was her chance.

'Yeah, obviously it won't happen again,' she said.

They'd done it. It was out of her system. And she'd keep telling herself that until it was true.

Alice stared at her, her expression inscrutable. 'But… I don't want us to go back to being at odds either. I feel like we're in a place where we could be friends again. If that's something you'd want? I mean—'

'Sure,' Briar said, interrupting what she was sure would be a painful rejection and squashing the feeling that she was making a terrible mistake. Alice was leaving in a few weeks anyway. Surely Briar could stay sane for that long.

Chapter 16

Briar

After their morning conversation, things were surprisingly easier between them. It was like the thing that they'd been avoiding since meeting again was now out of the way, and they could move on. They loaded up Briar's car with supplies, stopped at Alice's house to get her bag, and then were on the highway headed back to camp before noon.

Briar only lasted an hour in their not-quite comfortable silence, before turning off the highway.

'Where are we going?' Alice asked, turning off the GPS so it would stop chirping at them to turn around.

'You'll see.'

Minutes later, they pulled into the parking lot of The Grand Ole Diner, a staple from their counselor days. Alice clapped excitedly when the building came into sight. It was a quaint place, overlooked by most in favor of the more convenient fast food places closer to the highway. They walked in and were immediately met with the sickly-sweet smell of syrup and powdered sugar. Briar's stomach growled as they sat in a booth and immediately ordered caffeinated drinks.

'So, how's London?' Briar asked, hoping that hearing Alice talk about her life would cement the fact that she would be returning to it. She was determined to make it until the end of the summer, be friendly, and part amicably, so that Alice would go back to being someone Briar only wondered about when she couldn't sleep.

Alice smiled up at the server dropping off their drinks before turning back to Briar. 'Oh, um, it's great!'

'Where do you live?' Briar asked, sipping her coffee.

'Shepherd's Bush,' Alice said, pouring milk into her tea. 'It's a bit of a commute to Oxford, but when Tess moved to London it seemed like the right thing for me too. She thinks it's mad that I'm still in school, but at least in the city, I have her.'

Briar nodded, pushing away any jealousy towards Tess, and instead tried to remember where Shepherd's Bush was in relation to her dad's.

'I always knew you'd be in school for as long as humanly possible,' Briar said. 'I've never met someone who likes to learn as much as you.'

Alice shrugged. 'I like knowing things.'

'I know.'

There was a beat of silence, and Alice thumbed the edge of her mug. 'You were good in school, too.'

Briar snorted. 'No, I wasn't.'

'Yes, you were. I cared more maybe, but only because you had an actual life.'

'*You* were my life outside of school,' Briar said, regretting the words as soon as they were out.

Alice didn't seem to notice. 'Everyone loved you,' she said, ducking her head. 'You were the reason I got invited to parties. Even teachers only tolerated me because we were friends.'

Briar stared into her coffee. Alice hadn't said anything untrue, but while Briar may have been well liked, she'd only had one real friend. There had only been one person who knew her fully, who she could have shared anything with.

'You were the one with the boyfriend,' Briar pointed out instead.

Alice flushed. 'Yeah, well,' she muttered, 'that was the only thing I had going for me.'

'Says Miss DPhil from Oxford.'

'And now we're back to my being good at school,' Alice said. 'See, I've never been cool.'

Briar paused, her mug poised against her lips. She didn't know how to say that she'd always found Alice cool, that her favorite thing in the world until she was eighteen had been listening to Alice talk.

'Are you ready to order?' Their waitress had returned and Briar glanced at the menu, realizing she'd forgotten to even look.

'Can I have a stack of chocolate chip pancakes with scrambled eggs, bacon, and a side of hashbrowns?' Alice jumped in. 'And some orange juice, please.'

The waitress scribbled the order. She turned to Briar, who stared at Alice in wonder.

'I'll have the same.'

The waitress took their menus, and Alice shot her a look. 'What is it?'

'I can't believe you remembered our order,' Briar said.

Alice shrugged. 'When I was really homesick, those first few months, this is what I thought about.' She closed her eyes, breathing deeply. 'The smell is exactly the same.' Her eyes snapped open. 'I even got the curtains right.' She thumbed the blue gingham, and added, 'I'd think about this place a lot.'

Briar swallowed. 'Me too.' It was a small concession, but it felt monumental.

'What about life in DC?' Alice asked.

She didn't know where to start, how to catch Alice up on the last decade.

Sticking to the easy stuff, Briar regaled Alice with stories of her different jobs over the years. She told her about the shows she'd seen ushering at a local music venue, the horrendous customers she'd had as a barista, and the funniest pickup lines tried on her at the bar.

Alice laughed so hard at one story that she nearly choked on her orange juice. In turn, she told Briar all about her research, the dissertation process, and how she was only one of three women in her program. Briar couldn't help but admire the light in Alice's eyes when she talked about her work.

'Seems like you're really busy,' she said when Alice stopped to breathe. They'd finished their food, but Briar hadn't even noticed the time passing. 'Doesn't leave a lot of time for dating.'

It had been a stupid thing to say. They'd recovered spectacularly from the awkwardness of the morning and now she was veering towards dangerous territory again.

Alice pursed her lips. 'It doesn't.' She swirled her spoon in the puddle of syrup on her plate, not looking up at Briar. 'What about you?'

'Well, being a bartender might get you hit on a lot, but it doesn't lend itself to starting relationships.'

'But you *have* dated…' Alice trailed off.

Briar shrugged. 'Yeah. There was Riley in college. First girlfriend, first of mostly everything…' She cleared her throat. 'We broke up when my mom got sick. We were in different places in our lives.' She didn't mention that Riley had tried to convince her to stay in school. In the end,

Riley hadn't been able to understand the lengths Briar would go to for her family.

Alice hummed. 'That sounds hard. I can't imagine.'

She reached out and grasped Briar's hand. Briar knew that Alice wasn't talking about the breakup, but about Susan's cancer, about Briar having to drop out of school – and she couldn't talk about that yet, not with Alice. If they only had the summer to be friends again, she didn't want to spend it stewing over how different her life would have been if Alice had been around for the hard parts. She looked away from their overlapping fingers.

'And then there was Miles,' Briar said, moving into easier territory. 'He was nice.'

It was a terrible summary of her last relationship. She and Miles had dated for just over a year, and he had been there for a very low point in her life. Her mother had been in remission, but Briar had been stuck, unable to make any decisions without having a panic attack at the thought that her mother would die without her there.

'Just nice?' Alice asked, sipping her tea.

'He was safe,' Briar said, not loving that descriptor either. Miles had supported her through her mom's move closer to camp, Briar finding and losing several jobs, and her preoccupation with the twins' college admissions process and RJ's job search. He had been a stable presence and had made Briar feel saner, but then he'd gotten a promotion to Chicago, and she hadn't gone with him. She hadn't been able to leave her mother.

He'd accused her of never completely letting him in, which was eerily similar to what Riley had said during their breakup. And Briar couldn't deny that. She hadn't let anyone fully in since she'd lost the person who had meant the most to her. Neither of them had known about Alice, but both had seemed to sense that hole in her life.

Alice nodded, seeming to accept that answer, and Briar jumped at the chance to take the focus off of her.

'And you and Tess?' she asked, managing to make the question sound light-hearted.

Finding out about Tess had been one of the worst moments of Briar's life. Seeing Alice's post on Instagram with her face pressed against another woman's, smiling for the camera, had broken Briar's heart all over again. Briar had been desperately trying to convince herself that the problem between them had been Alice's inability to accept her sexuality. But the post made it clear that coming out hadn't been the issue, she just hadn't wanted Briar as anything more than an experiment.

Alice grimaced. 'I suppose we just decided we were better off as friends?'

It wasn't a good enough explanation for Briar, who had built the idea of Tess up in her head for so long. She was the one who got to date Alice while Briar watched from an ocean away. Briar had spent countless nights looking at the photos of them on Alice's Instagram, finding Tess's Tumblr in second semester and poring over her poetry wondering which ones were about Alice. She had combed through the details of every line, looking for Alice's influence.

'Who decided?' she asked, wondering if Alice had treated Tess the same way she'd treated Briar, brushing off whatever they'd had without a backwards glance.

'She did,' Alice said, then shook her head. 'I don't know, maybe it was mutual.'

Briar raised an eyebrow, and Alice sighed.

'She knew I wasn't in a place to be dating anyone, emotionally speaking,' Alice said, looking at their hands again. Briar fidgeted, moving her hand away under the guise of grabbing her coffee.

'You didn't agree?' Briar asked.

'Not at first,' Alice said. 'But eventually, yes. She was right; what I needed was a friend.'

Briar's heart clenched uncomfortably. Part of her wanted to point out that she had been Alice's friend, that she would've continued to be, even after everything, if Alice had just let her.

'Right,' she said instead. 'And there hasn't been anyone else?'

'Nope,' Alice said. 'Too busy, as previously noted.'

Briar nodded, not fully satisfied with that answer, but not wanting to push her luck. She glanced at the bill between them and finally picked it up. 'We should head out. I hate driving at night.'

'I remember,' Alice said, slipping out of the booth.

Chapter 17

Briar

They got back to camp in time for dinner.

'Our fearless leaders have returned,' Freddie shouted from one of the mess hall tables, saluting them. It was Sloppy Joe night, something Cook always made for the British holdovers in between sessions.

Briar smiled at the children munching on their sandwiches, red sauce dripping all over their hands and faces, as Alice examined the food in mild horror.

'What, you're too good for Sloppy Joes now?' Briar asked, fixing herself a plate.

'I think I prefer beans on toast,' Alice grumbled, taking the seat next to her.

'Don't let Cook hear you,' Briar murmured close to her ear. She caught Sierra staring at them and quickly moved away.

After dinner, Freddie kept the kids occupied with an elaborate Settlers of Catan tournament, leaving Alice and Briar free to plan for the next session at a nearby table.

'Okay, so if we move the Joshes to rotation 5, we'll have enough counselors on shift to cover duties. That way everyone gets a night off, and we'll have one rotation on standby to fill in where needed,' Alice said, drawing out a diagram. 'Then you, me, Sierra and Freddie can serve as shift leads,' she said, still scribbling. 'We'll have to find someone to lead the last one, but we can figure that out tomorrow.'

'Carly could work, she's in rotation 4 and she's been here nearly as long as Sierra,' Briar suggested, and Alice added the name to the list.

'Okay, and then between you and me, whoever's not on active shift will man the main office, answer calls and deal with any disputes,' Alice said. 'Does that sound good? This way you'll have at least a few hours free each day, if you need to go handle any, um, business.'

Briar cringed, remembering the last time they'd talked about her plans to sell the camp. 'Thanks.'

Alice didn't seem to notice. 'Well, I don't want to jinx anything, but I think the next session has a chance of not going completely horribly.'

Briar laughed. 'With confidence like that, I don't see how we could fail.'

'You two look like you're in a good mood,' Sierra interrupted, walking by them.

Alice glanced hesitantly at Briar. It was an unspoken question what the hell they were supposed to tell people about the shift in their dynamic.

'Just a much-needed rest,' Briar said.

Sierra eyed them suspiciously but dropped it. It was bedtime for the campers anyway, so she and Freddie shuffled them out of the mess hall and to their cabins while Alice and Briar helped Cook clean up.

Afterwards, Briar followed Alice back to the director's cabin. She stared at her, tracing the lines of her tank top up to her freckled shoulder blades. Briar had done well today, pushing last night out of her head. But it was harder now. Knowing that they would be sharing a room again, having Alice so close, was bringing everything back. She shivered, not able to stop the memories of the night before from flooding back in, a low thrum beginning in her stomach. The lights of the cabin twinkled into view, and Briar opened her mouth to say something – probably something stupid, but being back at camp made her feel like it wouldn't be.

And then Briar stopped in her tracks, taking in the tall frame lounging on the porch swing.

'What are you doing here?'

Noah stood, grinning. 'Sorry, I should've called, but I didn't want you to talk me out of it. I'm here to help, in any way I can. I can teach music, or art, or swimming. Did I mention I'm lifeguard certified…?'

'Oh,' Briar said, wondering how long he'd been waiting out on the porch, and how Harper would manage without him. There had been reasons she didn't want Noah giving up his summer for her, and seeing him in front of her brought them all back up.

And irrationally – because nothing was happening between them – it felt like it would change things with her and Alice now that they had gotten better. As much as she loved Noah, he had always complicated her friendship with Alice.

'That's really nice of you,' Alice jumped in, when it became clear Briar wasn't going to say anything more. 'It's late, so maybe we'll work it all out tomorrow, and you stay with us tonight?' She looked to Briar for confirmation.

'Yes,' she said automatically.

Noah and Alice headed into the cabin with Briar trailing behind. It was tight when it had just been Briar and Alice, but with Noah's oversized limbs the place seemed incredibly cramped.

Noah scratched his neck awkwardly. 'Sorry, I clearly didn't think this all the way through. Harper said it was a good idea, so I just hopped on the bus. I should've called first.'

Seeing Noah looking uncomfortable freed Briar from her stupor, and she pulled him into a hug.

'Hey, no. I'm really glad you're here,' she said into his chest. 'I'm sorry I'm so weird about asking for help. It just feels like a lot sometimes, when you drop everything for me.'

'You'd do the same,' Noah said, pressing his face into her hair. She didn't reply, because she couldn't explain how it was different when she did it.

'Take my bed,' Briar said instead, gesturing to the cot. 'Alice and I can share.'

'No way,' Noah said. 'I can take the floor.'

'Don't be silly,' Alice said.

'Yeah, dude, it's fine,' Briar said, pulling off her jean shorts and climbing into Alice's bed.

Noah shrugged and excused himself to the bathroom. Once he was out of the room, Alice slid into bed too and Briar turned to face her.

'Are you alright?' Alice asked.

'Just being silly,' Briar said. She couldn't explain why Noah offering to help was so hard without admitting it was Alice who had taught her that she shouldn't rely on other people.

Noah walked back into the room, and Alice took her turn in the bathroom.

'Everything good?' Noah asked Briar, folding his T-shirt and jeans and stuffing them into his backpack. 'You and Alice seem different.'

'We talked at the party,' Briar said, throwing an arm over her head. It had always been difficult to lie to Noah, and Briar had learned that not looking at him made it easier. 'We've called a truce.'

'That's great!' Noah said, and Briar smiled to herself at his enthusiasm. He truly didn't have a petty bone in his body. The prospect of his best friend and ex-girlfriend patching things up could only be a good thing in his mind. Briar wished she could have his untarnished perspective.

'Hey, Noah?' she said, sitting up.

'Yeah, Bri?'

'Thanks for coming.'

'Literally any time,' Noah said, climbing onto the cot. His feet hung off the end of it, and Briar grinned at the sight.

'Good night,' Noah said, pulling his knees up to his chest.

'Good night.'

Alice crept in a few minutes later, flicking the overhead light off. The bed shifted as Alice got comfortable, the warmth from her body seeping into Briar bones as she drifted off to sleep.

Chapter 18

Alice

Alice woke up in a tangle of limbs. It took her a full minute to figure out where she was and who she was curled around. She was used to waking up in the same bed, in the same flat, alone. Since Tess, she hadn't slept in the same bed as another person.

Then everything came back to her, and heat crept up her neck as she suddenly felt every place where Briar's body was touching hers. She turned her head, keeping her body as still as she could, to look at Briar's face.

Her lips were slightly parted, her bangs messy and her legs curled up to her chest in the same way that they always were.

The idea that her brain had stored all of this useless information was either alarming or impressive – she wasn't sure which. She didn't remember anything from her senior year biology project, but she remembered the exact rhythm and cadence of breathing that marked her sleeping in the same bed as Briar. The worst part was that it didn't feel strange at all. It felt comforting, like no time had passed at all. It felt, in a way, like she was home.

She shook the feeling off, gently removing Briar's arm from around her. This wasn't meant to be that kind of sleepover, just one borne of necessity when Noah had showed up. Briar had made it clear after the last night they'd spent together how much she'd regretted it, and Alice couldn't blame her.

She had known as soon as she'd seen Briar afraid to come back to bed that sleeping together had been a mistake. Like always, Alice had only been thinking of herself, what she wanted, and had ignored that Briar was in a vulnerable state. So, she'd done what she'd failed to do when they were eighteen: she'd owned up to her mistake and apologized. It had seemed to result in a positive turn in their relationship. They had easily slipped into something resembling friendship – not what they'd had before, but definitely progress. Alice's tested hypothesis had yielded promising results. If only she didn't want to throw away the whole experiment to be able to touch Briar, really touch her, again.

Briar stirred beside her, slowly opening her eyes. 'Hi,' she croaked.

'Hi,' Alice said, smiling despite herself. It should have been awkward, after everything, but instead it felt normal, like they'd done this hundreds of times before – because they had. Then Noah let out a loud snore from the other bed and Alice tensed. 'Breakfast?' she whispered.

Briar nodded eagerly.

'Hey,' Freddie greeted them before they had made it past the flagpole. 'We have a situation.'

Immediately, Alice's stomach dropped. 'Is it Robin?'

'No, Cook's sick.'

'Cook doesn't get sick,' Briar said, echoing Alice's thoughts. She had always assumed that Cook had some sort of deal with the devil that granted him constant good health. She'd never so much as heard him sneeze before.

'Which is why it's a situation,' Freddie said grimly. 'He won't let me touch him, threatened to cut off my fingers if I tried, but he definitely has a fever. Still, he's insisting no one else can make a passable meal for the campers arriving today.'

Alice and Briar exchanged a worried look. This situation might require an actual medical professional, showing the gaps in their staffing situation once again.

'What's up?' Noah's voice came from the director's cabin, and Alice turned to see him on the porch.

'Cook's sick,' Briar said, and it hurt Alice to hear her sound so deflated after things had seemed to be improving.

She couldn't believe she'd been optimistic about the session up until this moment, that she'd thought her tentative friendship with Briar could fix the problems from the first session.

'Give me a sec,' Noah said, going back inside.

'I'll deal with corralling Cook back into his room,' Alice said. 'Unless you think we should bring him to urgent care?'

'Couldn't get a good enough look at him to say,' Freddie said.

'Damn,' Briar said. 'Usually he'd have sous chefs, but I couldn't find anyone to replace them. He swore he'd be fine on his own.'

'It's not your fault,' Alice said. 'And I'm sure he'll be fine, he just needs some time to rest.'

The lines in Briar's forehead eased slightly. 'And I can cook dinner tonight.'

'*We* can cook,' Alice corrected her. 'We know Cook's system, where he hides everything.'

'That leaves me and Sierra to handle the check-in,' Freddie said, sounding uncertain.

'You've got this,' Alice said to Freddie. 'We'll go over the cabin assignments again tonight.'

Just as she said it, Noah emerged again. 'Harper's coming,' he announced, walking down the steps.

Briar's eyes went wide. 'Oh, Noah, you didn't ask her to drive all the way here on her time off, did you?'

'No,' Noah said. 'I told her what's going on and she volunteered to come. She *is* the only nurse we know.'

'Thank you,' Briar said quietly.

Noah hugged her. 'Anything for you.'

'Okay,' Alice said, clearing her throat. 'We have opening duties to go over. You can't just rely on your fiancée; we're putting you to work too.'

—

Alice and Briar spent the morning in the kitchen prepping dinner. They were making mac and cheese, and cooking for such a large group involved more chopping and cheese grating than Alice could've imagined. Her arms were sore by the time noon rolled around and the campers came into the dining room for a buffet of Uncrustables, pretzels, carrots and bananas.

Sierra popped her head in the kitchen. 'There's some girl here, says she's Alice's sworn enemy.' Alice whirled around to see Harper standing in the doorway.

'I didn't say that,' she clarified, her cheeks reddening.

Sierra nodded. 'It's true, I made it up because I thought it would be funny to see Alice's reaction. And I was right, it was.' She disappeared back into the dining room.

Briar, who had just settled with a plate of food, stood. 'Thanks for coming.'

'I've got it,' Alice said, gesturing for Briar to sit.

Alice guided Harper up the steps to Cook's room.

'How's Briar?' Harper asked, after a moment.

'Oh, you know,' Alice said. 'Can't really say she's doing well, but I hope she's a bit better than she was last week, at least. I've been trying to not be a total bitch, which seems to be helping.'

Harper huffed out some air, and Alice couldn't tell if she was annoyed or trying not to laugh. 'And how are you?'

Alice frowned. 'Me? I'm fine.'

Harper's eyes cut sideways towards her. 'I know you were close with Briar's mom.'

'I was,' Alice said, surprised both that Harper had noticed and cared enough to ask. 'But being here is keeping me busy. It makes it easier, when I feel like I'm being useful.'

She had no idea how she would feel if she was back home, but she suspected Tess was right, that she would be sad no matter what. At least this way she wasn't avoiding it but living through it. She'd never felt closer to Susan or missed her more, but she was doing everything she could to carry on her legacy.

Alice opened the door to Cook's room. 'Cook,' she called out into the darkness. He'd pulled the blinds over his skylight. 'I've brought my friend Harper. She's just going to make sure you're already on the mend, as you've told me several times you are. Not that I don't trust you, of course.'

She heard some grumbling that sounded like *bloody buggers*.

'You should get back to cooking,' Harper murmured. 'I'll be fine.'

Alice eyed the lump in the bed dubiously. 'Are you sure?'

Harper put a hand on her hip. 'I'm a nurse. I've dealt with difficult patients before.'

'If he threatens you, you should know that he doesn't actually have any knives up here. I confiscated them.'

Harper nodded as though this were par for the course, and Alice returned to the kitchen. She found Briar staring sleepily into the distance, a half-eaten Uncrustable in one hand.

'Coffee?' Alice offered. She started on the French press, packing the ground coffee into the bottom and putting the kettle on. 'Harper seems utterly unfazed by Cook,' she said after another minute of silence.

Briar smiled. 'Yeah, she's a real force. She reminds me a lot of you in that way.'

Alice tried not to be offended, reminding herself that Briar liked Harper and had probably meant it as a compliment. 'How did you two become so close, anyway?'

'We ran into each other at a party a couple months into freshman year. Noah and I had the same Intro to Education class, but I hadn't seen Harper at all.' She paused and Alice looked over at her, but she was staring at the wall in front of her, expressionless. 'She said she wanted her own friends, that she was feeling sick of being the person she was in high school.'

'Doesn't everyone?' Alice asked, pouring the boiling water into the French press. 'That's what college is for.'

Briar frowned. 'I didn't mind who I was in high school.'

'Well, of course you didn't,' Alice said. 'You were always the coolest person in the room. You never cared what anyone thought of you.'

Alice had always envied that about Briar. Everything Alice did was carefully calibrated to the reactions of her peers and her parents. She suspected that was a large part of why it had taken her so long to figure out she was a lesbian. She had never taken a moment to investigate who she wanted to be, separate from the constant need for acceptance.

She'd been jealous when Briar had come out in their junior year of high school, and at the time she'd had no clear explanation for the feeling. She had ended up attributing it to the fact that Briar was so fearlessly herself. And with a mother like Susan, how could she have been anything else?

Briar didn't respond for a minute. 'Well, I'm definitely more of a mess now than I was then. So maybe I'm one of those shitty people that peaked in high school.'

Alice stirred in the sugar, bringing the coffee to Briar and sitting across from her. 'You didn't peak in high school,' she said, resisting the impulse to take Briar's hand.

Briar took a sip of coffee. 'I guess I just imagined my life as an adult differently, and it sometimes feels like every decision I make is just rolling with the punches.' She took another sip and then said in a flat tone, 'There have been a lot of punches.'

'If it helps,' Alice said, 'you're the same person to me now that you were then.'

As she spoke, she wasn't sure if that was actually true. Yes, Briar was still the person who understood her better than anyone else. But this new thing between them, the one that they were refusing to talk about, changed things for Alice. Briar was suddenly so much more to Alice than she'd been before, and having to ignore it was torture.

Briar kept quiet, seemingly lost in thought. Then she gulped down the rest of her coffee and stood.

'We should get started prepping sides.'

Alice stood too and passed Briar a mountain of broccoli before turning to mince garlic. 'I still make this recipe all the time,' she said, trying to distract Briar. 'The garlic in the roux makes all the difference.'

Briar nodded, chopping the broccoli. 'We always had wild garlic in the garden my mom needed to use up.'

'There was no feeling as good as getting off school on a Friday and going over to yours to cook,' Alice said. On those nights, the Elwood home had rung with laughter from Briar's siblings, who had taken turns pestering them as they cooked. It had made Alice wish she'd had siblings – their home had felt alive in a way hers never had. 'I looked forward to being an adult, to having a house like the one you grew up in and someone to share it with. Simple things.'

The bungalow had been filled to the brim with memories, from screen-printings done by Briar's grandma to glasswork Susan had collected from the local Renaissance fair. As soon as you walked in the door, you knew exactly who the inhabitants were. Alice had aspired to that, yet had somehow ended up in a bare flatshare in London with a broody grad student and not a single piece of art on the walls.

Briar nodded. 'Having you around made it fun, like it was our own place.'

The words mimicked Alice's thoughts so closely that she felt entirely transparent. After having been around colleagues who hadn't been able to read her for so long, there was something surreal in the existence of a person who she'd shared everything with once.

'Yeah,' she said softly. 'It did feel like that. I thought that was what being an adult would feel like, but it never has.'

Briar cleaved a head of broccoli neatly in two. 'No, it hasn't.'

They had made so many plans when they had been younger, about the lives they would live side by side, the places they would go and the people they would become. None of them had come true. Alice was to blame for that.

'Shit,' Briar hissed, and Alice turned to see that she'd sliced her finger with the knife.

Alice grabbed for her automatically, examining the cut as blood dripped onto their hands.

'We need to put pressure on it,' she said, trying to project confidence. Briar had always been better at treating wounds than her, since she got queasy at the sight of blood. 'Cook has a first aid kit somewhere.' She whirled around and rifled through the cabinets until she found it on a shelf opposite the stove.

'I can do it,' she said, and Briar placed her hand in Alice's more tentatively this time, eyeing her warily. 'What? You don't trust me?'

'I'm a little worried you'll faint,' Briar admitted.

'I'm not going to faint,' Alice said, though honestly, Briar's doubt in her was propelling her forward more than anything else. She pressed a piece of gauze into the pad of Briar's thumb, taking tape in one hand and winding it around the finger.

'Are you...?' Briar trailed off, the corner of her mouth quirking up.

'Thinking about the scene from *Pirates of the Caribbean* where Elizabeth bandages Will's hand?' Alice huffed out a laugh, giddy on the feeling of sharing every point of reference with someone again. She knew this was Briar's way of distracting her, and she was grateful. 'Of course I am.'

Briar looked up at her from beneath slightly wet lashes. '"My heart's always belonged to you",' she recited solemnly.

Alice knew Briar was just quoting the movie, but her racing pulse hadn't seemed to have figured that out. She bit her lip, staring at Briar, caught in some sort of spell.

'It's still bleeding,' Briar said, her voice a whisper now.

'Oh,' Alice said, looking down. She applied more pressure and Briar grimaced in pain. 'Sorry.'

'It doesn't feel that bad, honestly,' Briar said. 'You're doing a good job.'

Alice didn't want to examine how Briar's praise made her feel, so she cleared her throat, wrapping the tape tightly to secure the bandage. 'How's that?'

'Good.' Briar's voice was barely audible, her gaze locked on Alice.

'How's it looking in here, ladies?' Freddie came through the swinging doors and Alice dropped Briar's hand like she'd been burned. They both washed their hands before returning to their prep stations. Freddie squinted at them. 'The hungry swarm descends in an hour.'

Chapter 19

Alice

'Everyone,' Alice called, gesturing for the campers to come closer, 'welcome to the decomposition lab.'

Running the decomposition lab had been Alice's favorite part of her summers as a counselor. She would bring the campers to the compost bin weekly to take a look at where their food scraps went and how they broke down. Now that she had some free blocks of time, she was determined to bring it back.

The group of eight-year-olds observed the giant compost bin with trepidation, none of them taking a step forward.

'Don't be shy,' Alice said, grabbing a shovel to use as a pointer. 'Come one, come all, and deposit your scraps into the bin.'

She raised the lid and the campers dumped their trays of lunch scraps, matching looks of disgusts on their small faces.

'It stinks,' one of them said, and the others laughed.

'That's right, it does stink.' She closed the bin. 'Can anyone tell me why?'

'Because it's rotten food?'

Alice smiled encouragingly at the girl who had answered. She'd forgotten in her years of dealing with undergraduates what it was like to teach children so young. She loved that they were still discovering themselves and their interests, that they still viewed the world with wonder. She missed feeling that way herself.

'Yes, but can anyone tell me why rotting food smells so bad?'

Nobody said anything. Alice gave the bin a whack with her shovel, enjoying the looks of delight on the kids' faces. This wasn't the kind of curriculum they had in the classroom and she had their rapt attention.

'This bin is filled with tiny little organisms called bacteria. The bacteria break down the food, and that breakdown releases gaseous waste.'

'Like a fart?' a kid asked, while another blew a loud raspberry into his elbow.

'Exactly,' Alice said, unfazed. 'Can anyone tell me the name of this breakdown?'

Robin, who'd been standing off to the side of the group, raised his hand. 'Decompotision?' Robin had mixed up the syllables, but she nodded anyway.

'Right, decomposition. The bacteria in this bin are called decomposers. Can anyone name any other decomposers? I'll give you a hint: think of things that live in the dirt!'

'Bugs!'

'Exactly! Some bugs are decomposers, like centipedes, millipedes and sow bugs. What else?'

'Worms!'

'Yes! If you look closely,' Alice said, pointing the shovel at the level in the compost bin where the food scraps met dirt, 'you can see some worms wiggling around.'

The group leaned in, no longer grossed out. 'There's one right there!'

'Can anyone think of any other decomposers? I'll give you a hint, your parents might eat them on pizza.'

'Eat them?' The kids traded horrified expressions. Alice nodded seriously.

'Olives?'

'Artichokes?'

'Barbeque sauce?'

'Mushrooms?'

Alice pointed at the boy who got it right. 'Mushrooms! Most mushrooms are decomposers, from the kinds that grow on trees high over your head to the ones you can buy at the grocery store.'

'Woah.'

'Decomposers are very important,' Alice said, turning the handle of the compost bin to mix up the green and brown matter. 'Just like you and I need nutrients to live, plants need nutrients to grow big and strong. Decomposers help put those nutrients back in the soil for the plants.'

'And then we eat the plants.' Robin had a familiar expression of awe on his face.

'Woah,' the boy beside him said, looking sideways at him and smiling.

Alice beamed at them. 'Exactly, it's a cycle. One of the most important cycles in our natural world. So... who wants to learn more about it?'

When Alice ended the lesson, asking the children to look out for any interesting mushrooms around the woods and to report their findings back to her, she noticed Briar leaning against a tree not far away.

The campers dispersed and Alice put her hands on her hips, turning to Briar. 'Observing my lesson?'

Briar smiled slyly. 'Don't worry, you earned full marks. And I've got good news, Sierra's covering your Cook shift. Thought you and I could sneak away.'

Alice felt giddy at the look on Briar's face, like the two of them were sharing a secret.

'Where are we going?' she whispered, though there was no one around to hear.

'I've got some extra work for you,' Briar said, gesturing for Alice to follow her.

'Oh, because I haven't been working enough,' Alice grumbled, playing along and continuing on the route she now recognized would bring them to the parking lot. According to the schedule they'd created, Briar had the afternoon off to deal with her mom's estate. Alice decided her choices were either to submit to this kidnapping or to not see whatever it was that Briar wanted to show her. So she got into Briar's car without further complaint. They drove to the main road, and then in a direction Alice had never been in before.

She stared at Briar's side profile, the red-gold color of her hair striking in the midday light. Allowing herself to really look for the first time, she drank in the familiar sight of Briar driving.

'You look good,' she said, because she hadn't slept much the night before and therefore was prone to blurting out her thoughts. 'Better, I mean. Better *rested*.'

A blush crept up Briar's neck. 'Oh man, these campers are really running you ragged, huh?'

'Yes,' Alice said.

Briar glanced sideways at her, smirking, and Alice felt like something had shifted. There was a tension between them which had been there, underlying everything for the past few days, but now felt out in the open. After an agonizingly long silence that Alice knew was probably less than five minutes, Briar pulled into the driveway of a weathered Victorian house. It was a bright lilac that Alice immediately recognized as Susan's favorite color.

'Your mom's house?' she asked.

'Yeah,' Briar said, cutting the ignition.

Alice followed Briar up the stairs, careful to avoid a loose nail jutting out of one of the steps. Briar jammed the key into the lock, and Alice got her first glance at the interior.

'Well, it's got lovely bones,' she said. It was true, but it was also the most charitable comment she could have made. Lovely bones beget rotten wood.

'It's a shithole,' Briar grumbled. 'I tried to convince her not to move out here. Almost all of our fights were about the house in some way. But you can imagine how those arguments went.'

'Like talking to a wall?' Alice guessed, trying to remember if she'd ever successfully changed Susan's mind about anything.

'Yup,' Briar said, narrowing her eyes critically at a crack in the wall to their left. 'I need to fix it up before I sell it, but I'm behind on repairs and I thought I could do some catching up today.'

'You want me to help you?' It felt like a turning point. 'What do you need to do?'

'Clean out the gutters, take down the Christmas lights – I refused to let her go onto the roof and do that herself when she wanted to in January – and fix a leaky faucet. The banister is unstable, so that's a hazard.' Briar ticked the items off on her fingers as she went. 'That's just off the top of my head, I'm sure there's more.'

'Maybe we could write them down?' Alice suggested, pulling out her phone and taking notes. 'What about the crack in the wall?'

Briar eyed it with a grim expression. 'Just another symbol of my fractured world.'

'Then let's tackle that one first, shall we?' Alice said. 'Where's the paint?'

Briar led her into the dining room, where she opened the loose door to a closet and gestured inside.

Alice pulled out her phone, adding the door to the list, and then grabbed a can of paint, brushes, spackle, and a scraper.

'Good thing you know an artist,' she teased.

'You still draw?' Briar asked, taking one of the brushes and heading back into the living room.

'Never,' Alice admitted, following her. 'Sometimes I doodle mushrooms in the margins of my to-do lists, if that counts.'

'Are they as good as mine?' Briar asked. Her eyes flitted to the spot behind Alice's right ear where a tattoo artist had etched in her illustration of a *Cortinarius violaceus*, in honor of Alice's camp name. Alice felt the skin there tingle.

'Better,' she said, wrinkling her nose at Briar. The drawing had come out looking more like an ear than a mushroom – Alice had been asked on more than one occasion if it was meant to be ironic.

'Snob.' Briar layered spackle on the wall and practically attacked it with the scraper.

'When did this crack appear?' Alice asked, gently prying the scraper from Briar and employing it with a steadier hand.

'Oh, you know, around the time my mom's cancer came back and she neglected to tell me anything was wrong.' Alice turned to look at her, but her eyes were fixed on the wall. 'She got really frail and she couldn't keep up with things around the house. I begged her to come back to DC.'

'I'm so sorry,' Alice said, dropping her hand from the wall for a moment. 'The cancer came back in February, didn't it? I heard from her around then, but I didn't get the impression that anything was wrong. She sounded in good spirits. It wasn't until her last note that I realized how things had progressed…'

Briar's lips twitched and Alice realized that her emails with Susan were still a sensitive subject.

'Yeah, well, I'd already given up everything for her once, and I would've done it again. Maybe she finally figured that out. I'll never be sure.' She paused, frowning. 'But then again, she went and foisted the camp on me after all of that, so maybe she didn't care about derailing my life.'

Alice knew that defending Susan wouldn't go over well, but it was instinctual for her. She had loved and admired Susan so much, had thought of her as something like a mother. And she also sensed that being angry with Susan, while it might help in the short-term, wasn't going to help Briar get through this. But she didn't know how much she could push Briar, with their tentative friendship being what it was.

'She must have thought that running the camp would be good for you, in some way,' she tried, finishing with the crack and putting down the scraper.

Briar sighed, and Alice was glad that she at least didn't look angry.

'It hasn't been *all* bad,' she said, glancing in Alice's direction.

Alice felt a smile grow on her face. The words were simple, but the rush of them made her lightheaded. It was pathetic that none of her recent accomplishments gave her the same floating feeling as one sentence from Briar.

'But I can't do it again. I'm not cut out for it. I mean, you've seen how it is, the level of organization that's required to keep things running. I've never had that. Always needed you to keep me on track.'

Alice remembered the days after school where she'd go through Briar's calendar and write in when each of her assignments was due and which ones she would have to work on when. She would text reminders if they weren't at Briar's house working on the homework together, which they usually were.

'I'm not going to tell you what to do when it comes to selling the camp,' she said carefully. 'I understand why you're doing it, I just don't want to talk about it.'

Briar laughed, leaning against the wall. 'Should we make a list of things we're not talking about? *Noah, Harper, summer 2015, me selling the camp, you caring about my mom more than me...* What am I missing?'

She was lightening the mood, and Alice was grateful for it. Whatever was happening between them couldn't survive under pressure. And lately, any time they were alone, Alice felt like she could hardly breath with the weight of it.

'I'm sure we can find things to add to the list,' Alice said, turning back to the wall. 'It didn't seem like you loved me talking about Tess.' She glanced sideways at Briar, wanting to see her reaction.

'Exes,' Briar said, eyes crinkling in amusement. 'Added.'

'Hmm, what else?' Alice asked, turning to Briar fully. She was closer than Alice had realized, and the flutter of Briar's eyelashes made her forget what she was saying. 'Um, the other night?'

Briar glanced down at Alice's mouth. 'Yeah. Definitely not.'

Neither of them moved. The air felt charged, like all Alice needed to do was lean in and she would get exactly what she wanted. What they had agreed not to do again.

Alice turned back, painting over the same section again and willing her heartbeat to return to normal.

'I'm glad we had this talk,' she said, still tense. 'When I leave at the end of the summer, I want to count myself as made up with you. And Noah.' Her voice went up at the end of the sentence, inflecting it like a question.

It was the wrong thing to say. Whatever softness had been in Briar's expression before was gone now.

'I'm honored to have made it as a stop on the Alice Hughes apology tour,' she said.

Alice didn't know how Briar had managed that – to go from someone she knew better than herself to a stranger in a millisecond.

Chapter 20

Alice

In honor of their first non-disastrous week of camp, Alice and Briar hosted a poker night in their cabin.

Alice arranged a spread of snacks they had confiscated throughout the summer: bowls of barbeque-flavored crisps, chocolate-covered pretzels and matcha-flavored KitKats. As she did, her eyes were drawn to the other side of the room, where Briar was stirring hot chocolate on a burner. She was flushed from the combined heat of the summer evening and the bubbling pot in front of her, and she looked perfect. Alice wished she could take a picture to capture the moment and bring it back to London with her.

Briar opened a bag of marshmallows, popping one into her mouth. The white powder stuck to her lips in a way that derailed Alice's thoughts entirely. She watched in equal parts horror and awe as Briar licked her fingers clean.

'What?' Briar asked innocently.

'Nothing,' Alice said, shaking her head. 'You ever have one of those moments where you think, in hindsight, you really should've realized you were gay sooner?'

She refrained from mentioning that she meant all the times she'd watched Briar eat marshmallows and had a funny feeling in her stomach. At the time, she'd attributed her queasiness to Briar's seemingly endless capacity for sweets. Now she recognized the want for what it was, an ache low in her belly.

Briar shot her a funny look. 'All the time.'

'Like,' Alice ploughed on, determined for Briar to not figure out what had prompted this train of thought, 'our obsession with the middle school English teacher who was definitely a lesbian.'

'Ms. Monroe,' Briar said, smiling fondly as Alice reminded herself not to stare at the dimples in her cheeks. 'Man, she was *really* into the gender roles in Shakespeare.'

'And that phase we had where we would only watch foreign movies that just happened to be gay,' Alice added, thinking about their legs tangled together in Briar's bed, watching movies on her laptop.

'Well,' Briar said sarcastically, 'that was *obviously* because we were incredibly cultured teenagers, and not for any other reason.'

'Do you remember when they scissored in *Blue is the Warmest Colour* and we had to immediately Google if that was a real thing?' The scene had fascinated teenage Alice, and she hadn't been able to stop thinking about it for weeks afterward.

Briar laughed. 'Yeah, because I'd just come out and needed to make sure I was an expert in all the gay shit in case people came to me with questions.'

'Are you guys talking about *Blue is the Warmest Colour*?' Noah's voice came from the doorway, and Alice turned to see him and Harper there. 'The movie you made me watch with you like five times the summer before senior year, even though I fell asleep every time?'

Alice had felt a spark of magic the first time she'd watched the movie with Briar and proceeded to try to recreate it again and again without success. She'd wondered what was wrong with her for the longest time, that watching a movie with her boyfriend didn't feel as good as watching it with her best friend.

'You just didn't appreciate *film* the way we did,' Briar teased.

'Or maybe I wasn't as gay as either of you,' Noah said, then looked at Alice. 'Sorry, am I allowed to call you gay? I know Briar is okay with the umbrella term—'

'Yes,' she cut him off before he could work himself up. 'I'm very gay, thanks.'

'Babe, you can't just ask someone if they're gay,' Harper said, settling onto the floor and looking around. 'This place looks nice.'

Briar and Alice had pushed the desk to the side of the room and laid blankets and pillows on the floor for people to sit on, trying to make the space cozy for their guests.

'I hope you lot are ready to get smoked,' Freddie sang as he and Sierra entered. 'Mama needs a new leather jacket.'

'Sorry,' Sierra said, as they settled on the floor. 'We did tequila shots, and you know what they do to him.'

'Yeah, they make me awesome.' Freddie grabbed the cards and started shuffling.

'Pretending I didn't hear that,' Alice said, sitting between Briar and Freddie. Her thigh rested against Briar's in the cramped space, and she tried to ignore the heat between them.

'It's our night off, let us live,' Sierra said. 'What are we betting? Chips or clothes?'

'Chips,' Alice and Briar said in unison, trading a glance. A half-naked Briar wouldn't help Alice's barely existent self-control. Noticing Briar's flushed face, she wondered in a way that felt strangely like hope if Briar was facing a similar dilemma.

Sierra and Freddie both booed.

'I'm game,' Harper said, surprising Alice. If someone had suggested this in high school, Harper would have been the first to protest. 'I'm totally comfortable with my body.'

'You've got a great body, sweetheart,' Noah said, squeezing her arm.

'Okay, gross,' Briar said.

'You're outnumbered, darlin',' Freddie said, imitating a Southern drawl as he dealt the cards out. Alice chanced a glance at Briar and prepared herself for a very long night.

An hour later, Sierra had swept them all out of their pocket money and most of their clothes. Alice had been the first out of the game, having refused to take off her bra and underwear even when heckled. She was now nursing her hot chocolate, watching Briar and Noah put up a valiant effort to win back some dignity.

'I'll cover your kitchen shift,' Noah said to Sierra, thumbing his cards. He'd just lost his pants and was resorting to more creative betting.

'What about your boxers?' Sierra asked, waggling her eyebrows.

'Stop trying to get us to take off our underwear,' Alice admonished. 'That was a ground rule!'

Freddie sighed, leaning heavily against Alice. The tequila had hit him hard in the second hand and he'd been completely useless ever since. His weight shifted Alice even closer to Briar, and she struggled to resist the gravity that was pushing her practically into Briar's lap. Alice silently thanked the universe that Briar hadn't lost her shirt yet, because she wasn't sure she could stand the sight of Briar in just a bra. It had been hard enough when she'd lost her shorts in the last hand.

'Kitchen duty it is,' Sierra said, not skipping a beat. She turned to Briar. 'You calling?'

Briar frowned at her cards, then shook her head. 'I fold.'

Sierra whooped, momentarily waking Freddie, who gave a sleepy pump of his fist in celebration. 'Take it off!'

Briar rolled her eyes, grabbing the hem of her oversized T-shirt and pulling it over her head. Alice had mentally prepared herself to see Briar in a bra, but she hadn't expected the plunging black mesh – *that* seemed engineered specifically to make Alice crazy. Briar's nipples were just barely visible through the thin fabric, and Alice's face felt very hot all of sudden.

Harper whistled. 'Since when do you own lingerie?'

Briar stuck out her tongue. 'Bite me.'

'Yeah, yeah, Briar has tits,' Sierra said. 'Let's get back to me winning.'

She splayed her hand on the blanket, revealing two kings and an ace. Noah's face lit up.

'Three jacks! Take that!' Noah said, throwing down his cards and raking in the pile of cash. 'We're rich!'

'That's like two hundred dollars,' Briar pointed out, laughing.

'Yeah, but on his salary...' Harper trailed off when Noah frowned at her. 'Sorry.'

Alice sensed tension in the air as Noah and Harper exchanged glances. She wanted to look at Briar, to see if her expression gave anything away, but she couldn't trust herself to glance anywhere in Briar's vicinity right now.

'I think we're gonna call it a night,' Noah said, after a moment.

'Please,' Freddie said, shaking himself awake. 'These kids have ruined me. I'm knackered.'

'Yes,' Alice said wryly, 'the kids and nothing else have made you tired.'

Sierra looked up from counting her other winnings. 'My work here is done.'

The others stumbled back into their clothes and said their goodbyes, leaving Briar and Alice still half-naked and alone. Alice stood purposefully, keen on setting the office back to how it had been and going immediately to bed before she did anything stupid.

'We should move the desk back,' she said, grabbing blankets and pillows and throwing them across the hall and into their bedroom. 'Tidy up.'

'Okay.'

She heard Briar moving behind her. Alice hoped that the way she was staring at the opposite side of the room seemed normal. Her eyes caught on the CPR poster in the corner.

'Thinking of getting recertified?' Briar teased. Her voice came closer. 'It's probably like riding a bike.'

'I could have forgotten,' Alice said indignantly, refusing to turn around. She wished she had thought to put her clothes back on. Then she wouldn't feel like this, like her skin was on fire, prickling over every inch exposed to Briar's gaze.

'And it's very important to remember CPR, obviously.'

Alice turned to face Briar. She was standing very close now, and something rooted Alice to the spot. 'Exactly. What if a camper is struck by lightning?'

Briar huffed, and Alice focused on maintaining extremely careful eye contact, not letting her gaze dip.

'I know CPR. Brains *and* a great rack – really, I'm the whole package.'

Alice's cheeks burned. She'd hoped Briar hadn't noticed her fleeting glances during the game of strip poker, but she was sure now that Briar had been paying close attention. Maybe they'd been trading those same fleeting glances for the past week.

'I haven't noticed anything related to your… um…' Alice blinked rapidly, trying to think of something to say to defuse the tension but also wanting more than anything else to just give in. It felt like Briar was testing her, and she desperately wanted to ace the test.

'Yeah?' Briar asked, making a disbelieving sound in the back of her throat. She took a step forward, and Alice instinctively stepped back, her thighs hitting the desk they were meant to be repositioning. 'Is this where I make a joke about mouth-to-mouth?'

'Ha,' Alice said, so close now she could count every freckle on Briar's face. She hadn't even realized she'd leaned in. 'What are you—'

Briar cut her off with a kiss, and Alice let herself dissolve into it. She savored the sensation of Briar's body pressing against hers, trying to memorize each detail that had previously escaped her drunken mind. She would never drink alcohol again if it meant that she would remember the exact feeling of Briar's skin forever.

She ducked her head, sucking at the juncture of Briar's jaw, moving across her exposed clavicle.

'Think I might be too old for hickeys,' Briar said, her voice breaking. 'God, Alice, you make me…'

'Me too,' Alice whispered, grasping at Briar's hips. They stumbled, crashing back into the desk. Briar lifted her onto it, pushing between Alice's knees.

It would be easy for Alice to lose herself in this, to get swept up in the scent of Briar, the touch of her hands, and to think of nothing else. But she couldn't, not after Briar had regretted it the last time.

Alice leaned away. 'We should talk about this.'

Briar ran a hand over her face in frustration. 'I was enjoying not talking.'

'We need to be practical,' Alice said.

'I knew you were going to say something like that.'

'I just think,' Alice said, charging ahead, 'we can't fool ourselves that this isn't going to happen again. It's becoming a bit of a pattern with us. So why don't we plan for the most likely outcome?'

'The most likely outcome being that we have sex again?' Briar asked wryly.

Alice was overcome by a wave of self-doubt. 'Unless, um, you think that's not the most likely outcome. And I'm just being stupid.'

Briar gave her a look. 'You're never stupid, Ally.'

She hadn't called Alice by her old nickname the whole summer. That, and the glint in Briar's eye, gave Alice the confidence to press on.

'So, how do you want to handle this?'

Briar cocked her head, considering the question for far longer than Alice had anticipated. 'I don't want anyone to know.'

It wasn't the first thing Alice had expected to hear from her, and it stung. 'Oh. Yeah. Of course.'

'It would complicate things with Noah. And we're co-directors. It looks… messy.'

Alice knew that Briar wanted to be perceived as a competent camp director more than anything, so she tried not to take it personally. But it still left her with a familiar pain – of not being capable of earning the pride she was sure she should be worthy of from at least one person in the world.

'But it's not messy. Right?'

'Right,' Briar said. 'I mean, it's just friendship and sex. Neither of us wants anything else from this.'

'And no one gets hurt,' Alice said slowly.

Briar nodded slowly, holding her gaze. 'No one gets hurt.'

It shouldn't have been hard to agree to. Alice hadn't given anyone the power to hurt her in a long time. Still, it took her a moment. 'Are we shaking on it?'

'I'd rather kiss on it,' Briar said, her hands coming back up to rest on Alice's waist.

'That can be arranged,' Alice said, and leaned in.

–

When Alice checked her inbox for the first time that session, she found fifty unread emails. She groaned, cradling her head in her hands. It was the longest she'd gone without checking her email since the beginning of the summer.

Feeling a pit in her stomach, she scrolled past a few from Jeremy pointing her to different grants and instead started with the ones from her flatmate. Each was shorter and even more direct than the previous. The final one just read: *Alive??? Your plant isn't. –AHR.* He had attached a picture of her fiddle leaf fig, dead.

Scrolling back to the top of her inbox, one of the emails from Jeremy caught her eye, this one titled: *FW: something to think about…*

He'd sent an email chain with one of his colleagues at the Royal Botanical Society.

Wouldn't want to take her away from you… Ken from their research department had written, to which Jeremy had responded, *Alice has been ready for a role like this since I met her.*

Her eyes scanned the page in disbelief. She was up for a job – a fully funded job – starting in the fall.

She'd known it was something she'd have to think about soon, but school had seemed endless. This felt real, like a permanent decision. A commitment to her life in London.

Well, she had already committed. She'd committed ten years before, when she hadn't come home for the holidays, telling her mom she'd see her the next time she was in Europe.

The interview was two days after camp ended, and Alice had no idea how she was going to be ready in time. She'd never felt less like the person she'd left in London, who would have ruthlessly carved out time in her diary to prepare. Instead, the Alice at camp wanted to savor her final moments in her favorite place in the world.

'Yo, you good?'

Alice's head snapped to where Sierra was leaning against the door jamb. 'Yes, fine. What's up?'

Sierra squinted at her, then shrugged. 'Kylie had a family emergency. Think you can cover art?'

Alice nodded, relieved for the distraction. She could put off replying to Jeremy until tomorrow.

Her turn subbing in for the art counselor went considerably better than her stint teaching theater. As her class on flower pressing drew to a close and the campers filed out of the cabin, Robin beckoned her over to the table he was sharing with his new friend, Sam. They had bonded in her decomposition lab and had taken to foraging in the woods together in their free time. Alice's heart swelled whenever they asked her to come look at an interesting mushroom.

'What is it?' she asked.

'My flower pressing is for you, Violet,' he said solemnly. 'It's like our own friendship bracelet.'

'Friends forever?' she asked, holding out her finger.

He took it in his own. 'Yes.' He and Sam filed out of the classroom with the rest of the campers, leaving Alice to arrange the flower pressing kits off to the side of the room to reveal to the campers at the end of the session.

'Hey,' a familiar voice came from behind her, 'I'm here for a lesson? I heard there's a hot art counselor?'

Alice turned to Briar. 'Who told you that?'

'Oh shit,' Briar said, 'I thought you were someone else. My bad.' She leaned against the table closest to the door, lips tilted in a smug half-smile that Alice found painfully sexy.

Alice checked her watch. 'The next group will be here in… twenty minutes.'

'That's plenty of time.' Briar strode over to Alice. 'Don't you think?'

'I don't know—' Alice said, but was cut off by Briar kissing her, quick and hard. When they pulled apart, they were both flushed. 'I love the mural,' Briar said, as though it was an explanation for what had come over her. 'Am I your muse?'

'I forgot about that,' Alice admitted. Something like uncertainty flashed across Briar's face, and Alice explained, 'It feels like forever ago when I painted it, pestering Freddie with questions about your life. But I guess my best work has always been a bit inspired by you.' She touched the tattoo on Briar's forearm. 'That's my favorite drawing I've ever done.'

It almost hurt to admit to Briar that she had meant so much to Alice, even after everything. She didn't know if Briar had figured out what had taken her so long to accept: that years of their friendship hadn't been platonic at all. At least, not on her end.

'You should start drawing again,' Briar said. 'It's a waste of talent not to.' The words sounded so much like something Susan would have said that Alice couldn't argue.

'Okay,' she said, leaning in to kiss Briar again so she wouldn't have to think about what she was agreeing to. It wasn't exactly like she had any time to spare for art.

'No, I'm serious,' Briar said, stepping back to avoid Alice's distraction. She was reminded of why it was nice to not have someone who could read your mind around – they could be pesky about wanting the best for you. 'You can't sideline this forever.'

'I'll have more time eventually,' Alice allowed. 'Assuming I don't get a job or anything.' She forced the email from Jeremy out of her mind, leaning in for another kiss.

'Why wouldn't you get a job?' Briar demanded, taking another step backward. Alice was starting to feel rejected, which was unfair because Briar was the one who had put ideas of kissing into her head. 'As far as I can tell, you're publishing some of the most original research in the field.'

'What do you know about mycological research?' Alice asked, taken aback.

'Oh…' Briar's cheeks went pink and she ducked her head. 'You know, I've read some of your stuff here and there…'

Alice frowned. 'But I've only been published in some niche journals, and my undergrad thesis through St Andrews Press.'

'All of which is available online, for the casual mushroom fan...' Briar said, looking at her again, her gaze soft and a little bit shy.

Alice kissed Briar again. Looking at her now, her lips slightly parted and her bangs sweaty against her forehead, Alice was acutely reminded of being a teenager with a crush.

'You're a mushroom fan?' she teased.

'Shut up,' Briar mumbled. 'I guess if I was an incredible artist *and* one of the foremost experts responsible for the reclassification of the Basidiomycota division, I would also have trouble making time for both. Thank god I'm a fuckup and don't have that problem.' She rolled her head forward, resting it in the crook of Alice's neck.

'You're not a fuckup,' Alice said, running a hand through Briar's short hair, admiring its silkiness. Then she brought up something she didn't expect to go over well, 'Do you know what you're going to do when the summer ends?'

She needed to hear the answer, to know what Briar would be doing when she wasn't around to see it for herself. If she felt confident Briar had things sorted out here, maybe she could start thinking about her own future.

Briar blew a breath of frustration onto Alice's collarbone. 'None,' she admitted. 'Back to the bar, I guess.'

'Do you like it?' Alice asked, twirling the hair at the nape of Briar's neck.

'Sure,' Briar said, tilting her head to look at Alice. 'I like my coworkers, and the regulars too. I learn a lot every shift, just talking to people about their lives.'

'Then why aren't you sure you'll go back?' Alice asked.

Briar sighed. 'I just haven't been thinking about it. Trying to get through the summer at the moment.' She paused. 'Why?'

'When I'm back in London, I want to be able to picture your life in DC,' Alice said.

Briar frowned. 'Why would you want to do that?'

Alice felt embarrassed by the admission, but ploughed on anyway. 'For years, I had an idea in my head of what your life here looked like. And it was true in a lot of ways, but also not. Understanding things better now, it's… nice.'

Briar straightened, looking at her like she had grown a second head. Alice wasn't sure if her reaction would have been better or worse if she'd shared the whole truth: not just that she wanted to know what Briar's day-to-day looked like, but also that Briar was okay.

'I can send you some Snapchats if it makes you feel better,' Briar joked.

Alice didn't smile back. She imagined herself poring over books late at night, her stomach rumbling and her body shaking with too much caffeine, getting a Snapchat from Briar and questioning every decision she'd ever made. It was certainly a distraction her research-addled mind wouldn't be able to resist, which made it dangerous. Being miles away from Briar, studying her life through social media, had been one type of pain. She didn't know if she could handle having a sliver of her and not the whole thing.

So she cleared her throat, steering the conversation in another direction. 'What do you like about your coworkers?'

'I dunno... they sort of remind me of the counselors. Just good kids who are eager to learn. I've been there the longest, so they always come to me when they have issues. It makes me feel capable.' She snorted. 'Capable as a bartender. I can add it to my resume.'

Alice raised her eyebrows. 'From the bar to camp, you're always surrounded by adoring fans. You inspire that in people.'

Briar shook her head. 'Like I said, I've been at the bar a long time, so people trust me. And here people trust me just because I'm the daughter of the camp's founder. Not exactly anything I accomplished myself.'

'Oh, please,' Alice said, frustrated by having to explain to Briar just how special she was, by the idea that people didn't constantly remind her. 'You must notice the way you captivate a room when you walk in. I don't see any of your siblings having the same effect around here.'

'No,' Briar said, 'but that's because I encouraged them to pursue their own passions.'

Alice wanted to argue that Briar had other passions as well, that she had a life outside of her mother's camp. But maybe that was the difference between the Briar she had known and the one in front of her. That Briar had been full of potential, and this one couldn't see that she still was.

'What about going back to college?'

Briar scrunched her nose. 'I couldn't.'

'Why?' Alice asked.

'It's embarrassing, isn't it? I'm too old to be finishing my bachelor's degree, let alone the master's I would need to become a teacher. I mean, you almost have a terminal degree.'

'And I didn't have a dying parent at any point during that process,' Alice said gently. 'I couldn't have gotten through school if I'd had a family to look after, or even a functioning social life.'

'Self-deprecating isn't a good look on you,' was all Briar had to say to that. 'You're a genius. You would have gotten through school no matter what. We're not the same.'

'But—'

'Look,' Briar said, putting a hand on her hip, 'I came in here to make out a little. Do you realize how absolutely annoying it is that you insist on trying to improve my already perfect life? Look around' – she gestured to the dusty classroom sarcastically – 'we're in *paradise*.'

Alice giggled. 'Is it sad that I honestly agree with that?'

Briar smiled again, drawing her closer. 'You think this is paradise?'

'Well,' Alice said, 'you're here, aren't you?'

'That's such a line,' Briar scoffed, but pulled her in for a kiss anyway.

Chapter 21

Briar

Briar drifted into consciousness slowly, vaguely aware of the sound of footsteps. She took in light coming from the hallway, then glanced to her right, finding Alice's side of the bed empty. The world outside was dark.

Briar quietly crept across the bedroom. The footsteps were coming from the office, and as Briar entered, she almost ran into Alice.

'Ally?' she grumbled, squinting against the onslaught of overhead light.

'Oh,' Alice said, starting. 'Sorry, I didn't mean to wake you.'

The insomnia had begun in high school. Alice would arrive to school late, heavy concealer under her eyes and a dullness about her that Briar had detected instantly. Between first and second periods, Briar would sneak out to get Alice coffee from the shop across the street. Alice would sip on it until lunch, when she would lean on Briar's shoulder and let sleep claim her for a few minutes.

'It's fine,' Briar said. Alice was still in her pajamas and she was clutching what was possibly the thickest book Briar had ever seen. 'What are you doing?'

'Reading,' Alice said, glancing down. '*Every Living Thing*, have you read it? Susan sent it to me when I got accepted to Oxford.' She thumbed the page. 'This must have been her copy.'

'You nearly ran into me while… reading?' Briar asked, sure that her brain was simply too tired to make sense of what was going on.

'Yes,' Alice said. 'I pace while I read. Tire my brain and my body at the same time. It's efficient.'

Briar imagined Alice pacing late at night, alone in her dorm room. She wished Alice would have just picked up the phone, that she could have been there for her.

'What's wrong?' she asked, knowing Alice's insomnia always worsened before exams or big presentations.

'I got an email from my advisor,' Alice said, sighing and walking over to the desk. She put the book down and slumped into the chair.

'Bad news?' Briar slid into the opposite chair. Alice steepled her fingers together, squinting at nothing in front of her. It was a familiar gesture, from countless late night study sessions where Alice would quiz Briar before a test.

'No.' She sighed, rubbing her eyes. 'He's recommended me for a position with the Royal Botanical Society.'

'That sounds like good news,' Briar said.

'Yes,' Alice said faintly. 'I suppose it is.'

'Do you not want the job?'

'It's everything I've been working towards,' Alice said firmly, then sighed. 'I just didn't expect it to happen so fast. I'll be interviewing as soon as I get back, and then I've got to defend my dissertation. Jeremy says it just needs some final tweaks, but it's nowhere near ready.' She was working herself into hysterics. 'And I just don't know if I'm ready to be done with school yet. I feel like I have so much more to learn. I'm not re—'

Briar got up and crossed over to Alice before she could finish. She grabbed Alice's chin and tilted her face up.

'It's going to be okay,' Briar said. 'The real world isn't that scary. Trust me, you're going to be fine. Not just fine, you'll be incredible.'

Alice's eyes were glassy as she wrapped her arms around Briar's waist. Briar squeezed her back just as hard. They stayed like that for a while, until Alice was able to breathe normally again.

Briar slowly disentangled herself and looked Alice in the eye again. 'We're going to make sure you ace that interview. If you need time to prep for it, we can work it into the schedule. But' – she grabbed Alice's hands and pulled her up – 'that can all wait until morning.'

Alice let Briar guide her back to bed, didn't complain when Briar made her drink a whole glass of water, and, when Briar slipped into bed, gratefully clung to her.

'Now,' Briar said, wedging a thigh between Alice's knees and slipping a hand under her tank top, 'tell me all the different subspecies of mushrooms in the Mid-Atlantic.'

It was an old game they had played when Alice couldn't sleep. Alice smiled and leaned in, pressing her lips against Briar's softly before retreating to her own pillow again. 'Alphabetical?'

Briar nodded.

'Scientific names?'

'Naturally.'

Alice kissed her again before closing her eyes and starting: '*Armillaria gallica, Armillaria mellea, Armillaria solidipes, Cortinarius caperatus, Coprinus comatus, Coprinopsis variegata...*'

They both were asleep before Alice finished the Gs.

The next morning, two of the counselors woke up with some kind of rash. How they'd contracted it, and subsequently infected each other, Briar didn't want to know. She sent them off to see Harper and brought their campers to the lake for a swim lesson.

Noah was lifeguarding the empty lake diligently. His face lit up when he saw the nine- and ten-year-olds bumbling towards him.

'Well, hello there, sailors,' he said, grabbing a stack of kickboards. 'Today, we're gonna see who can kick the hardest.'

Briar watched them from the beach, enjoying the quiet.

Without any distractions, her thoughts inevitably turned to Alice. That sweltering poker game had frayed the last of her nerves, and she hadn't been able to resist anymore. It was just like high school again, the same desire coursing through her every time she looked at Alice. Only now it was worse. Because now, Briar knew what Alice looked like sprawled out beneath her, knew what her lips felt like on Briar's skin, knew the sounds Alice made when she came.

It had been driving Briar insane. Every touch, every glance, every second alone together seemed to be pulling her closer. And so, she'd kissed her. Damn the consequences, damn however much it was going to hurt when Alice left. It was the chance to have everything her teenage self had ever wanted, and Briar had taken it.

And then the night before had happened, and now it was impossible to ignore that Briar was once again giving too much of herself. It was supposed to be just sex, not late-night conversations where Briar soothed Alice's fears of the future, or held her while she cried. It wasn't supposed to be falling asleep in each other's arms. Briar needed to be better about putting a wall between her feelings for Alice and her attraction.

'Earth to Briar.'

Her head snapped up to see Harper.

'Oh, hey.'

'You good?'

'Fine,' Briar said, making room on her towel. 'So, what's the diagnosis?'

Harper put her bag down and sat. 'Crabs.'

'No,' Briar said, scandalized. 'How did that happen?'

'Apparently, David went to a white party over the Fourth and brought back souvenirs.'

Briar grimaced. 'So him and Josh…'

'Are sleeping together? Yup,' Harper said. 'Josh is *pissed*. And I got to hear all about it while examining their junk, so yay me.'

'I guess it's a good thing I stocked up on that lice shampoo.'

Harper shuddered. 'Anyway, they're having it out, so I figured I'd come ogle my half-naked fiancé. How's he?'

'Spectacular, as always,' Briar said, resting her arms on her knees and digging her toes into the muddy sand. They sat in silence, watching as Noah played a version of sharks and minnows that pitted him against twenty children.

Harper's presence was always calming. The ease Briar felt now put the uneasiness she felt with Alice in stark relief. Being with Alice was constantly being on edge, the air between them charged. It was like waiting for the floor to fall out from under her.

She wished she could be honest with Harper.

'I'm glad you're here,' Briar said instead. 'Thanks for coming back. And letting Noah be here. I know—'

Harper raised a hand to stop her. 'Don't do that. We love you, and we want to help. I'm just sorry I can't be here all the time with my work schedule.'

Briar chewed her lower lip, glancing sideways at Harper and taking in her exhausted expression and the book poking out of her bag: *Adult Children of Immature Parents*. Briar raised her eyebrows. She knew she had missed things over the past few months, but now it felt like the source of the tension between Harper and Noah was obvious. When it came down to it, the problems between them were always related to Harper's parents.

Harper noticed her expression and shoved the book deeper into her bag. 'It's for work,' she muttered.

Briar clicked her tongue. 'Sure.'

Harper softened. 'I'm just stressed with wedding planning.'

'Is that all?' she asked. 'Noah said you were being weird. And he's right.'

Harper blew out a sigh. It had taken Briar years to learn how to get Harper to talk to her, but now it was one of her best skills.

'My parents...' Harper started, rolling her eyes at Briar's obvious glance at the book in her bag.

'...hate Noah,' Briar supplied.

'They don't *hate* Noah. They hate that he's a music teacher.'

'Ah,' Briar said, not surprised. This was an old fight, one that Harper had had with her parents many times. 'So what?'

'So,' she said, 'is it too much to ask that my parents support me on my wedding day?' At Briar's confused look, she added, reluctantly, 'They're refusing to pay for the venue.'

'What?' Briar said. 'But they offered you the money when you booked it!'

Harper nodded grimly. 'I know, but we had this massive fight a few weeks ago and all this shit came up again. How if I hadn't started dating Noah, I wouldn't have switched from pre-med to nursing. That I'd be nearly done with my residency now.'

Harper's shoulders shook with anger, and Briar reached out to soothe her. She knew that particular comment hurt Harper the most. What her parents didn't know was that Harper's pre-med courses had driven her into a depressive episode so intense that Noah and Briar had slept in her dorm room for three weeks to make sure she didn't fail out or do something much worse.

It had taken years of therapy for Harper to stop seeing her nursing career as a consolation prize. Her parents just weren't there yet.

'You save people's lives every day,' Briar said seriously. '*And* you're not an asshole. So you're already better than them.' She paused. 'Are you going to tell Noah?'

Harper shook her head. 'It would just upset him. There's nothing he can do.'

Briar shrugged. 'Maybe not, but you know he'd be there for you, if you let him.'

Harper reached out and squeezed her hand. 'I'll think about it.'

Chapter 22

Briar

Briar found Alice in their bedroom donning a bright blue bandana and smirked.

'So I've been sleeping with a river rat this whole time?' she asked, grabbing the face paint she'd left out and wiping two green streaks under her eyes to mark her as a member of the opposing team. It was the day of the traditional game of Capture the Flag which divided the camp into teams: the River Nymphs and the Forest Elves.

Alice smiled wryly. 'Who knows what secrets I've tricked out of you in your sleep.' She slipped a finger up Briar's arm suggestively. Briar shrugged her off, refusing to be drawn in. Since the last session's game had gotten rained out, there was even more pressure to win.

'Joke's on you,' Briar said, pulling her hair into two short braids. 'Freddie won't tell me where he hid the flag.'

Alice laughed. 'You're not in the inner circle?'

The blue of Alice's tank top matched her eyes, making them look impossibly big. Briar glanced down at the rest of the outfit, which included jean shorts perfectly molded to Alice's thighs. She had the urge to grab Alice's waist, skim her hands up to her ribcage, and take the damned tank top off. She swallowed.

'He knows I'm the weakest link.'

As soon as they started, Freddie sent Briar to guard their team's jail, a patch of grass in a clearing with white lines drawn around it. The job was reserved for the youngest campers. Briar tried not to be offended.

An hour into the game, they'd jailed fifteen of the blue team.

'Guys,' Briar called out to the campers guarding the jail. 'Remember, you gotta give them at least five feet.'

Her teammates grumbled but moved away from the line.

There was a cry in the distance, and suddenly Freddie came running through the clearing. His shirt was drenched in sweat, his eyes wild. 'Keep an eye out. There's a plot afoot,' he yelled as he darted back into the trees.

'Be normal,' Briar called after him. The campers around her giggled. 'Everyone get ready! They must be trying for a jailbreak.'

She scanned the trees for movement, her heart quickening with adrenaline. She heard a stick crack nearby and whipped her head around to see a flash of blue. Without thinking, she took off, racing into the woods after her opponent. She would recognize that shiny ponytail anywhere.

Alice tried to cut left but stumbled over a root and Briar crashed into her. They fell together, sprawled on the forest floor.

'Okay, ouch,' Alice said breathlessly, shifting so that Briar slid off of her. 'It's two-touch, not tackle.'

'I'm sorry,' Briar said, giggling at the state of Alice's hair, which was tangled with twigs. She reached up to pull a few out. Alice was trying her best to look stern, but the glint in her eyes was overwhelmingly fond as she swiped her thumb across Briar's lips, the pad of it coming back pink with blood. Briar blinked in surprise and ran her tongue over her bottom lip, tasting metal.

'Ow.'

Alice glanced around before leaning in for a kiss. She pushed Briar down into the brush, slotting their bodies together. Briar kissed her back just as hard, pulling at Alice's hair. Her other hand slid into Alice's back pocket. Alice gasped into her mouth, biting Briar's bottom lip.

'Ow.' Briar broke away with a wide grin, then felt her lip split further. 'Oh, fuck. Okay, no more kissing.'

Alice laughed, standing and then helping Briar. 'I'll take the request into consideration, but I'm not sure I can be in full compliance.'

Briar tried to glower but couldn't wipe the smile off her face. 'I'm gonna have to haul you in.' She grabbed Alice's hand and walked her back towards the jail. They were nearly there when Briar heard the telltale horns that signaled the end of the game.

She shot a questioning glance at Alice, who looked too smug for her liking.

'This was a distraction?' Briar asked, putting it together. Alice beamed back at her, looking particularly angelic in the light streaming through the tree canopy. 'You're evil.'

Alice pulled her hand out of Briar's grasp, skipping back to the center of camp. 'I'm competitive.'

At that moment, she reminded Briar so much of her younger self that she didn't care about losing.

—

Of the VHS tapes Briar had picked up, the campers selected *A League of Their Own* for movie night. They lay in their sleeping bags on the mess hall floor, watching the giant projector screen at the end of the room, as the counselors watched from the back. Cook, who had fully recovered, was in such a good mood that he was passing out bags of popcorn and chocolate chip cookies.

Briar smiled into her cup of Sunny D, her eyes skipping around the room before finally settling on Alice. She was in a corner with the counselors from Cabins 5 and 9, talking quietly but animatedly, her hands waving wildly as she spoke. Watching her sparked something warm in Briar's abdomen.

'Whatcha looking at?' Sierra sidled up to her, and Briar quickly covered her smile by taking a sip of her drink.

'Just enjoying the movie,' Briar said. 'Trying not to think about what could go wrong next week.'

Sierra eyed her like she saw through the subtle verbal parry.

'Yeah, this session is going much smoother,' she said finally. 'You and Alice make a good team when you're actually working together.'

Briar nodded, tight-lipped, suddenly nervous that even talking about Alice would give them away.

'We do,' she managed.

'So... why aren't you trying to kill each other anymore?' Sierra asked, sensing a bruise and poking it.

Briar shrugged. 'We're just making it through the summer.'

And that was the truth. Maybe Briar didn't want anyone to know about Alice because she knew that it was stupid to have started something with her in the first place. Alice was leaving in two weeks. Whatever was going on between them had a clear expiration date, and yet, Briar couldn't help herself. Her crush from high school had come back in full force.

Alice came to save her then, raising her cup to Sierra. 'Cheers, River Nymph.'

'Cheers.' Sierra clinked her cup.

'I can't believe we fooled you,' Alice said, grinning at Briar.

'I'm out of practice,' Briar said. 'Should've seen your jailbreak for the Trojan horse it was.'

'It's funny how Alice was so sure you'd go after her,' Sierra said, a knowing glint in her eye.

Briar's face was now permanently flushed. 'I guess my competitive streak got the best of me.'

'I came here to see if you want to review the schedule,' Alice said smoothly. 'I think I've worked out how to cover for Josh and David.' Briar stood, following her outside.

'Can't wait to see this timetable,' Briar said as they walked towards their cabin. 'I know you're just dying to show me, you geek.'

Alice huffed. 'I was lying about the schedule.' Briar raised an eyebrow at her, and she shrugged. 'I just wanted to get you alone.'

Briar grinned and, with a quick look over her shoulder, took Alice's hand. The night air was humid as she led them down the path. But before they reached the cabin, Alice pushed Briar against a nearby tree, grabbing Briar's hips.

'Hi,' she said, mouthing at her neck, making Briar gasp. The rough bark bit at her skin, pain coupled with the sharp nip of Alice's teeth on her clavicle. Her hand fisted in Alice's hair, pulling her head back for a kiss.

'Inside,' she gasped, breaking away, but Alice caged her back in. Her lips never left Briar's skin, skirting across her cheeks, her nose, her eyelids, mouthing along her jaw, and biting the lobe of Briar's ear. 'Please.'

Briar breathed out the word, and Alice trembled against her, her head finally lifting to meet Briar's gaze. She looked wild, her eyes dark and heady, and Briar lost her ability to think.

Alice dragged her the final few yards to the cabin. They pulled at each other's clothes, stripping bare and falling into bed. Briar's hands skimmed over Alice's curves, unable to get enough of her.

'You have no idea how many times I've thought about this,' Alice murmured, her thumb rubbing along Briar's lower lip where it had split. Giddiness filled her at the words. Briar had thought about it too, too many times to count. But she'd never expected to hear the admission from Alice.

She parted her lips obediently, and Alice's eyes flashed as she dipped her thumb into Briar's open mouth. Briar sucked, tasting the saltiness of Alice's skin, and couldn't stop herself from moaning.

'I've got you,' Alice whispered, kissing her neck. Her hands drifted down Briar's body, leaving fire in their wake. And wherever her hands went, her mouth followed.

Not a single inch of Briar's body was left untouched, except for the one place she needed it the most.

'Ally,' she begged, running her hands through Alice's impossibly soft hair, tugging on it, trying to get Alice to move from where she was biting a mark into Briar's hip. Alice glanced up at her wickedly. 'Please,' Briar groaned, feeling like she might burst.

And then, finally, *finally,* Alice's mouth met her center, and Briar lost all sense of herself. Her hands fisted into the bedsheets, feeling like she was being held together by Alice's fingers, her impossibly hot hands holding down her hips and keeping her tethered to the world.

Chapter 23

Briar

Alice was gone when Briar woke up, and she wasn't in their cabin when Briar returned from breakfast, either. Just as she was about to go find her, the phone rang.

'Hello, Briar speaking,' she said.

'Oh, Ms. Elwood,' came a British voice from the other end. Dread immediately set in. 'I've been trying to reach you.'

'Mr. Lavish, how are you?' Briar said, injecting false cheer into her tone.

Mr. Lavish was the lawyer who'd been handling her mom's estate. Briar had been dodging his calls since he'd met with the appraiser the week before.

'I'm well, dear,' Mr. Lavish said. 'I've found you a buyer.'

Briar blanched. 'Really?'

She'd convinced herself there was no harm in going through the motions of selling the camp: appraising it, consulting Mr. Lavish and discussing it with her family. But at no point had she considered that there would be a buyer so soon. Her mother hadn't even been in the grave for two months.

Mr. Lavish pressed on, oblivious to Briar's spiral. 'He's a local businessman from Virginia. He saw the photos and he's excited to use the land for his hunting parties. Says he's willing to offer five per cent over asking.'

'Hunting parties.' Briar's voice was an octave higher than usual. She glanced around the hallway, trying to imagine what it would look like with taxidermized deer heads hanging from the walls. 'Wow.'

'He wants to see the property. Is there a time that works best for you?'

'Um,' Briar said, trying not to think about the rabbits currently making a home in the stump outside being strung up for sport. 'The session ends August first.'

'Perfect,' Mr. Lavish said. 'I'll send the details. Sorry, I've got to run. We'll talk soon.'

Briar listened to the dial tone for a moment before taking a breath and dialing a new number.

'Bri?' Laurel's tone was bright on the other end of the line. 'How are you? Haze, come here.'

'We're in Bath!' Hazel announced.

'I've had some news,' Briar said, not able to soften the blow. There was a long pause, and Briar knew the twins were exchanging a look, silently conversing in a way that had always made her jealous. 'There's a buyer.'

'Oh,' Hazel said. Briar wished she could see them, cursing the landline for being her sole connection to her family. She wanted nothing more than to be with them right now. 'I mean, Dad said there might be, but I thought it'd fall through.'

'Well, it didn't.' She sighed, pinching her nose and gritting her teeth through the next sentence: 'I think I'm gonna do it. Sell it—'

'No, don't! We'll move back,' Laurel cut in.

'Yeah, we can run the camp together,' Hazel said.

Briar shook her head. 'Absolutely not. What about making the next big video game? You guys have careers ahead of you, you can't give that up.'

Briar felt close to tears. Telling the twins was always going to be the hardest part. She'd raised them when her mother had been too busy, and then too sick, to do it herself. But her fear of disappointing them was far outweighed by her fear of not providing for them.

'You dropped out to take care of mom,' Laurel said. 'Why can't we do this?'

'Because I said so,' Briar snapped, then immediately felt awful. She never yelled at her siblings. But they didn't know what they'd be agreeing to give up. Briar had no direction, no plan. For the last six years, she'd been barely a person. Her entire life had been on hold, waiting for her mother to recover, then worrying she'd get sick again. And now she was dead, and Briar had nothing.

She let out a breath slowly. 'Did you finish your exams yet?' There was another long pause, and Briar sighed. 'Is Dad there?'

'Yeah,' Hazel said.

'Put him on.'

Briar listened to the twins locate him and press the phone into his hands.

'Briar! How are you, my dear?' His voice boomed.

Her mess of feelings crystallized into anger at him, for not being there when her mom had gotten sick, for not taking care of his children when Briar had struggled for years, for swooping in when it was far too late and taking the twins from her. Part of her wished he'd taken her too, that she could feel like a child with a parent looking out for her.

'You can't keep jetting the twins all over England like they're on some grand tour,' she hissed. 'They need to finish their schoolwork. They need to re-enter the real world. And eventually, they need to realize that their mother is dead.'

Briar found it difficult to swallow.

'Trust me,' her father's tone was clipped, 'they are very aware she's dead. I've got it all sorted.'

That was the final blow for Briar. She hung up and stalked to her bedroom, falling into unmade sheets, grasping a pillow and pulling it tight against her torso. She screamed into it.

—

It was dark when Alice found her there.

'Wassup,' Briar croaked. Alice's figure was haloed by the glow of the hallway light, and she couldn't make out her expression.

'You missed dinner.' Alice flicked on the bedside lamp, and Briar saw that she was holding a plate of pizza. Her stomach rumbled. 'Are you alright? You slept for a long time.'

Briar grabbed the plate from her. 'Just tired,' she said between bites. 'And my dad is a dick.'

Alice nodded as if those two thoughts made sense together. 'I'm sorry.'

Briar finished inhaling her first slice, and she finally had enough energy to process the time. 'Shit, I'm sorry. What did I miss? I can—'

Alice held up a hand. 'It's all good, everything's done. I'm quite capable, I'll have you know.'

'Oh, I know,' Briar said. She wanted to kiss her, but something inside her felt too raw, like if she kissed Alice now, she'd be confessing something she wasn't ready to admit.

'You should come outside,' Alice said, standing. 'It rained earlier, so it's cooler.'

Briar nodded slowly, staring at the remaining slice of pizza. Alice grabbed the plate. 'This will be waiting for you.'

Briar dragged herself out of bed and into the bathroom. She splashed some water on her face, letting it wake her. Her hair was a complete mess, and she teased the knots out with her fingers to make it presentable.

When she pulled the shower curtain open, she screamed.

'What?!' came Alice's voice as she raced into the bathroom.

'Kill it! Kill it!' Briar shouted, balancing precariously on the toilet seat.

Alice looked around. 'Kill what?' she asked frantically.

'Spider,' Briar said, pointing. 'Oh my god, Ally, kill that motherfucker right fucking now!'

Alice paused and laughed, kneeling and sticking her hand into the shower.

'Don't!' Briar's voice was high and shrill. 'Don't *touch* it.'

'Bri…' Alice had the audacity to sound stern. She straightened, a daddy longlegs crawling across her index finger. 'It's harmless.'

'It's evil,' Briar muttered. Alice walked out of the bathroom, the hand carrying the insect cradled against her torso.

'It's not even a real spider,' Alice explained. 'No venom, no pincers. It's more afraid of you than you are of it.'

'I seriously doubt that.' Briar held the screen door open for Alice, then watched as she descended the porch steps. Alice put her hand against one of the nearby trees and waited patiently for the daddy longlegs to crawl off.

'You were very brave,' she teased. Briar rolled her eyes and took a bite of pizza to avoid having to respond. They settled on the porch swing, listening to the water drip off the leaves above them and onto the cabin's tin roof. There was a cool breeze blowing, tickling the hairs on the back of Briar's neck. The sun was down, and the receding light was a deep purple, casting everything in shadow.

'I'm going to miss this.' Briar sighed, surprised to hear the words come from her own mouth. Not because they were untrue, but because she'd sworn not to talk to Alice about any feelings concerning their arrangement.

Alice didn't react at all, just stroking along Briar's spine. A faint hum was the only confirmation that she'd even heard.

'I'm not going to try to persuade you not to sell it,' Alice said. Briar turned to look at her. Alice was gazing out at the forest, where fireflies were flitting around, glowing yellow-green. Leave it to Alice to be utterly oblivious to how Briar felt about her.

'I've thought about keeping it,' Briar admitted, trading one heartache for another. 'I just can't run this place. I'll never be my mom.' She felt tears prick at her eyes, and she scrubbed at them, frustrated that she still had tears to shed. 'But letting it go also seems wrong.'

Alice slid closer, her hand drifting down to tuck Briar into her side. Briar let her head fall onto Alice's shoulder. The tears kept coming, but for once she didn't mind crying in front of someone else.

'I just...' she continued, 'I don't know why she made it my decision, as if I didn't have enough to deal with. She didn't trust me enough to tell me her cancer came back, but sure, I'll know what to do with her entire legacy.' She let out a humorless laugh. 'It's so typical of her: big ideas, leave the details to me. I'll sort it out.'

'It's not fair,' Alice murmured.

'No, you know what's not fair?' She pulled away from Alice's grip. 'That she told you she was dying before she told *me*. You know what's not fair? Her cancer coming back after five fucking years and killing her in a matter of months. You know what's not fair?' Briar choked on her breath, gritting her teeth against the grief threatening to overwhelm her, needing to voice the thought that had been haunting her all summer. 'That I didn't do more to save her.'

'Oh,' Alice said. Her eyes were wide and searching as she reached up to grip Briar's cheeks in both hands. 'There wasn't anything you could've done.'

Briar's lower lip trembled. Her throat was dry, a large lump making breathing difficult. She wanted to close her eyes, to cut herself off from Alice's gaze, but she couldn't. 'I just— I put my whole life on hold. I was right there. I was ready. And it didn't matter. In the end, she didn't even tell me what was happening.'

'I know,' Alice said, tucking Briar back into the crook of her shoulder and squeezing her arms around her tightly.

Briar wasn't sure how long she cried, only that slowly she was able to focus on all the places she and Alice were pressed together, the soft touch of their knees, the heat of Alice's skin under her cheek, Alice's fingers digging into her waist. She felt calmer, her mind clearing.

The profound exhaustion that only came from a full-body cry threatened to overtake her. She raised her head, glancing at Alice and dreading any reaction from her. Briar couldn't handle pity, or understanding, or grief. She had no more room for anyone else's emotions.

Alice's expression remained impassive, taking in Briar's red, snotty appearance as if she were cataloguing changes in a petri dish. She rose, guiding Briar back to their bedroom. Alice stripped the tear-stained tank top over Briar's head and replaced it with the ratty T-shirt Briar liked to sleep in. She gently pushed Briar onto their bed before shuffling around the room, turning off lights and closing drawers. Briar's eyes slowly closed, comforted by the sound of Alice's footsteps.

A warm, damp cloth was placed on her forehead, soothing the tension headache that was forming. Alice swiped the towel along her face, and down the sides of her neck. She scrubbed Briar's left arm and then the right, the pressure of her fingertips releasing tension Briar didn't even know she was holding. Alice moved onto her legs, cleaning her thighs and around her knees, kneading at her calves in a way that made Briar groan softly. Her moans turned to giggles as Alice reached her feet, dragging the washcloth between her toes before finally washing away the grime on the bottom of each foot.

She snuggled beside Briar, folding easily around her and drawing the top sheet over them.

Something important had shifted between them, but sleep claimed Briar before she could name it.

Chapter 24

Alice

The summer was ending.

It had always been like this. There would come a time when Alice would realize fall was impending, and her brain would flip to prematurely mourn the end of camp and the return to real life, counting the days as though she was facing the worst kind of sentence upon returning home.

But somehow, this time, she hadn't been expecting it, and as she sat with the campers around the bonfire, her limbs grew heavy with bittersweet emotion.

Robin and his friends giggled as they stuck marshmallows on sticks to roast. Seeing them together, Alice was hit by a wave of nostalgia for the bonfires of her own youth, for the feeling that there were so many opportunities ahead of her.

At the time, high school had felt like just another place where Alice had to be perfect. Now, she wondered if it was the freest she would ever feel. She'd come so far – left home, come out, pursued her dream career – and somehow felt just as trapped as she had at eighteen, but with no real means of remaking her life again. She'd taken too many steps down one path before realizing that there were no diverging trails ahead.

The bonfire marked the start of the last week of camp. After that, they would spend a week packing up. And then she would go back to London, interview for a job, and start the next stage of her life. A stage 4,000 miles away from these woods, from this summer.

She looked at Briar, sitting with a group of campers, and was overwhelmed by the wrongness of leaving her all over again. The first time, it had been an impulse, a reflex to prevent her heart from breaking any further. That heartbreak had blindsided her, upending the life that she'd known. This time she was willingly walking into the heartbreak, eyes wide open. Freddie cleared his throat meaningfully from beside her.

'Look, I don't want to put something else on Briar's plate,' he said, looking down. 'But I was wondering if you know whether she can hire me in the fall.'

Alice studied him, confused. 'I thought you had a job.'

'They can't sponsor my visa anymore. So I asked Briar if she'd be willing to take me on, just for the year.' His expression was unusually grave.

'Oh,' Alice said. 'Honestly, I'm not sure what she's thinking when it comes to the fall...' She trailed off, unsure if it was her place to tell Freddie that Briar was almost certainly selling the camp. It felt like Briar's news to share.

Freddie nodded. 'That's fine, I'll give her more time. I know it's a big ask.'

Alice grabbed his hand, squeezing it. 'Hey, we'll figure it out.'

'*Bri-ar, Bri-ar, Bri-ar,*' the kids who Briar was holding court with started chanting, and Briar stood. Everyone fell silent.

'Okay, okay,' Briar said, holding her hands up in defeat, 'I'll sing something, but only if you promise to be on your best behavior for the rest of the night.' Her gaze swept across the group, landing on Alice for a moment. Alice wanted to bottle the feeling of Briar looking at her like that, like the two of them were sharing a secret, forever.

Noah handed Briar his guitar and she played a few chords, testing them out.

Alice watched her, trying unsuccessfully to clear her mind of all of the unproductive thoughts that surfaced at the sight of Briar in the firelight, at the knowledge that she was going to hear her sing one last time.

Something had changed between the two of them in the last week, and it felt like they couldn't go back to how they had been at the beginning of the summer. It should have been a good thing, but instead it just made Alice sad.

She wanted so badly to go back to when Briar had given her the friendship bracelet that very first summer, to savor every moment. When it had seemed like anything was possible, with Briar at her side. When she couldn't fathom there would ever be an ending.

'This is one of my favorites,' Briar said, looking at Alice again. 'Apparently Paul McCartney wrote it when he was fourteen, so all you fourteen-year-olds out there, take notes. You could be world-famous musicians one day.'

She played the first notes of 'When I'm Sixty-Four', and Alice felt a tightening in her chest that could only mean she was about to cry.

She was grateful to camp, in a way, for making her act so irrational. She never would have kissed Briar all those years ago if it wasn't for camp, a place where she had always been reckless. And she never normally would have quit her real life to spend a summer trying to apologize to a friend, but love seemed to evoke strange responses from her.

Briar had learned how to play this song when they were twelve. It was the summer Alice had skipped her art classes to take extra music ones alongside Briar. Alice had discovered that summer that she was completely tone deaf, and that Briar had the voice of an angel.

As Briar sang the song's final stanza, Alice allowed some tears to escape. By letting a few out, she hoped that she could act like an actual functioning human for the rest of the campfire, and not a mess. Everything in moderation.

Once she was back in London, these feelings would stop, she was sure of it. She'd managed to move on once before.

Briar handed off the guitar to Noah, who performed a spirited rendition of 'Yellow Submarine'. Alice expected Briar to return to the campers she'd been with before, but instead she sat next to her.

'Hey,' she said, resting a hand on Alice's knee. 'What's wrong?'

'Nothing,' Alice said. 'I forgot how good you are.'

'Remember when you tried to learn it too?' Briar asked, grinning.

Alice swatted at her arm. 'No need to lord it over me.'

Briar put a hand on her chest in mock affront. 'I would never.' Alice narrowed her eyes. 'Oh, well, if you insist…' She broke into a quiet rendition of Alice's nasally singing voice.

'Fuck off,' Alice said, smiling.

Briar brought her face even closer to Alice's. 'I just wanted to see if I could make you say *fuck*.'

Alice laughed. 'You're such a child.'

The campers around them erupted into applause and they turned back to Noah, who was giving a theatrical series of bows to his fans. Freddie stood next, gesturing for quiet.

'Back by popular demand,' he announced, 'it's your favorite duo! What do you think' – he turned to Sierra – 'can they handle it?'

Sierra nodded. 'I don't see any fainters.'

Freddie broke into song.

'He has such a beautiful soprano,' Alice muttered to Briar, and she was rewarded with Briar's laughter, which had once been, and had again become, Alice's favorite sound in the world.

Freddie and Sierra continued, the performance somehow morphing into Sierra giving an educational lecture on indigenous history as Freddie did an interpretive dance in the background.

'Andddd remember, kids, imperialism is *not* giving. Or whatever it is you all say nowadays,' Sierra said, as they reached what Alice supposed was the end.

'Should we have let them do that?' Alice asked out of the side of her mouth.

The final piece of self-control that was keeping Alice composed broke at the sight of Briar hunched over, red-faced and giggling. She laughed at the sound of Briar's laughter.

'Definitely—' Another peal of laughter overtook Briar. 'Definitely not.'

'We're terrible camp directors, aren't we?' Alice asked, wiping a tear from Briar's cheek with her thumb. 'Are we scarring these children permanently?'

'They'll bounce back.'

'What about us?' Alice asked. 'I don't think I'll ever get the image of Freddie doing the splits while Sierra sings "This Land Is Your Land" un-ingrained from my hippocampus.'

'We're long past any chance at normalcy for you, I'm afraid,' Briar said.

'Are you okay? I've never known you to *giggle*.' Freddie plopped himself down next to Alice. 'Actually, you two have been laughing an awful lot recently.' He looked between them for a drawn-out moment. 'Anything you want to tell me?'

'No,' Briar said.

'Are you getting high on Cook's supply?' he accused.

'No!' Alice said, still laughing, catching Briar's eye and reveling in the feeling of having a shared language with her again. She felt a pang of recognition, as if this scene had happened before. That was what it meant to have a best friend like Briar – someone who had shaped the way Alice's brain worked in ways she would never be able to understand the extent of.

She knew now that her heartbreak at eighteen hadn't been teenage angst. She'd loved Briar then, and loved her now. Maybe she'd never stopped.

Alice was propelled to her feet. 'I need to talk to Noah and Harper.'

She wanted to give Briar one last magical moment of the summer, something she could look back on positively despite what came next. And she would need help to pull it off.

Alice made her way around the fire pit to where Noah and Harper were talking in hushed tones. There was a hint of tension that reminded Alice of the poker night.

'Hi,' she said awkwardly, wishing she'd timed her bright idea to not interrupt what was clearly an important conversation.

'Hi,' Noah said, easily turning his furrowed brow into a clear expression. Harper's frown didn't fade as quickly.

'Briar's birthday is in ten days—' Alice started.

'We know,' Harper interrupted.

'Right, of course you do. I was just thinking it would be nice if we could surprise her with a party.'

'I think that's a great idea,' Noah said.

'We should get the old crew down here, anyone who's able to come on short notice: Rafa, Zach, Sonya. And you guys can get in touch with her college friends, maybe? Her roommates?'

Harper nodded. 'Sure.'

'Should we have it here?' Noah asked. 'Or back in DC?'

'My idea was to do it at Susan's house. I have a list of projects that need to get done. I don't want Briar to have to do all of them in the fall, when she'll have so many other things to catch up on. So we could fix it up as a surprise.'

'I *am* pretty handy,' Noah said.

Alice nodded. 'We can enlist Freddie, Sierra and Cook too. The kids are so much better behaved than the first session, we can do with less coverage. I think they could smell our fear.'

'Like sharks,' Noah agreed.

Harper looked up at him. 'That's blood, not fear, babe.'

'Thanks for taking my plan in stride.'

'Oh, there was a choice?' Harper deadpanned. Noah nudged her with his elbow. 'Kidding!'

'If this is about apologizing,' Noah said, gesturing toward where Briar was trying not to be obvious about observing them, 'I don't think you need to anymore. I feel confident that you're forgiven.'

—

'It's time!' Briar said cheerily, intercepting Alice as she was making her way back to their cabin after a clandestine party planning meeting with Noah, Harper and Cook.

'Huh?' Alice said, feeling caught out. 'I was just… walking!'

'Yes, I can see that,' Briar said. 'Are you ready to prep?'

'Oh. The interview.' Briar had been insisting they make time for it for the past week, but Alice had been procrastinating. 'Maybe tomorrow?'

Briar linked her arm with Alice's, pulling her toward the mess hall. 'First, fuel.'

Once they had raided the kitchen, Briar laid out a series of index cards on one of the mess hall tables. Alice stared at her in wonder.

'I still do this when I prep for job interviews,' Briar explained. 'The Alice Hughes Method, patent pending.' Alice felt her cheeks go pink. 'Now, write out your responses to each question while I make popcorn.'

Briar disappeared and Alice got to work writing responses.

'Ready?' Briar asked, returning. She collected the cards, shuffling them and then sitting across from Alice. 'Tell me about yourself.'

Alice cleared her throat. 'I'm entering my final year of a DPhil in mycology at Oxford University. I've been Dr. Jeremy Beecham's research assistant for the past three years. Prior to Oxford, I graduated with a degree in biology with first-class honors from St. Andrews.' It was an easy recitation of her resume, something Alice had done thousands of times at networking events.

Briar cocked her head to the side. 'Why mushrooms?'

Alice blinked. 'That wasn't on any of the cards.'

'Gotta be able to think on your feet,' Briar chided.

'I spent a lot of time in the woods as a child,' Alice said wryly, since explaining this to Briar felt like the most pointless exercise in the world. 'I grew attached to the forest floor, playing in the dirt.' Getting dirty had been a novel experience for Alice. So much of her life was pristine: the sterile house she shared with her mother, the platinum blonde hair she meticulously maintained and the grades she received. Having one sliver of mess in her life was her only rebellion. 'I came across a beautiful mushroom one day, and I showed it to my camp counselor. She opened a new world to me, the world of decomposers. I was fascinated with the way that something could become nothing, all because of this small and seemingly innocuous thing.'

'What's camp?' Briar joked.

'Fair point,' she said. 'I'll just say it was for school or something. Tell him I found a picture of a mushroom in a book and was taken by it and asked my teacher what it was.'

The thought of encountering a mushroom for the first time in a classroom felt wrong, a betrayal of the girl who had sat in the dirt studying them her whole childhood, but she pushed that aside.

Briar nodded, flipping to the next card. 'Why do you want this job?'

Alice's mind went completely blank, forgetting everything she'd written down. The only thing she could think of was how it would feel to tell her parents about it. Her mom would congratulate her on a job well done, and her dad would return her email with encouragement.

'This job aligns perfectly with what I've envisioned for my career,' she said, reciting the words that Jeremy had put in his email to her. 'The Royal Botanical Society will give me the resources to put more time and energy into my research. I'll be at the cutting edge of the field, not just citing others but being cited.'

It wasn't as gratifying a thought as she had expected it to be. The citations would mean something to her parents and her peers, but the job itself would mean even more hours poring over books, working with men who would never fully respect her, presenting at conferences to bored academics. It would mean less time outside. It would be a life like the one she'd left behind in London, a life she now realized she hardly missed at all.

'You missed a few points on that one,' Briar said, oblivious to Alice's racing thoughts. 'You'll want to make it more personal and grounded in your day-to-day, so your passion comes across. Obviously, it's not all about the prestige for you.'

Alice nodded. 'That makes sense.'

She was overwhelmed by the thought of more prep. She hadn't left herself the time, hadn't even thought of the interview when she'd had the idea to fix up Susan's house. Camp had taken away some of her edge, softening her in ways she hadn't known she'd had to look out for. To go back to academia, she would need to sharpen up again.

Briar flipped to the next card. 'What accomplishment are you most proud of?'

Again, Alice couldn't remember the words she'd written. Looking into Briar's hazel eyes, she felt proud that she'd stuck around when she'd wanted to leave midway through the summer. She felt proud that she was going to be able to take some of the burden of fixing up the house off her. She felt proud of Robin for making friends. She felt proud of herself, for introducing him to what she hoped would be a lifelong love of decomposers.

She searched desperately through her academic accomplishments, her research, trying to think of an anecdote to answer the question.

She recited a story about winning departmental honors for a project she'd worked on with Jeremy.

The interview didn't leave Alice's head for the rest of the day and into the night. As she listened to Briar's steady breathing, she hated her brain for not being able to shut off. She needed to do something, to talk to someone. But it would be too early for Tess.

She found herself at the phone, dialing her dad's number, before she realized what she was doing. She'd done it in high school sometimes when her insomnia had made her lonely, picking up the phone and talking to him about school, about her assignments. It had been years since she'd called him this late, but she doubted his routine had changed much.

'Hello?'

Alice couldn't remember the last time she'd heard his voice; it had been at least a year. 'Hi, Dad. It's Alice.'

'Oh,' he said, and she could tell she had startled him. 'Is everything alright? What number are you calling from?'

'Everything's fine,' she said, though it felt like a lie. 'I'm at Camp Lakeside. Where I used to go?' It came out as a question; she couldn't be sure her father remembered anything about her life.

'Oh?' His tone was distracted.

'I've been helping out this summer. Because Susan died.'

'I'm sorry to hear that.' Alice hated how she couldn't tell if he knew who Susan was or if he was just humoring her. 'You're not in London?'

'I'm going back in a couple of weeks.' She squeezed her eyes shut. 'I'm interviewing for a job when I go back. It's a prestigious one, at the largest research organization for mycology in the UK.'

'So, you'll be staying in London, then,' he said, not a question but a statement.

Alice blinked. He almost sounded sad. 'I suppose so, if I get it.'

'What does that mean for the wedding?'

And then his concern made sense. 'Oh, nothing.'

Her dad sighed. 'Your grandparents have been asking about you. And I think it would be good for people to see you there.'

'Good for people to see me...' Alice repeated slowly. He meant he wanted the opportunity to play at being a good father, to explain her existence as the distant but doting daughter, rather than the truth: that she hadn't seen him in half a decade. 'Is it not enough for them to see your *other* children?'

There was silence on the other end of the line. Alice had never spoken like that to him before, and she didn't know if it had made her feel better or worse.

'I'll give you some time...'

'I don't need time,' Alice said. 'I'm not coming. And you can give people whatever excuse you want.'

'I guess there's nothing I can say to that, is there?'

'You could apologize,' Alice said, feeling bold.

He sighed again, as though Alice were sucking the life from him by asking him to do anything at all. 'Would it make a difference?'

For years, she'd waited for him to come visit her in DC, to take her out to lunch, to tell her that he knew what he had done had been wrong. To admit that he hadn't just betrayed her mom, but had ruined Alice's life in the process.

For years, she'd wondered if she was exactly the same as him, destroying everything she touched, leaving a wreck in her wake.

'I don't know,' she admitted quietly.

'Good night, Alice.'

'Good night.'

She sat, staring at the phone, unsure of what she had just done. It wasn't clear to her if she had altered the trajectory of her relationship with her dad forever, or if the thing it had always been was now just out in the open. She'd been the perfect daughter her whole life and had destroyed it in a second.

She walked out of the cabin and down the path towards the mess hall, thinking a cup of tea might help. But when she entered the kitchen, she was surprised to see Harper already standing over the stove.

'What are you doing here?' Alice demanded, annoyed that she couldn't sulk in peace.

Harper started, turning. 'Making hot chocolate. What are *you* doing here?'

Alice sighed, dropping into a chair and rubbing her eyes. 'Tea.'

'Couldn't sleep?' Harper asked, her tone softer. When Alice looked up, she saw that Harper was pouring boiling water into two mugs. 'What kind of tea?'

'Peppermint, please. It's in—'

'I got it,' Harper interrupted, opening Cook's tea drawer as though she'd done it a thousand times before.

Alice's eyes narrowed. 'When did you become so familiar with this kitchen?'

Harper pursed her lips. 'When are you going to stop thinking everything I do is some sort of plot against you?'

Alice huffed out a breath. 'I guess you haven't done anything that terrible to me this summer.'

'Nothing that terrible?' Harper repeated incredulously. 'I've saved your ass. Multiple times.'

'Yeah, okay,' Alice admitted. 'I'm sorry.'

Harper eyed her suspiciously for a moment more, as though Alice was going to say something mean.

'Apology accepted,' she said, sliding the tea to Alice.

'Why are you being nice to me?' Alice asked, watching Harper prepare her hot chocolate.

Harper snorted. 'Why would I be mean to you?'

'You were pretty mean in high school,' Alice said.

Harper didn't answer immediately, busying herself with wiping cocoa powder off the counter.

'It wasn't that deep,' she said finally. 'I was sixteen and jealous.'

'You were jealous of *me*?' Alice asked, incredulous. Harper had never once given her the impression that she had looked upon her with anything other than disdain. She'd made Alice feel like she didn't belong in their group, like she was missing some innate social knowledge that every other person had. It didn't make sense for her to have been jealous when everyone had liked her and no one had liked Alice.

Harper cocked her head, sitting across from Alice. 'You're at Oxford and you didn't put together that I had a crush on my fiancé when you were dating him?'

'I mean...' Alice said, blowing on her tea, 'I guess I knew, yeah. I just thought you separately hated me for unrelated reasons.'

Harper let out a surprised laugh. 'Well, it didn't help that you were smarter than me.'

Alice shook her head. 'I wasn't smarter. I just studied more.'

'No, you definitely were.' Harper hummed thoughtfully. 'It used to really piss me off. I'd get a 96 on a test and you'd get a 98. It was like no matter how good I was, you were always better.'

Alice shrugged, not sure what to say to that. 'Sometimes I felt like it was the only thing I had going for me,' she admitted. 'You were popular. I wasn't.'

'Are you being nice to me now?' Harper asked, feigning shock.

'Only for now. You haven't said why you know where the tea is, so I'm still suspicious.'

'I've come in here a few times when I couldn't sleep,' Harper said, staring down at her mug.

'Something wrong?' Alice asked.

'No,' Harper said quickly. Then, looking at Alice's face, she added, 'Weddings are messy. Anyway, why are *you* awake?'

'I called my dad.' Alice couldn't explain it further.

Harper considered her for a moment. 'He's a dick, right? Left your mom?'

'You remember that?'

'Know thy enemy,' Harper said.

'Yeah, he cheated on her,' Alice said. She thought back on how harsh she'd been with him, but no longer felt bad about it. 'I asked him to apologize.'

Harper nodded. 'I get it. I've tried to get my parents to apologize for a lot of things.' She grimaced. 'It never goes well.'

'They're still together?' Alice asked.

'Unfortunately,' Harper replied, running her finger over the lip of her mug. 'I think they thought staying together would be better for me. But it was a lot of pressure. Like I needed to succeed to make it worth it for them.'

Alice wondered if her parents would be happy now if they'd stayed together. She couldn't picture it.

Harper sighed. 'It was better when I went to college. No, actually, it was way worse, but then it got better. Having Briar and Noah was good for me.'

'Yeah,' Alice said. She knew what it felt like to be surrounded by people who cared about her. It was something she'd spent the last decade of her life convincing herself she no longer needed.

'They remind me that I didn't have to be anything more than myself,' Harper said. 'Is that corny?'

Alice smiled. 'Only a little.'

Harper shrugged. 'Whatever. They're my best friends. I can be corny for them.'

Alice's chest ached at the declaration. It was a glimpse into what her life could've been if she'd never left; it was another reminder that no matter what happened this summer, she would leave again. She reached over and squeezed Harper's hand. 'I'm really glad that Briar has you.'

Chapter 25

Alice

Alice had devised a schedule for fixing up the house, breaking down every task to match each person's capabilities until all the projects were scheduled to be completed exactly on time. She had also created cover stories for the majority of the excursions, although for some of them Freddie and Sierra were just supposed to keep Briar too distracted to notice the missing staff.

Physical labor was a great distraction from her now hard-to-ignore feelings. And Noah proved to be an invaluable asset, both in his strength and his high spirits. When Alice's energy flagged, when she just wanted to give up, go back to camp, and wrap her arms around Briar, he was quick to remind her that it would all be worth it when they got to see Briar's face at the party.

By the third day, they'd fallen into an easy familiarity with each other, joking around as they worked to reattach the closet door, with Noah holding it while Alice tackled the screws.

'Are you sure you know how to use a screwdriver?' Noah asked, his arms shaking from the weight.

'Yes, I'm sure,' Alice said, blowing a strand of hair out of her face. 'Would you like to try?'

'I'm just the brute strength, you're the brains.'

'Mind over matter,' Alice muttered, working the hinge open. 'Distract yourself, so you don't think about your arms hurting. Talk about something.'

'Okay, um…' She pictured him closing his eyes, focusing. 'Harper refuses to acknowledge her parents' disapproval of our relationship. And I don't know how to talk to her about it, because I'm technically not supposed to know.' He paused. 'And our venue coordinator called me last week and told me the final check, the one her parents were supposed to write, hasn't arrived.'

'Woah, okay,' Alice said, as she finally managed to get the hinge tight enough. 'You can let go of it now. It should stay in place.'

'I just wish she'd tell me. The wedding's in a few months. If we're finding a new venue, she needs my help.'

Alice stood and brushed off her pants. 'Noah, your parents are the best.'

Noah looked confused. 'Yeah?'

'Harper's parents are assholes, and you don't understand what that's like. Which is amazing, but sometimes limiting.' She paused, and he looked at her like he was realizing something. She continued quickly, 'Admitting that your parents don't care about your happiness… it feels like a personal failing. Surely, if you were good enough, if you were lovable, then they would love you, right?'

She thought she'd said it unemotionally, logically explaining human psychology. Based on his expression, Noah didn't seem to feel that way.

'Oh, Alice,' he said softly.

'This is about Harper,' she insisted. 'You have to be patient with her. This isn't about you, or how much she trusts you. It's about how she feels about herself.'

Noah nodded. 'Thanks for telling me that,' he said seriously, and Alice felt like she was going to cry for the millionth time that week.

Just then, Harper walked through the front door. 'Hey, guys,' she said. 'FYI, there's a case of scabies going around. So that's fun.'

Alice shuddered 'How's Briar coping?'

'Oh, fine,' Harper said. 'She said anything's better than lice.'

'She *was* scratching her head for weeks.'

'I think she's in better spirits now too,' Harper said, coming over to give Noah a kiss on the cheek. 'Might have you to thank for that, Alice.'

'Would it be pushing your gratitude to ask you to learn plumbing?' Alice asked.

'Most definitely.'

She sighed. 'Noah?'

'On it!' he said, retreating to the kitchen. 'Bringing out the big guns: dudes on YouTube who refuse to spend money on handymen.'

'I have another task for you,' Alice said, looking at Harper. 'I need your help with a group text.'

'What are you so scared of?'

'I don't know,' Alice said drily, 'that people might be mad that I've ghosted them for a decade?'

'Everyone will be happy to see Briar. Just focus on that.'

Alice showed the text to Harper for approval.

> Hey all! Alice here. Sorry for the long time, no text. Noah, Harper & I are planning a party down at Briar's mom's house in Virginia for her birthday on 8/3 @ 3 p.m. There will be food & booze. Hope you can make it!

Alice pressed send. Before she could worry that no one would respond, a ping sounded.

'See?' Harper said, when Alice showed her. 'Keep expectations of your behavior low, and you'll always meet them.'

But Alice worried that she didn't want to keep expectations of her behavior low anymore, that she now wanted the impossible. To be known as someone who showed up, who was a loyal friend, and who fought for her relationships instead of letting them go as soon as they became difficult. And she knew she couldn't be that person. In two weeks, she would once again be the girl who left.

–

On the final night of the session, Alice didn't make it back to the cabin until late. She'd been making the rounds, ensuring suitcases were packed, stuffies were secured, and pickup plans were memorized. It had been a hard night of goodbyes.

'Bri?' she called out as she climbed up the porch steps. There was no answer.

Alice crept into the hallway, catching the door before it could slam behind her. She tiptoed into the bedroom, listening for Briar's light snores, but there was only silence.

Alice felt arms sneak around her waist, pulling her backwards into a warm body.

'Jesus, you scared me,' Alice said, trying to turn around, but Briar's hands tightened on her hips, keeping her still.

'What took you so long?' Briar murmured into her ear, kissing the back of her neck. The sensation shot goosebumps down Alice's back.

'There was a lot to do,' Alice said, her voice growing weaker as Briar kissed across her shoulder, slipping the strap of her tank top down. 'Why are all the lights off?'

Briar laughed, her breath tickling Alice's skin. 'I wanted to surprise you.'

There was a rustling behind her, like Briar was digging around in her pockets, and then the room was cast in a low pink glow. Briar had hung fairy lights all around the room, ones that faded from pink to purple to blue and then back again. It gave the room a magical glow.

'Oh,' Alice said, touched.

'I thought we could celebrate surviving the summer,' Briar said, her lips brushing the sensitive skin under Alice's jaw.

'Like a party?' Alice asked coyly, grinding back, enjoying how Briar's fingers tightened on her hips. 'Should I invite the others?'

Briar bit sharply at Alice's jaw, making her gasp. 'I'd rather you didn't.'

'Why's that?'

'Because I wanted to thank you,' Briar said, then spun Alice around in her arms. Their faces were close, and Alice's body was practically vibrating with anticipation. She leaned in, but Briar kept her lips just out of reach. 'Properly.'

Then Briar kissed her, groaning as she tugged at Alice's hair.

Alice melted into her, hooking a leg around Briar's calf and nearly toppling them. They broke apart, and Briar fell to her knees.

'What—' Alice started, only to be hushed by Briar.

'Just let me take care of you,' Briar said, pulling at the laces of Alice's boots, taking them off, followed by her socks. She kissed Alice's knees, her fingers drifting up the back of her thighs. Alice felt unstable, like if Briar wasn't holding on to her, she'd collapse.

Briar undid the front of her shorts, pulling them down and leaving Alice in her tank top and panties.

'This seems hardly fair,' Alice breathed. 'You're still dressed.'

'This is about you,' Briar said, kissing up her thigh.

'And if *I* want to see you?'

Briar paused as if she were considering, then dropped a final kiss to Alice's hipbone before standing. Alice reached for Briar's shirt, pulling it over her head, then fumbled at the drawstring of her shorts.

Briar huffed out a laugh, swatting Alice's hands away. 'So impatient.'

'Well, stop teasing me,' Alice said, biting at the side of her neck. She sucked at the skin there, selfishly wanting to leave a mark, wanting there to be some proof of her having been there, even after she was gone.

Briar pushed her, and Alice fell onto the bed with a gasp. She only had a second to recover before Briar was on top of her, grinding a knee between Alice's thighs. The friction was torture, lighting a fire low in her abdomen. Alice claimed Briar's mouth with a kiss, snaking a hand down to grab her ass and bring their bodies together.

Briar broke away, her expression making Alice shiver. Briar was even more beautiful like this, her bangs sweaty and stuck to her forehead, her lips wet and swollen from kissing, her eyes dark and dangerous.

'You're distracting me,' Briar said.

Alice blinked, trying to figure out why they weren't kissing anymore. 'Sorry?'

Briar grinned at her, chest heaving. 'This is meant to be a thank you. So if you don't mind…'

She ducked her head, lips trailing down to Alice's chest. Briar pushed up Alice's tank top, mouthing at Alice's abdomen and lower still.

Finally, Alice's brain caught up with Briar's words. 'You don't have to— Oh, holy shit.'

And then she couldn't argue anymore.

—

'What are you thinking about?' Briar asked her afterwards, playing with Alice's hair.

'That I didn't get a s'more at the campfire,' Alice said wistfully. 'The campers wouldn't leave me alone. They needed to tell me every detail about the mushrooms they found during their hike.'

'They love you,' Briar cooed.

'No, they love mushrooms, which is honestly better,' Alice said. 'I hope I've just created a new crop of mycologists.'

'I'd study mushrooms if it was you teaching.'

A few seconds passed and then Alice sat up suddenly.

'Oh no,' Briar said, but a smile was blooming on her face. 'That's your scheming face.'

'Do you want to sneak into the kitchen and make s'mores?' Alice asked, grinning at her. 'Like we used to?'

Briar shook her head slowly, but Alice could tell she was just playing the part. 'I'm too old for those sorts of unlawful activities. I'm reformed now. No one can pull me into the world of crime again.'

'Not even me?' Alice asked, tracing Briar's collarbone with a finger.

'Well...' Briar breathed.

'Come on,' Alice said, pulling her out of bed.

They pulled on semi-presentable clothes and made their way to the mess hall without a flashlight, not wanting to be caught. It felt like they were kids again, the adrenaline pumping through Alice's veins, making her feel giddy.

'You know we have a key, right?' Briar asked as she boosted Alice through the mess hall window.

'But it's more fun to break in.'

There was only one problem: when they got into the kitchen, Robin and Sam were already there, making s'mores over the stove.

'What's this?' Alice said reproachfully. 'You already had s'mores! While you were pestering me with questions!'

Robin shrugged, unconcerned by being caught. 'We wanted another.'

'Why are you here, anyway?' Sam asked, his eyes narrowing on Alice and Briar.

'We got a tip-off,' Briar said, very convincingly, 'that there had been a kitchen break-in.'

'These sorts of trespasses have to be dealt with by the highest authority,' Alice said.

Briar glanced sideways at her, and Alice could tell that she was almost on the verge of breaking the act and cracking a smile. 'That's us. The authority.'

It took everything in Alice not to laugh, picturing Robin and Sam watching them squeeze through the window – a feat that had been much more easily accomplished when they were smaller.

'Then why did you break in?' Robin asked suspiciously.

'We were testing out the potential entry points,' Alice said.

'We just came in through there,' Sam said, pointing at the ajar door to the mess hall.

Alice made eye contact with Briar, knowing exactly what was going through her head. That Cook had *completely* gone soft if he was leaving doors unlocked now.

'We'll let this go, as long as you go back to bed now without any fuss,' Alice said.

The boys shrugged. 'Okay.'

'But we'll be confiscating that,' Alice said, taking the s'more out of Robin's hand as he walked out the door.

'You're not going to make sure we go to our bunk?' Sam asked, turning back.

'We have to secure the entry points,' Briar said.

'And we'll know,' Alice said, pulling her face into a frown, 'if you don't go back to your bunk. We have eyes *everywhere*.'

Sam nodded gravely, and the two of them disappeared out the door of the mess hall. Alice and Briar dissolved into laughter as soon as they were out of earshot, falling to the floor with heaving breaths.

'Stop—' Alice got out. 'Stop making me—'

'I'm not…' Briar wheezed.

'I just want to eat my s'more.' Alice pouted, and Briar managed to collect herself, her eyes on the ceiling.

Alice ate in silence, relishing every bite. 'I'm just so happy he made a friend,' she said, trying to explain the feeling of lightness, of absolute freedom, that she was experiencing for the first time in years. 'And he makes a perfect s'more. There's nothing left for me to teach him.'

Briar grabbed Alice's sticky hand, squeezing it. 'I know,' she said, and Alice was sure she understood every unsaid word.

'I wish we could stay here forever,' Alice said. 'Live in this exact moment and never wake up in the morning.'

'We can't,' Briar said, turning to face her, their noses touching. 'But we can watch the sunrise, if you want.'

So they did.

—

With the campers no longer there to distract her, Briar finally caught Alice, Cook and Noah sneaking off.

'Where are you going?' she asked, narrowing her eyes at them and then at the car they had been about to get into. 'Alice, aren't you meant to be clearing some trails? For the fourth time this week?'

'I got Lee to cover for me,' Alice said smoothly, naming a British counselor who was, in fact, covering for her. 'An emergency came up.'

'What emergency?' Briar asked, hands on her hips.

'Those eejit raccoons got into me oven,' Cook supplied quickly.

'It's unusable now,' Noah said, employing his best wide-eyed innocent expression.

'There's a store a couple of hours away,' Alice said.

'There's a Home Depot in Frederick,' Briar said, her eyes on Alice. 'You should go there, you'll be back sooner.'

It took everything in her to continue the farce. She knew that Briar needed the party, the house fixed and off her mind, much more than a few more hours of Alice's company. She was doing the right thing, it just felt wrong when Briar was looking at her like that. Like she was depending on her.

Alice swallowed, her whole body constricted by the expectations that Briar had seemed to develop for her. When Alice hadn't been paying attention, they had slipped into a relationship she would miss terribly in the coming months. She just had to hope Briar didn't feel the same way, that at least one of them would come away from this unscathed.

'Cook wants a specific one, and they only have it in Alexandria,' Alice finally managed, her voice coming out uneven. 'We'll be back as soon as we can.' Briar nodded reluctantly.

When they pulled onto the highway, Alice cleared her throat. 'I hope she's not onto us.'

'I don't think she is,' Noah said, glancing at Alice in the rearview mirror.

Alice closed her eyes for a second. She wouldn't have minded Noah knowing about her and Briar, but now that they were this far in, it felt impossible to come clean. If Briar wanted her dalliance with Alice to be kept a secret, Alice could only follow that directive and try not to think about why Briar was so insistent on it.

'She must be stressed about the end of the summer,' Alice said finally.

Noah's eyes flashed to hers in the rearview mirror again. 'About you leaving, you mean?'

'No,' Alice said, hoping she was right. 'When the summer ends, real life starts.'

'She's not scared of real life – she's done this a million times before, finished camp and gone back to school or jobs. She's scared of real life without you.'

'She's scared of real life without *Susan*,' Alice corrected.

'That's part of it,' Noah agreed. 'But as the person who saw her through you leaving the last time, I think you should trust my judgement when I tell you she's going to miss you.'

Alice swallowed. 'I don't know why you're telling me this. My life is in London.'

'Aye, and he's saying ye have a life here too,' Cook said quietly.

Noah frowned. 'Just don't pull a disappearing act again, okay?'

'I'm figuring it out,' Alice said, focusing on folding her hands tightly in her lap. 'I don't want to hurt her again, believe me.'

'I believe you,' Noah said, cracking a smile, his easy demeanor returning. 'I had to bring out the tough guy act. She *is* my best friend, after all.'

'I'm glad she has you,' Alice said, staring through the window.

When they pulled into the driveway, Cook whistled. 'This place is looking ship-shape,' he said admiringly. 'Alice Hughes, you're a miracle worker.'

'It's all Noah,' Alice muttered sheepishly.

'How much is she selling for?' Cook asked, as they got out of the car.

'I don't know,' Alice said, walking up the porch steps. She was proud to note that it did look significantly nicer with a structurally sound railing. 'Briar seems too focused on fixing it up to think of anything beyond that.'

'You know,' Cook said, 'I have a bit of retirement saved up. And a small fiefdom in northern Scotland bequeathed to me by a duke…'

He kept talking, but Alice barely followed the dizzying details of Cook's almost certainly fictional story, which seemed to involve a duke disguised as a pirate, lovers separated by circumstance, and a badly behaved lion.

Chapter 26

Briar

Briar watched from the parking lot as the counselors closed the cabins up for the summer, dragging mattresses into storage and deep cleaning the bunks. How children got so sticky was still a mystery to Briar, but the phenomenon required thorough scrubbing of all surfaces.

She might be giving them pointless work to maintain a camp that was soon to become hunting grounds. In minutes, she would be showing the potential buyers around, while hopefully avoiding anyone finding out. It was hot, and sweat dripped out of every pore on her body. There was no place she wanted to be less.

As a car appeared in the distance, Briar wrangled her emotions into less complicated shapes, pulling herself into the charming persona she used at the bar.

'Hey there,' she called to the man who stepped out of the car. He was tall, dressed simply in khakis and a blue shirt, but the fit of them screamed custom tailoring. His wife wore a large woven hat and a dress so white it was hard to look at in the direct sunlight. Neither of them had broken a sweat yet, and Briar felt disgusting in comparison.

'You must be Ms. Elwood,' the man said, his voice booming with a Southern twang. He put out his hand for Briar to shake. 'I'm Sonny Randolph and this is my wife, Gladys.'

'Nice to meet you,' Briar said. 'Mr. Lavish said you wanted a tour. Anything in particular you wanted to see?'

'Just want to get a sense of the land,' Sonny said. 'Whatever you want to show us.'

'I'd like to see the kitchen,' Gladys said.

Briar nodded, trying not to cringe at the thought of bringing them into the thick of the action. 'Sure, okay.'

She led them towards the cluster of cabins off the main green.

'So, I'll start with the mess hall. It's got a full chef's kitchen. It's also the only building that's winterized.'

She glanced back, trying to discern if the thought of having to install heating units in the cabins made any impact on their opinion of the property, but Sonny's opaque aviators made it impossible to tell.

She pulled open the doors to the mess hall, which was thankfully empty. The tables had been folded and stacked against the far wall, making the room look bigger.

Gladys clapped her hands. 'Oh honey, look at the skylights!'

Briar smiled tightly. 'Yeah, it's a good space. We can fit 150 in here for meals. Of course, that's children, so it will be fewer with full-sized humans.'

She'd meant it as a joke, but they ignored her, walking into the middle of the room.

'What do you think?' Gladys asked, pointing to the far side of the room. 'We can add the wet bar and dining table over there and leave this side for the living space.'

Briar squinted, trying to picture the room with real furniture and not donations from local elementary school cafeterias.

'Let me show you the kitchen,' Briar said, guiding them. When she opened the door, she was surprised to see Cook, since he should've been at least six hours into his twenty-four-hour post-camp nap. They blinked at each other before Briar realized she was blocking the Randolphs.

'Um, this is our cook,' Briar said, stepping aside. Cook gave the Randolphs a withering look.

'How do you do?' he asked, bowing his head. Briar was pretty sure only she could tell he was doing it mockingly.

Sonny smiled and clapped Cook on the back. 'An Englishman! Amazing.'

'I'm Scottish,' Cook corrected, but Sonny didn't seem to hear.

'The Randolphs are thinking about buying the camp,' Briar said awkwardly, and Cook's eyebrows almost disappeared into his hairline.

'Are they now?' he said, sizing them up more aggressively. Briar knew she only had a few moments before Cook went feral.

She began ushering the Randolphs away from him. 'Like I said, this kitchen could feed a small army, so you should have everything you need.'

Gladys evaded Briar's herding, surveying the room. 'I think we'll have to gut it.'

Briar gritted her teeth, refusing to look at Cook. 'Right,' she said brightly, grabbing the Randolphs by the shoulders and spinning them out the door.

'Your cook's quite a character,' Sonny said.

'Haha, yeah.' She couldn't get the image of Cook's face when she'd mentioned selling the camp out of her head.

Briar took them along the path to the lake, then reversed direction skillfully as she spotted Freddie. He was another person she didn't want to meet the Randolphs — she still hadn't figured out what to do about his visa.

Looping around, she pointed out the archery range and the greenhouse as they made their way towards the camp entrance.

The last stop on the tour was the director's cabin.

'This is the smallest of the residential cabins,' Briar said, showing them into the hall. 'Bedroom to the left, office to the right.'

'I think we could keep the rifles here,' Sonny said from the office doorway. 'Build custom shelves along that back wall.'

Briar blanched, her stomach flipping at the thought of her mother's books and furniture being replaced by guns, ammo and neon orange beanies.

'Well,' she said, clapping her hands together, 'is there anything else you needed to see?'

The Randolphs took the hint and followed her out the door. She led them back to their car and shook their hands again. Sonny said he'd put an offer in on Monday.

'I think you'll be pretty pleased with the number,' he said, winking as he slid into the driver's seat. Briar repressed the urge to scowl as she watched them drive off, the wheels kicking up a dust storm down the drive.

—

'Bri,' came a small voice on the other end of the line. 'I messed up.'

'What happened?' Any residual tiredness from being awoken by the phone ringing at 3 a.m. left Briar at the sound of her sister's panicked voice.

'I got the date wrong,' Hazel said. 'I thought I had another week, but my bio final is due today and I haven't even started.'

Before Briar's brain could fully understand the problem, she said, 'We'll figure it out. It's gonna be okay.'

'I can't fail this,' Hazel cried. 'I won't graduate.'

'You're going to graduate,' Briar said emphatically, her gaze flicking up at a creak in the floor, catching Alice's eye as she peered into the hall.

'You said it was a bio final?' Briar said, as Alice came over. 'Luckily, I happen to know an expert.'

Alice took the phone from Briar, turning the speaker on. 'How can I help?'

Hazel launched into a complex explanation of spore patterns, talking so fast it made Briar's head spin. But Alice just nodded along, slipping into the office to grab a pencil to take notes. Briar left them, heading toward the mess hall.

She heated water on the stove, then rummaged through the pantry for snacks. She stuffed what she could into a bag and poured the boiling water into a mug, grabbing teabags on her way out the door.

By the time she returned to the director's cabin, Alice was wide awake, pencil tucked behind her ear and hands steepled as she rapidly dictated into the receiver. From the furious clicking sounds on the other end, Briar could only assume that Hazel was typing every word.

She laid out her bounty on the floor. Alice's face brightened at the sight of Twinkies, and she made a grabbing motion. Briar tossed it over.

It occurred to her that she should probably be angry. She'd reminded the twins they needed to finish their schoolwork, and she'd raised them to understand that leaving it until the last minute was irresponsible. But hearing Alice's calm tone made it impossible to feel anything but safe; she knew everything would work out. Briar could be disappointed in Hazel at a more reasonable hour.

She pulled a knee up to her chest and rested her head on it. Tiredness returned to her bones, and her eyes slowly shut as she listened to Alice's voice.

'Briar?' Briar hummed in response, just on the edge of sleep. She felt a hand on her shoulder. 'Hey, go back to bed. I got this.'

Briar blinked up at Alice. The light in the hall had shifted slightly, and Briar had no sense of how long she'd been asleep.

'Haze?'

'I'm still here,' Hazel's voice sounded small over the speaker, but there was no longer any panic in it. 'Ally gave me an outline. I think it's gonna be okay.'

'It definitely will be,' Alice said, grabbing Briar's hand and pulling her up. 'You basically had all the research done. You were in a much better position than you thought. You just needed some help organizing it.'

Briar's heart clenched at the warmth in Alice's tone, her sleepy brain supplying her with pictures of Alice working with her students, of what her life in academia must be like. She found herself jealous of Alice's future Royal Botanical Society colleagues, of the people who would benefit from her brilliance every day. They didn't know how lucky they would be, how they had taken her from someone an ocean away.

Then she crawled back into bed, wrapping the blankets tightly around her and hugging a pillow to her chest, feeling safer than she had in years, but at the same time, intensely scared of what she was about to lose.

Chapter 27

Briar

'Ally,' Briar groaned, leaning her head against the car window, sure the cool glass was the only thing saving her from heatstroke, 'it's too hot to have sex.'

Alice laughed as she sped down the highway. 'Who says you're getting any?'

'But it's my birthday,' Briar grumbled. She didn't mention that it was Alice's last day. They'd successfully avoided discussing her flight the next morning, though it left a weight in Briar's stomach.

Alice tutted. 'There's still work to do on the house.' She reached over and grabbed Briar's hand, giving it a squeeze. 'I'll take you out for ice cream afterwards.'

'Oh, boy,' Briar deadpanned. She'd been in a foul mood since the tour. Sonny had been true to his word, and Briar was getting inundated with calls from Mr. Lavish, trying to discuss the offer.

She had spent the last week feeling like she was nursing the worst hangover of her life: bleary-eyed, often nauseous and plagued by an aching sense of dread that wrapped itself around her chest and squeezed tighter with each passing day.

It had been a relief when Alice had finally taken pity on Briar by suggesting a drive. Briar had assumed they were going to her mom's house. The to-do list taunted her from the office bulletin board, so if she was in for a day of manual labor, it wouldn't be the worst thing.

Alice pulled into the driveway, and they climbed out of the car. As Briar squinted at the monstrosity that had eaten away at all her free time for the summer, she couldn't help but think it didn't look anywhere near as bad as she remembered.

She followed Alice up the porch stairs, in through the front door, and—

'Surprise!!!'

Looking out at a sea of people, she couldn't fully comprehend what was happening, even as she read the banner with *Happy Birthday, Briar* in bold letters.

Alice pushed her into the crowd, where Noah immediately enveloped her in a bear hug.

'Oh, we soooo got you,' he said with a booming laugh.

'Rafa? Zach? Oh my god, Sonya?' Briar pulled her high school friends into hugs. 'What are you guys doing here?'

'Alice texted us,' Sonya said, with a look that said she had been as surprised to get that text as Briar was to see her there. 'We wanted to come. We love you, man.'

'Totally,' Rafa said, slinging an arm around her. 'You're the best.' He planted a wet kiss on her forehead.

'Sorry,' Zach said, freeing Briar. 'He hit the punch a little too hard. Just like sophomore year homecoming.'

'Alice,' Sonya called. 'Get over here! It's so good to see you.'

Alice smiled at her and then, after a moment's beat, brought her arms up for a hug. It was so awkward and endearing that Briar almost cried.

'We'll be right back,' Alice said to them. 'Sorry, I've just got one more surprise for Briar.' She grabbed Briar's hand, leading her into the kitchen.

'Briar!' Hazel and Laurel immediately pounced on her, and Briar spotted RJ and her dad leaning against the kitchen counter behind them.

'Oh my god,' she said, swiping at the tears that were suddenly spilling onto her cheeks. 'I can't believe you're here.'

'We wouldn't miss your birthday,' Laurel said.

'Or the camping trip,' Hazel added. 'Dad and RJ are coming too.'

It was a tradition their mother had started when they'd aged out of camp. No matter what summer plans they'd had, the Elwood siblings were to report during the second week of August for a camping trip to the nearby lake. Briar hadn't been planning on continuing with it this year, assuming it would be too painful for everyone.

'We want to scatter mom's ashes at the lake,' Laurel said.

'I took the whole week off,' RJ said. 'So I can help with anything else you need.'

She was surprised and touched that her siblings had coordinated the end-of-summer trip without her. Her mom's ashes were just another thing that she had been putting off thinking about until camp had ended, and it was a relief to have a plan made for her.

Briar put a hand to her heart, feigning shock. 'But won't the stock market collapse without you?'

'Ha,' he replied, unamused, and the twins quickly hopped on the ribbing-RJ-about-his-job train, the conversation devolving into nonsense.

She avoided her father's questioning gaze as the twins switched subjects to recount their travels. Briar didn't want to give him the opportunity to bring up the estate and ruin her good mood. Her birthday had always been the one day a year when Briar could be selfish, and she was glad Alice had given her the opportunity to do so.

At some point, Alice and Noah pulled her away to give her the full tour, walking her through each room to show off everything they had done. A warm feeling settled in Briar watching Alice in her mom's home – the house that had caused Briar so much stress was finally what her mother had always dreamed of, thanks to Alice.

'Briar,' her dad called out as they walked back to the kitchen. She groaned and leaned into Alice, any of the goodwill she'd developed for her dad in the last few hours evaporating immediately at his tone.

'If I give the signal,' she whispered in her ear, 'get me the hell away from him.'

She turned to her dad and RJ. 'What's up?'

'Mr. Lavish gave me a call,' her father said, arms crossed. She sensed that she was meant to be contrite. 'He says you've been hard to reach.'

Briar nodded. 'Yeah, it's closing week. I haven't been in the office much. And you've seen the state of the landline, it's a wonder calls go through at all. Right, RJ?' She looked to her brother for support.

'Bri,' RJ said gently, 'I get that it's been a lot. And I should've been more involved, but legally, it's up to you to make this sale happen. I mean, you *do* still want to sell the camp, right?'

Briar huffed out a laugh. 'As you've both explained, it would be irresponsible for me to keep it.'

Her father put what she assumed was meant to be a comforting hand on her shoulder, but the constricting feeling in her chest was back. 'We're not trying to force you into anything.'

'No, of course not,' Briar said, shrugging him off. 'You're just telling me exactly what to do.'

'Look,' RJ said, seeming to realize their dad wasn't getting anywhere, 'I don't want to watch you sacrifice everything for someone who isn't here anymore.'

Briar had never heard her usually stoic brother express concern for her before. 'I didn't know that was how you felt.'

'It is,' RJ said firmly. 'Look, my therapist says I need to be more direct, so here goes.' He took a deep breath. 'I know I said it was just about the money, but it's not. I figured it'd be easier for you, if you were doing it for me and the twins. But really, I want you to give it up for *you*. Please.'

The fight drained out of her at the look on her brother's face. Thinking about how the twins had planned the annual camping trip, how RJ and her dad had discussed selling the camp, she realized how far removed they were from the time when things would have fallen apart if Briar hadn't been dedicating everything to keeping her siblings on track.

In a way, running the camp had been just another thing on the long list of responsibilities that had transferred from her mom to her over the years. And Briar knew now that she could figure out something else, something better, to do with her time than to shoulder another person's legacy. Even if she didn't know what that was yet.

'Okay.'

'Okay?' her father asked, and Briar nodded.

'I'll sell it.' She looked around for Alice and met her gaze. 'I'll call Mr. Lavish back tomorrow.'

Alice was at her side the next moment. 'Sorry to interrupt, but I need Briar's help in the basement.'

They descended the rickety stairs, and Briar was immediately grateful that Alice's excuse had brought them somewhere cooler. The unfinished basement was still a little dingy, housing her mom's old potting bench, a few storage boxes and an auxiliary fridge.

'Are you alright?' Alice asked.

Briar turned into Alice, nuzzling her neck. The sensation of her skin against Briar's was the only thing drowning out the panic and relief fighting inside her.

Alice's arms wrapped around her. 'How did that go?'

Briar hummed in a way she hoped conveyed her unwillingness to talk about it. Instead, she kissed Alice, crowding her against the bench and hoisting her onto it.

'At your birthday party?' Alice teased, already pulling Briar closer.

'It *is* my party,' Briar said, ghosting her hands up Alice's thighs.

Alice's reply was lost as Briar kissed the spot on her neck that always made her breathless.

'It would be...' – Alice carded her fingers into Briar's hair – '...irresponsible to hook up here.'

'Totally,' Briar said, popping open the top button of Alice's shirt. She ducked her head to suck at her exposed collarbone.

'Everyone's upstairs,' Alice gasped, as Briar's hand snuck into the front of her shorts, tracing the lace edge of her panties.

'We will definitely be missed,' Briar agreed, breathing out hard as her hand crept even lower. Alice gripped her shoulders.

Briar pushed her lips hard against Alice's to stifle the moan she knew was coming.

Like a splash of ice-cold water, the lights in the basement flicked on and loud creaking footsteps came down the stairs.

'Blimey.'

'Woah.'

Briar froze, instantly knowing that voice.

'Noah,' she said slowly, turning. He stood halfway down the stairs, Freddie just behind him. The look on his face was inscrutable, his mouth pulled into a tight line.

Briar wasn't sure how long they stood there before Freddie cleared his throat uncomfortably. 'What's that, Sierra?' he called weakly before bolting up the stairs.

'Well,' Alice said, shifting uncomfortably, 'this is unfortunate.' She winced at her own words and Briar blew out a long breath, waiting for Noah to say something.

'How long has this been going on?' Noah asked, reaching the bottom of the stairs. He wasn't looking at Briar, but over her shoulder at Alice.

'Since the Fourth of July,' Alice said. Briar glanced between them, feeling like she was once again watching Alice and Noah's relationship from the outside. 'But it's casual.'

Hearing Alice say those words hurt Briar more than she'd expected. It didn't matter that she'd been the one to insist they didn't tell anyone, that she had wanted it to be casual in the first place. A part of herself she hadn't recognized until now had hoped she wasn't the only one getting lost in this thing between them.

The words were a helpful reminder of what they actually were to each other. Of course logical, unflappable Alice felt exactly what Briar had asked her to feel. She had thought she was doing things differently this time, but they had ended up in the exact same place. And it would end the exact same way: Alice gone, and her heartbroken.

'Casual,' Noah repeated. 'If it's casual, why didn't you tell me?'

Alice glanced at Briar. 'I—'

'We didn't want you to be mad,' Briar said, stepping between them. If she and Alice would never see each other again after tonight, preserving her friendship with Noah had to be her priority.

Noah shot her a quizzical look. 'Mad? Why would I be mad?'

'Your ex and your best friend...' Briar trailed off at the look on his face.

He snorted and shook his head. 'My best friend finding someone to support her through the toughest time in her life? Oh yeah, I'm pissed.'

'It would be okay if you were,' Briar said.

'I'm not,' Noah said. 'Honestly, did you guys really think I would care? High school was like a million years ago. I love you, and I want what's best for you. Always. Even if it's Alice.' He looked at Alice. 'Especially if it's Alice.'

Briar refused to cry. Instead, she hugged Noah, tucking her head into his neck as he wrapped his arms around her. 'Thank you.'

'I'm gonna go up,' Alice said awkwardly, already headed for the stairs. 'Someone should make sure Freddie's still breathing.'

Noah pulled a six-pack of beer from the fridge, which Briar assumed was why he and Freddie were in the basement in the first place. He tossed her a can.

'So... you and Alice,' he said, eyeing her. Briar popped her beer open, leaning against the gardening bench and hoping she looked nonchalant. 'Casual.'

'So casual,' Briar repeated.

'Uh huh.'

They stared at each other for a long time, not blinking. Briar caved first. 'Okay, maybe not so casual for some of us.'

Noah snorted. 'No kidding.' He messed with the tab of the beer can, and Briar could tell he was gearing up for a lecture. 'This started before the Fourth, didn't it?'

Briar swallowed hard. 'Um... I don't know how to answer that.'

'I mean, it started back in high school, right?' Noah asked, raising his eyebrows.

Briar squeezed her eyes shut. 'For me, at least, yeah.'

She didn't know what she had expected from Noah, but he just nodded thoughtfully, as though he'd figured out the riff of a particularly complicated song.

'I think I kinda knew,' he said. 'I mean, we were friends before, but that fall semester freshman year, I feel like I got to know the real you. And having someone who was going through the same thing was nice. It was the same, right?' He watched Briar's face carefully, and whatever expression she made he must have read as confirmation. 'You lost her like I did. Loved her like I did, didn't you?'

Briar could only choke out, 'Noah, I'm so sorry. I should've told you. I don't know why I didn't.'

'I wish you had.'

'There's one more thing...' Briar hesitated, not sure how much to share, but not wanting to keep secrets anymore. 'Alice leaving was my fault. We kissed at the end of camp. That's why she left, because she couldn't handle that she had cheated on you.'

After years of thinking about that night, of making sure no one else would ever know, telling Noah felt unnatural. But once she had, she knew it was something she'd needed off her chest.

'Do you want me to be mad about that?' Noah asked, sizing her up. 'Do you think you deserve it?'

'Yes.'

'Well, I'm not going to be,' Noah said. 'It was forever ago. I'm getting married to the woman I love. And my best friend in the whole world is going to be standing up there with me.'

'Okay,' Briar said, amazed that he could just brush it off. Like that one moment hadn't completely changed her life, like she hadn't held onto it for years and years. He made forgiveness seem so simple.

'Now,' Noah said, grabbing the pack of beer, 'let's get back to the party, birthday girl.'

Briar followed him up the stairs, nearly running into him when he paused just before the basement door. He turned to look at her over his shoulder.

'Does she know?' he asked.

'Know what?'

'That you love her?'

'Oh,' Briar said, looking down. 'No.'

'Maybe you should tell her,' he said.

'It won't change anything.'

'It might.'

Briar didn't have the heart to tell him he was wrong.

Chapter 28

Alice

In her search for Freddie, Alice ran into Harper in the living room.

'Have you seen Noah?' Harper asked.

'Have you seen Freddie?' Alice deflected.

'He was here a moment ago,' Harper said, glancing around. 'He and Sierra disappeared somewhere.'

Alice collapsed onto the couch. 'Noah's downstairs. He and Briar are having a heart-to-heart.'

Harper nodded, sitting next to her. 'Yeah, they do that.' Neither of them said anything for a moment. 'Are you going to tell me what this heart-to-heart is about?' Harper asked finally.

Alice looked sideways at her. 'Why do I feel like you already know?'

The corner of Harper's mouth quirked. 'Maybe because you and Briar are terrible actors? I mean the amount of blushing alone… It's sickening. Honeymoon phase type stuff.'

'Can you have a honeymoon phase if you're friends with benefits?' Alice asked, genuinely curious.

Harper scoffed. 'You're not *friends*. Briar and I are friends, and I don't look at her the way you do.'

'How do I look at her?' Alice asked. It was relieving, to finally be able to talk about it with someone. With Harper of all people, who suddenly seemed to have the information Alice desperately needed.

Harper considered the question for a moment. 'Like she's going to make everything better again.'

Alice blew out a breath. 'Like I forgot what life was meant to feel like until she was in front of me.'

'So why hide it?' Harper asked.

She fidgeted in her seat. 'Briar wanted to keep it a secret.'

Harper nodded, as though she'd expected that answer. 'Because of Noah?'

'We kissed once, back in high school,' Alice admitted. 'Right before I left for school. Noah and I hadn't officially broken up yet. I never told him, and neither did Briar.'

'You were at camp?' Harper asked.

'Yeah.'

'And you hadn't talked to Noah in weeks?'

'A month.'

'And you guys had agreed you were breaking up before you left, anyway?'

Alice studied her. 'Why are you trying to let me off the hook for cheating on your fiancé?'

'I'm not,' Harper said. 'Of course it was wrong. But it was also ten years ago, and Noah is happy. So who's the victim here? Who's the person who let this kiss ruin their life?'

'Me?' Alice tried.

Harper smiled. 'I knew you were smart. Just not as smart as me.'

'Thanks,' Alice said. 'You're a pretty good friend, you know that?'

'I do.' And then Harper did something Alice absolutely had not seen coming: she hugged her. Alice tried to relax into the alien sensation of being comforted by Harper.

'Hiya,' Freddie said, appearing over Harper's shoulder with Sierra. 'Could we have a chat?'

'Yes,' Alice said, standing. She paused, turning back to Harper. 'Noah knows that your parents aren't paying for the venue. He wants you to talk to him about it.'

Harper's mouth formed a perfect 'O' before Alice followed Freddie and Sierra.

'I'd love some answers,' Freddie said drily. 'If you'll oblige.'

'Let's talk in the garden,' Alice said, heading toward the back door. This was her favorite change to the house – the weedy mess had been transformed by Alice's green thumb, and she'd strung up lights around the patio and bought outdoor furniture off Facebook Marketplace. Her talents were truly wasted on the measly five plants in her flat, which were now all dead.

'So,' Freddie said, turning to face her once they were out in the night air, 'why am I the last person to know about you and Briar?'

'You're not,' Alice said, confused. 'No one knew.'

'I knew,' Sierra said.

'You did?' Alice asked. 'Well, I guess that makes sense.'

'Sierra and I have just had a talk about keeping secrets from friends,' Freddie said. 'It's not nice to do, if you were wondering.'

'Well, telling you was complicated,' Sierra said, 'because of the whole Briar selling the camp thing.'

'What?' Freddie said, looking between them. 'Briar is selling the camp?'

Alice wished the earth would swallow her whole. 'I don't know if she's going to go through with it.' She grabbed his hand. 'Listen, no matter what, I'm going to find a way for you to stay. I didn't want to tell you about the possibility of the camp being sold and stress you out more.'

'What do you mean?' Sierra asked. 'Freddie's visa is being sponsored by his job starting in the fall.'

Freddie looked at the ground. 'So… there's something I haven't told you…'

'Oh my god!' Sierra exclaimed. 'No more secrets, do you both hear me?' She pointed an accusatory finger at each of them in turn. 'Let's just all be honest with each other.'

Alice laid a gentle hand on her arm, and her expression softened. 'The purple tips are a little 2014 Tumblr.'

Sierra cracked a smile, and Freddie laughed. 'What a mad summer,' he said, shaking his head. 'What would Susan think if she was looking down on us now?'

'She would hate the drama,' Alice said thoughtfully. 'But she would be proud of us for pulling it off, despite everything. And she'd be happy that the party went on without her.'

'Aye,' Cook said, stepping out from behind the shed and startling the three of them.

'Christ!' Freddie exclaimed. 'Have you been there the whole time?'

Cook dropped the still-smoking roach from his hand and squished it with his shoe. 'You lot are an entertaining bunch. Almost as good as the raccoons.' He smiled and then disappeared into the house.

'So, when the kids always insist that there's a camp ghost...' Sierra said, and the three of them doubled over laughing.

—

Alice stayed in the garden, chatting with the partygoers who came out of the packed house to smoke or cool off. Slowly, the guests trickled home as the hour grew late. When Briar finally came out, Alice guessed it was well past midnight.

'Hey,' Alice said, uncertain how Briar would be feeling after all the emotions of the party.

'Hi,' Briar said, gazing around the garden in wonder. 'This place looks amazing.'

'Thanks,' Alice said, taking Briar's hand and pulling her to lay in the center of the grass with her. She wanted to look at the stars together one more time before she left. 'Who's still around?'

'No one,' Briar said, propping up on her elbow to look at Alice. 'Noah and Harper just finished cleaning up and are headed back to camp.'

The crickets chirped, and the birds would be up before long. Alice knew there was no way she would fall asleep tonight, and Briar seemed to feel similarly.

Briar pressed a kiss to Alice's hairline. 'Noah didn't care.'

'Neither did Harper, if that was a concern. Or Freddie. Or Sierra — but she already knew. Or Cook.'

There was a long moment of silence, and then Briar said quietly, 'I think Noah's just glad you were here to keep me from falling apart this summer.'

'You could've done it without me.'

Briar nodded slightly, settling against Alice's side as the two of them gazed at the stars. 'I'm glad I didn't have to.'

'Why...' Alice struggled to get the question out, not sure she wanted to hear the answer. 'Why did you want to keep things between us a secret?'

'I was embarrassed,' Briar said, after a minute. 'Of what happened in high school. About how I fell apart afterward. Of how' – Alice felt her swallow – 'I needed you.'

'That sounds like something Susan taught you,' Alice said. 'Unseemly, to need someone.'

Briar lifted her head. 'I guess I thought that if people knew about us, they'd be watching me when you left, trying to make sure I was okay. And I couldn't stand that, not on top of everything else.'

'It's okay for people to see you struggling. I mean, not that I would be the cause for any sort of... you know.' Alice felt heat creep up her neck.

'You do cause a lot of problems for me,' Briar said, and Alice couldn't tell if she was joking. 'I think I've felt more things this summer than I have in a long time. And I don't have the strength anymore to pretend I don't care. Because I do, I care a lot. I...' She sat up quickly, facing away from Alice.

She wanted to reach out and lay a hand on Briar's shoulder, but something held her back.

'Why did you leave?' It was so quiet, Alice almost didn't hear her. She desperately wished she could see Briar's face, to get a sense of what she was thinking. 'I just want to know before you go again.'

'I was going to come back,' Alice said after a moment.
'What?'

She sat up too, and Briar turned to her. 'When I left for Noah's that morning, I thought I'd come right back and tell you that I loved you.'

She'd had every intention of returning, but in the car, reconsidering every moment of their friendship, trying to pinpoint exactly when she'd crossed the line, it had become impossible. After realizing her feelings, she couldn't face Briar again. She had rationalized it as being about cheating, but really, she hadn't been able to bear the thought of going back to being friends.

Briar's face contorted at the words.

'You loved me,' she repeated flatly. Alice tried to decipher what emotion lit Briar's eyes, but she couldn't. Briar had never felt more foreign to her than at this moment. 'If you loved me, you shouldn't have left.'

Alice shook her head. 'I didn't think it through.'

Briar's hands covered her face, and she made a noise that sounded alarmingly like a sob. Her whole body shook. Alice didn't know what to do. She'd never professed her love for anyone before, but was fairly certain this wasn't the optimal reaction.

'What if I stayed now?' The words came out without Alice thinking about them at all, but they sounded right. It was what she wanted. Everything in Alice had been waiting for the moment she could finally fix her misstep. The moment she could be someone Briar could rely on. Now was that moment. 'What if I didn't get on the plane?'

The shaking stopped. For a moment, Alice wasn't sure if Briar was even breathing. But then she lifted her head. 'Why would you do that?'

'Because I love you?' Alice hated how it came out like a question.

Briar scoffed. 'You don't.'

Blood rushed in her ears. 'Of course I love you. I've loved you since we were kids. I loved you even after I left.'

Briar stared at her, quiet fury etched in her features. 'Is that supposed to make me feel better?'

'I'm just trying to be honest with you,' Alice said, failing to find an explanation for Briar's behavior that wouldn't end in her own heartbreak.

'Why are you being honest *now*?'

'Because I want to stay. Because I love you.' It was the third time she had told Briar she loved her, and it seemed to make less of an impression each time. 'Don't you love me?'

Briar squeezed her eyes shut. 'Have you thought this through?' she asked, in a pained voice. 'How this would actually, logically work?'

'It would work,' Alice said, trying for confidence. She didn't understand how she'd gone from comforting to pleading in such a short time. 'It would work because I would make it work.'

'You would make it work,' Briar said disbelievingly. She stood, pacing, as Alice watched helplessly. 'What would you do? Where would you live?'

Alice's eyes pricked, her throat feeling dry. 'Details,' she said weakly. She knew that Briar was being the rational one. But she was trying to fix her mistake, and Briar was getting bogged down with the logistics. For once, Alice was throwing caution to the wind, and Briar seemed mad at her for it.

'Really?' Briar asked, her mouth curving into a twisted version of her usual smile. 'I shouldn't be the one telling *you* that you would have to figure out a hell of a lot of *details* to move to another continent and drop the degree you've been working on for six years.'

'I'll figure it out,' Alice snapped.

'But nothing's *changed*. You left me before, and I don't care if you had every intention of coming back. You didn't.'

'It's not the same now. Because I lo—'

'*Don't*,' Briar's voice was dangerously low, 'say it again.'

'But I do,' Alice insisted.

'You might think that,' Briar said. 'But if you stayed for me, you'd end up resenting me. Believe me, I know what that feels like.'

'I wouldn't,' Alice said, desperately reaching for any argument that would make Briar believe her. Something that would make Briar see that Alice was serious about staying, about being with her.

For the first time, she saw the full scope of the damage she'd done to their friendship, the trust she'd betrayed and lost.

'You can't fix this,' Briar said, with a finality that pushed every thought from Alice's mind, 'so stop trying. You're leaving in what? Three hours?'

Alice glanced at her phone, confirming the time. 'Yeah,' she croaked, exhaustion suddenly overtaking her. Briar reached a hand down to her. Alice looked at it warily before accepting the help. They stood like that for a moment, staring at each other, hands forgotten between them.

'It was only ever going to last the summer anyway, right?' Briar said. 'Let's not ruin it.'

Alice was certain that, despite Briar's words, something had already been ruined.

Chapter 29

Briar

That morning, after Briar said goodbye to Alice, she'd started packing. It was like she was possessed, as though now that Alice was gone the real world had come rushing back in. If she kept moving, it wouldn't catch her. If she kept moving, she couldn't think about Alice, about the things she'd said or whether she'd meant any of it.

Instead, she packed.

The only thing left was her mother's desk. She picked up the papier-mâché bowl she'd made in elementary school, wrapping it carefully in newspaper. She did the same with framed family photos, the twins smiling toothlessly at her as she packed them away.

She tested every pen, throwing away the ones that didn't work and bundling the ones that did with a rubber band. She found a stack of leather-bound notebooks that her mom would've kept her summer notes in and put them in the box. She packed away all the office supplies she could find and texted Noah to see if his school would take them.

Finally, she reached the bottom drawer of her mother's desk, the one with her laptop. When she logged in, it automatically opened to the email thread between Susan and Alice. After avoiding it all summer, the need to know finally overcame Briar's fears.

She scrolled to the beginning of their correspondence. Alice had written to Susan in September of freshman year.

> To: susan.elwood@gmail.com
> From: ahughes@standrews.ac.uk
> Subject: checking in
> Date: September 17, 2017
>
> Hi Susan,
>
> I hope you're doing well! I finally feel settled into my dorm and courses. I'm in Melville Hall, just like you were. My roommate seems nice enough, but I don't see her much as I'm in the library most of the time. I'm taking A Natural History with Prof. Davies and I'm loving it so far. Thank you for the recommendation.
>
> How's Briar? I saw the pictures from drop-off day. It was great the whole family was there to see her off.
>
> All my love,
>
> Alice

> To: ahughes@standrews.ac.uk
> From: susan.elwood@gmail.com
> Subject: re: checking in
> Date: September 20, 2017

My dear Alice,

I'm happy to hear you're liking St Andrews. Melville is just the place for you, but make sure you don't spend too much time in the library – get out and have fun! I know you already have Briar, but that doesn't mean there's not room for more friends in your life.

Dropping B off was harder than I thought. River didn't know what to do with me on the drive home; I was a blubbering mess. Don't tell B, she'd feel guilty about making her old mom cry.

She's joined the crew team! Can you believe it? Our girl is participating in a team sport. She's a coxswain. I think it'll be good for her to be in charge of eight men; she needs someone to boss around now that she's away from her siblings.

All my love,

Susan

To: susan.elwood@gmail.com
From: ahughes@standrews.ac.uk
Subject: re: checking in
Date: March 5, 2018

Dear Susan,

Thanks for sending the photos from your spring break! It looked lovely.

Maybe Briar told you already, but I figured you should hear it from me. I'm dating a woman. Her name is Tess. You remember the friend I mentioned going to a Halloween party with? That's her!

We've been dating for a few months now, so I thought I'd tell my parents. Their responses kind of surprised me. They weren't angry, or upset that I'm a lesbian, but they didn't seem to understand why I wanted them to know. It wasn't what I had expected, but it wasn't bad. It's funny to me that after all these years of being divorced, sometimes they still react the exact same way when I tell them news.

Anyway, I was thinking about when Briar came out to you junior year. She was never worried for a moment that you wouldn't accept and celebrate her exactly how she was.

How is Briar, by the way? Is she dating anyone?

All my love,

A

To: ahughes@standrews.ac.uk
From: susan.elwood@gmail.com
Subject: re: checking in
Date: March 25, 2018

Dear Alice,

I'm so glad you shared that with me. When you mentioned Tess in the fall, I wondered if there was something there. You speak very highly of her, and I'm sure when your parents get the chance to meet her, they will see why it was important for you to tell them. I would love to meet her myself!

I know you're deciding about coming home this summer, and I wanted to make it clear (if it wasn't already!) that you are always welcome to stay here. Briar and her siblings will be home for the summer. Of course, if you come all the way to the US, I'll also expect to see you at camp for at least one weekend! Deal?

Briar has been dating someone – I'm surprised she hasn't told you about Riley. She's come over for dinner a few times now. She always offers to help out in the kitchen, and she's quite the cook!

Anyway, just let me know about the summer once your plans are figured out. We'd love to have you.

Love,

Susan

To: susan.elwood@gmail.com
From: ahughes@standrews.ac.uk
Subject: re: checking in

Date: April 15, 2018

Dear Susan,

I'm sorry I didn't say anything sooner. I figured Briar had already told you.

I did something that I don't think she'll be able to forgive me for, and I made the decision to give her space. It hasn't been easy, and I won't lie and tell you that I don't miss her every single day, but I think this is the right thing to do. So, I won't be able to stay with you this summer.

I'm glad Briar has Riley, Noah and Harper. They look like they're having a great time in college, and I feel like I can live vicariously through the photos I see on social media :) Maybe one day things will be different and I'll come home again.

All my love,

Alice

To: ahughes@standrews.ac.uk
From: susan.elwood@gmail.com
Subject: re: checking in
Date: May 20, 2019

Alice,

Thanks for sending your newest research! It always makes me so happy to read anything you've written. You have such a gift for words.

It's gratifying to know that I've inspired a lifelong love of nature. I hope you'll consider again my offer to come stay in the bungalow or at camp this summer.

I'm sure you and Briar can mend things, if that's still holding you back.

I hope to see you soon, my dear.

Love,

Susan

To: susan.elwood@gmail.com
From: ahughes@standrews.ac.uk
Subject: re: checking in
Date: July 31, 2020

Dear Susan,

I'm so sorry to hear about your diagnosis. I have so many things to say – can I call sometime soon?

Maybe I can find a way to take a few days off from my research this summer to come see you. Would that be okay with you? I don't want to impose, and I know that your doctors might want to limit your exposure depending on your treatment plan... Anyway, let's discuss.

In the meantime, I'm sending you, Briar, RJ, Hazel and Laurel all of my love from across the ocean. If there's anything I can do to help, please just let me know.

Talk soon,

Alice

To: ahughes@standrews.ac.uk
From: susan.elwood@gmail.com
Subject: re: checking in
Date: May 20, 2021

My dear Alice,

Warmest congratulations on your graduation! I so wish I could have been there. This is one of those moments when the C-word becomes not just an inconvenience but damned annoying. I would give anything for the freedom to get on a plane and give you a hug and tell you I'm so, so proud of you.

I hope your parents behaved themselves for the weekend – I'm sure they played nice for such an important event.

I've sent a package which should arrive in a few days. In the meantime, let me know what you've decided for the summer!

Love,

Susan

To: susan.elwood@gmail.com
From: ahughes@standrews.ac.uk
Subject: re: checking in
Date: March 5, 2022

Susan,

I'm so glad to hear you're officially in remission! I have some news of my own, though it pales in comparison: I've been accepted to do a DPhil at Oxford!

I know I said I'd maybe be back in the States for the summer, but Professor Beechem has given me a research opportunity which is too prestigious to pass up. I hope to see you soon. I miss you all the time.

Briar's got a new man in her life? Please tell me more. Hope her apartment hunt is going well!

Alice

To: ahughes@standrews.ac.uk
From: susan.elwood@gmail.com
Subject: re: checking in
Date: September 21, 2022

Dear Alice,

Sorry for the radio silence over the summer – camp seems to get more hectic every year. Or maybe I'm just getting older.

I meant to wish you a wonderful start to your first trimester before it began, but alas, no better time than the present! Jer is a friend from college and I take comfort in knowing you'll have him looking out for you.

Love,

Susan

To: susan.elwood@gmail.com
From: ahughes@standrews.ac.uk
Subject: re: checking in
Date: August 28, 2023

S,

I know it's been a while, but I hope you're doing well. Another successful summer in the books?

Honestly, I've hardly been keeping in touch with anyone recently. I don't know what's wrong with me. I write texts and emails and delete them, thinking no one could want to hear from me anyway. I know you will tell me this is all silly, and you're probably right.

I moved to London last month. Tess convinced me it would make it easier to have a social life, to get out and date more (her goal for me, not mine, ha), but I think it's just made me even more aware that I have exactly one friend.

Sorry to be throwing a pity party, I know you can't stand that! But I needed to write to you, and this is how I'm feeling right now.

Did Briar make a decision about going back to college? I hope she doesn't let her worries about her friends graduating already get in her way. I know she'll be a brilliant teacher.

Love,

Alice

To: ahughes@standrews.ac.uk
From: susan.elwood@gmail.com
Subject: re: checking in
Date: January 24, 2025

Dear Alice,

Thanks for your New Year greetings, and sorry for once again being an inconsistent pen pal.

To be honest, I've been missing you terribly recently. Over the past month, I've spent a lot of time thinking about the best times of my life. You know that I loved college, but I think those summers where you, Briar and her siblings were all at camp will always top that. Nothing has given me more joy in my life than being able to bring you all to a place I love, a place I've put so much work into.

You know you're old when you're reminiscing about stuff like this! Anyway, how's school? Are you liking London any more now (aside from winter weather – oof)?

Love,

Susan

To: ahughes@standrews.ac.uk
From: susan.elwood@gmail.com
Subject: re: checking in
Date: April 13, 2025

Alice, my darling girl,

I have a confession: my cancer is back. There, I told someone. My doctors have been worried that I've been keeping this to myself, but frankly, I don't see the point in dragging anyone else into it. Still, it feels good to get it off my chest.

It's inoperable, unfortunately, and the prognosis is fairly bleak. Do keep this to yourself, dear. I'm still sitting with it.

All my love,

Susan

To: susan.elwood@gmail.com
From: ahughes@standrews.ac.uk

Subject: re: checking in
Date: April 14, 2025

My Susan,

I'm heartbroken to hear this news. Thank you for telling me.

I know you don't want to worry anyone, or have anyone dote over you, but I have to be honest with you, since I always am. I think you need to tell your children about this. They will want to be there to support you, especially Briar, and you need to let them. Now, of all times, your family needs to be together.

Sending all of my love & strength to you. You know what you mean to me, so I won't pain you by writing it all out.

Love,

Alice

To: ahughes@standrews.ac.uk
From: susan.elwood@gmail.com
Subject: re: checking in
Date: May 16, 2025

Alice,

If you're reading this, it means I'm dead. Excuse the melodrama. I would like you to speak at the funeral – you'll know what to say.

Be good to B, she's going to need you.

Love always,

S

Chapter 30

Briar

Briar woke up in a tent, bracketed by her sisters. Hazel's arms were a vice grip around her waist, and Laurel's breath was hot against the back of her neck. Smelling bacon, she disentangled herself carefully and unzipped the tent.

She found her father hunched over a camp stove.

'Wow,' Briar said. 'I didn't know you could use one of those things.'

'I'll have you know,' her dad said, 'that I was the first person to bring your mother camping.'

Briar snorted, sitting next to him. 'So, what? Everything she knew, she learned from you?'

He squinted at her. 'Absolutely not; she surpassed me immediately.'

'*That* I believe,' Briar said, wrapping her arms around herself for warmth. Her dad shucked off his fleece and offered it, and she took it gratefully.

'Breakfast's almost ready, if you want to wake them,' he said, pulling sausages off the griddle.

They ate breakfast in silence, then tidied the campsite and set off to do their mom's favorite hike.

Trudging down the trail, Briar couldn't stop thoughts of Alice from flooding in. There had been a time when she had come on these trips too. Susan had welcomed her into their family like one of her own.

Her mind went through the emails, over and over. She thought about Alice across the ocean, lonely and desperate, writing to Susan for news of Briar. And Briar had never known.

When she'd first stumbled across the emails, she had assumed they would be proof that Alice had never really cared about her, that she'd easily moved on. This time, she'd been searching for any shred of evidence for what Alice had declared that morning. The thing Briar had refused to let herself believe. She wondered now if she should have heard her out instead of shutting her down.

She tried to picture what Alice was doing at that moment, probably acing her interview. Despite everything, Briar hoped Alice would be happy in her new role.

The hike was five miles out and back, but they'd been doing it for so many years that it felt like it took them no time at all to make it to the lake.

They reached the familiar beach, staring at the placid water, feeling the absence of Susan acutely.

'This blows,' Hazel said.

'Totally blows,' Laurel agreed.

RJ and Briar exchanged a look, but it was their father who spoke. 'Yes, well. I know that this trip was always your mother's thing, but I thought...' He cleared his throat roughly, seemingly at a loss for words. No one spoke.

'I miss the way she would tell me not to bite my nails,' RJ said finally. 'She'd even know when I was doing it over the phone.' He held out his hands. 'They've looked awful all summer.'

'I miss how she'd always be able to tell us apart,' Laurel said, taking RJ's hand. 'Just by our voices, or by the way we walked. When we'd try to switch on her, she'd always catch us.'

Hazel linked their arms together. 'I miss her hot chocolate. I don't know how I'm gonna get through Christmas without it this year.'

Briar felt her throat close up. She'd been so focused on the summer that she hadn't let herself think about what came next. Alice leaving was only the start. The leaves would start changing, the world would keep spinning. And her mom would still be gone.

'I—' Briar cut herself off, trying to stifle the emotion but not quite managing it. It didn't matter anyway; she didn't want to hide her pain from the people who loved her – not anymore. 'I miss her in the greenhouse. Tending to the plants, snipping off dead leaves, propagating new ones.'

'I miss her calls,' her dad said. 'Your mother had a knack for always calling when I couldn't sleep. It was like she could sense it, even across the ocean.'

Briar stared at him. She hadn't known that her parents spoke regularly, but then again, she hadn't known a lot of things.

'She was a terrible cook,' Laurel said, and the rest of them laughed. 'Remember RJ's tenth birthday? She tried to make those meatless tacos.'

'Briar was the vegetarian,' RJ said, shooting a mock glare at Briar. 'I don't understand why the rest of us had to be subjected to it. It was *my* birthday!'

Briar had been thirteen at the time, and she and Alice had stopped eating meat after watching a documentary about factory farming. In the end, she hadn't even made it a full year, but Susan had been supportive, happy that Briar was taking an interest in the natural world.

'She was a good mom,' Briar said. It didn't fix any of the things Susan had done wrong. Briar still felt like she was failing her by selling the camp, still felt like there were a million things she needed to say to her and was still grappling with the fact that she never would. But in this moment, in this place, with her family, she could give her mom some grace. 'She did her best.'

They took in the view for a moment. Briar finally reached into her pack and pulled out a long bamboo tube. They all walked to the edge of the water.

'Well, mom' – she sighed, twisting off the cap and pouring out a small handful of ashes into her palm – 'here we are.' She looked to her family, pouring ashes into their outstretched hands. 'To Susan,' she murmured.

'To Susan,' they repeated. Briar let the wind sweep the ashes through the cracks of her fingers and out into the water. She watched them collect on the surface then sink, until the flecks were indistinguishable from the sand at the bottom of the lake.

Hazel leaned her head on Briar's shoulder, and Laurel did the same. Briar reached out, taking RJ's hand in her left, and her dad's in her right. They stood there for another long moment, listening to the rustle of the trees, the lapping of the water, the clicks of the cicadas, the caws of distant birds.

Chapter 31

Briar

One month later

Briar barreled down the steps of The Thirsty Crow.

'I know, I know, I'm late,' she said, shucking off her jacket and stuffing it under the bar.

Oscar nodded easily. 'No worries. It's been slow.' He continued wiping the spotless glass in his hands for several more seconds, his expression vacant.

'You good?' Briar said. He nodded again, finally putting the glass down and picking up another. 'The gummy hitting a little too hard?'

He flushed, finally glancing at her. 'Maybe...'

'Go take ten,' Briar said, grabbing the glass out of his hand. 'Maybe see if the kitchen will make you a cup of coffee. And if you see Shannon, don't talk to her.'

'On it,' Oscar said, his eyes still not quite focusing on her face. 'Good to have you back.'

Briar sighed as she watched him walk away. She quickly finished up the prep work for the night. It was only a Tuesday, but the trivia crowd could get rowdy, so it was best to be prepared.

The dive bar had operated in the basement of an old brownstone in Capitol Hill for several decades. Their ten-dollar beer and shot combo made it a local favorite among young staffers. And though it wasn't exactly Briar's scene, she'd missed it.

She nodded at some entering patrons, taking their orders and delivering drinks to their table. When she turned back to the bar, she caught sight of a familiar ponytail in the corner.

Briar stared, convinced she was seeing things. '*Alice?*'

'Hi,' Alice said. She sat with a manila folder and half-empty beer in front of her. It looked like she'd been there for a while. Briar walked over to her, blinking quickly, as though she might disappear at any moment. 'Do you want to sit?' Alice said, sounding exactly like herself and stubbornly not disappearing. 'I thought we could chat.'

'You're in London,' Briar said stupidly, still standing.

'I was,' Alice said. 'But I'm back.'

'I can see that,' Briar said, because she could, even if it didn't make any sense *why* she could.

'Aren't you going to ask me why I came back?'

'Um, okay,' Briar said, though she wasn't sure she wanted to know. Whatever it was would probably only break her heart all over again. 'Why?'

'Because I want to be with you,' Alice said. Like that fixed everything, like none of the problems that were insurmountable a month ago still existed.

'But—' Briar started.

'But I didn't have a plan,' Alice said, holding up a hand to stop Briar's protest. 'And now I do.'

'You do?' Briar echoed faintly.

She'd made peace with how they'd left things. She'd been doing fine without her for the past few weeks. But having Alice in front of her again, Briar ached with how much she'd missed her.

Alice nodded. 'Yes. First,' she said, 'you asked me what I was going to do. And I've decided to be the director of Camp Lakeside.'

Briar felt a pang of annoyance. She had almost let herself dream for a moment that Alice had solved their problems, that she was back for good. But of course not – that would have been too perfect for real life, something that only existed in Briar's imagination.

'I sold the camp.'

In the end, it had been simpler than Briar had imagined. She'd told Mr. Lavish that he could take the best offer he got, and it had sold a week later. Briar suspected the Randolphs were currently drawing up plans to fit the cabins with AK-47s or something equally upsetting. She wasn't sure how Mr. Lavish had managed it; probably it was the miracle fix-up job Alice had done, but he'd sold her mother's house, too.

'I know,' Alice said, tapping her manila folder as though that explained things. Briar frowned. 'Would you sit?'

Briar sat, arms folded, guarding herself against whatever Alice said next, knowing it wasn't wise to allow herself to be drawn in. Alice opened the folder, handing some papers to Briar. When Briar read them, the words didn't make sense.

'This is the deed to the camp,' she said, confused.

'It is,' Alice confirmed.

Briar squinted at the name at the bottom. 'Who's Matthew Blair, and why have you stolen his legal documents?'

'He handed them over willingly,' Alice said, taking a sip of her beer and making Briar wait an infuriatingly long time for her to continue. 'He's the very motivated buyer who ended up outbidding the Randolphs.'

'And he wants to keep an unprofitable camp?' Briar asked suspiciously.

'He has a *particular* interest in keeping it a camp.' Alice pulled out a few more documents, placing them in a spread in front of Briar. 'And he and I have spent the past few weeks developing a business plan to make it profitable.'

'Well, this all seems very official,' Briar said, impressed despite herself by the detailed plans laid out before her.

'Thank you,' Alice said, her cheeks going pink the way they always did when Briar praised her. 'I've barely slept pulling it together.'

'I assume there's more,' Briar said, eyeing the folder. Alice nodded.

'With the camp staying open for outdoor education trips during the spring and fall,' Alice said, 'I thought we'd need another full-time staff member. There's one assistant director in particular I happen to know is looking for a job.'

'Freddie?' Briar asked.

'The visa paperwork should be sorted in the next week.' Alice folded her hands on the table in front of her. 'Truthfully, that was a bit of a nightmare, but I think the consulate was just looking to get me off the phone at a certain point. I can be very annoying when I need to be.'

'I know,' Briar said.

Alice ignored that. 'And I'll have other support too. Matthew will be nearby if I need anything. He also bought your mom's house, and he's planning on living there.'

'Who is this mysterious benefactor?' Briar asked, narrowing her eyes.

Alice nodded to someone over Briar's shoulder. She turned and did a double take, her brain not computing the sight of Cook anywhere other than camp.

'Hiya, Bri.'

Briar stood and crushed him in a tight hug. 'Your name is Matthew?'

'Ay, it is.'

She pulled away, looking at Alice and then back at Cook. 'Where did you get enough money to buy the camp and the house? If I'd known you were interested and could afford it…'

'Nearly forty years' salary, with food and lodging provided.' Cook shrugged. 'I grow my own grass, so I've not had many expenses.'

Briar was sure her lungs weren't working properly. That was why her brain was getting all fuzzy around the edges. That had to be it.

She couldn't stop herself from looking at Alice again, from drinking in the sight of her, from hoping that maybe this was all real.

'So you've got it all figured out, huh?' she asked, failing miserably to strike a nonchalant tone.

Alice looked pleased with herself, and Briar wanted to kiss her more than she ever had before. 'I do.'

'Then what's next for me?' Briar asked.

'That's easy,' Alice said, stepping forward so that they were nose-to-nose. 'You get to do whatever the hell you want.'

'Is that so?' Briar said, finally letting herself break into the grin she'd been suppressing.

Alice nodded, snaking an arm around Briar's waist, pulling her closer. 'So… what are you going to do first?'

'I have an idea.' She wrapped her arms around Alice and kissed her deeply.

Epilogue

Briar

Eleven months later

'Hey,' Alice said from the doorway. 'When did you get here?'

'About an hour ago,' Briar said, stretching her arms over her head and snuggling deeper into the sheets. Alice had replaced the beds in the cabin with a plusher queen-sized mattress, which Briar often dreamed of sleeping on when she was home in DC.

Besides the bed, Alice hadn't changed the director's cabin much. It still had the same woodsy smell: old books, pine and honey. Nothing made Briar feel calmer.

Alice walked towards her, toeing off her sneakers and shucking her tank top over her head. 'You didn't come find me?'

'Figured you'd be busy with closing week.' Briar scooted over to make room for her.

'Too busy for you?' Alice said, sliding in. Her skin was sticky with sweat, but Briar hadn't held her in over a week and was greedy to touch her. Alice's fingers settled into the crook of Briar's hip, pulling her closer. Her mouth ghosted over Briar's shoulder.

Briar ducked her head for a kiss, sighing into it. 'Missed you.'

Alice grinned against her lips. 'Really? You didn't answer my call last night.'

'The guys took me out for a drink after my last shift,' Briar said, sliding a hand up Alice's spine. It still surprised her how much being in Alice's arms instantly pacified her, how the stress she didn't even know her body was holding slipped away. The whole world faded to the background and Briar could breathe a little bit easier knowing that Alice was there.

'How was it?'

'Good,' Briar said, swallowing. She wanted to hold on to the stillness for a little longer and didn't want to talk about anything serious.

Alice stared at her, eyebrows raised.

Briar shrugged, burying her face into the crook of Alice's neck. 'It's weird to be leaving.'

Alice ran her hands through Briar's hair.

'Of course it is,' Alice said, leaning down to kiss her forehead. Briar took a deep breath in, sitting up.

'It's more than just the job,' she said.

'Okay,' Alice said, sitting crossed-legged and lacing her hands together, waiting for Briar to continue.

Briar bit her lip, the unsettling feeling in her stomach that had been bothering her the whole drive to camp returning. She knew she needed to say something, that it was the only way Alice could help, but it was hard. Letting people in was still something Briar was learning how to do.

'I'm worried about what happens when I go back to school.'

Alice nodded. 'What do you think is going to happen?'

'That we'll break up,' Briar said automatically.

The thought had been nagging at her since getting her acceptance letter from William & Mary into their education program.

Alice looked surprised. 'Why would we break up?'

'Because we won't be together all the time.' Briar had tried long distance with Riley, and it hadn't ended well. She didn't want that to happen with Alice.

'We weren't together this summer and we made it work.'

'But this will be the longest time we'll have been apart since you came back,' Briar said, looking down at her hands.

'Right.'

Seeing she had stumped Alice, Briar continued, 'What if it doesn't work? This program is going to be hard. I'm going to have to study a lot to catch up. That means long nights and working on the weekends.'

Alice took Briar's hands and pulled them into her lap. 'I can work out a schedule with Freddie, and I'll come to you. It's only three hours. It'll be a little hard to start. But we're trying to hire more staff soon.'

Briar stared at their intertwined fingers. 'I don't want to lose you again.'

'You won't.' Alice said it so fiercely that Briar almost believed her.

'You don't know that.'

'I do, because I love you and I'm going to do whatever it takes to make you happy.' The look in Alice's eyes dared Briar to refute her.

'Oh,' Briar said, flushing. 'Is that all?'

'Yes.' Alice brought one of Briar's hands up to her cheek. 'And I'll keep reminding you of that anytime you're feeling unsure of us.'

Briar pulled her in for a kiss. 'That might be necessary.'

'Shall I start now?' Alice asked, skimming her hands up Briar's thighs. 'Reminding you of my devotion?'

Briar leaned her head to the side to give Alice more access as she kissed down her neck, letting herself be pushed back into the sheets. 'I mean, if you want.'

'Where should I start?' Alice mused, moving to straddle her. She picked up Briar's hand, kissing the inside of her wrist and making Briar shiver. She mouthed down Briar's forearm, biting playfully at the tender skin.

Briar gasped, her other hand reaching to grab at Alice's shoulder. She pulled her down and kissed her desperately.

When they broke apart, she asked, 'Are you going to seduce me every time I get nervous about our relationship?'

'I don't know,' Alice said, pulling at Briar's shirt, managing to get it and her sports bra over her head in one fluid motion. 'Is it working?'

Briar swallowed, mouth dry as Alice reached behind her back to unhook her bra. 'Maybe.'

'Well.' Alice lowered herself back down so that there was no longer any space between them. She brought her mouth to Briar's ear. 'I'll just have to keep testing out this theory, huh?'

'Gonna catalog my reactions?' Briar said with a breathless grin, grinding her hips in a way that made them both groan.

'If this is your idea of dirty talk...' Alice said with a laugh. Her cheeks were pink, her hair matted from Briar's fingers, and she was the most beautiful thing Briar had ever seen.

'Classify me like one of your mushrooms,' Briar deadpanned, and they both devolved into giggles.

They met Freddie the next morning, packing up the car together. As it turned out, the annual camping trip hadn't died with Susan, but had expanded to include more than just biological family. This year, Briar and her family were joined by Alice, Cook, Noah, Harper, Sierra and Freddie. Briar couldn't think of a more perfect way to end the summer.

When they reached the familiar stretch of road that marked the trailhead, Briar was practically buzzing with excitement. She caught sight of identical blonde heads and practically leapt from the car before Alice had fully stopped.

She squeezed Hazel and Laurel tightly. 'How was the flight?'

'Good,' Hazel said, struggling against Briar's vice grip. 'RJ and Dad should be here any minute.'

Briar caught sight of Sierra climbing out of the car she'd driven the twins in just as Freddie launched himself at her.

'I've missed you,' he cried. 'Having no service has been terrible. Please tell me you have the recent Paul Mescal photos I requested.'

Sierra nodded, handing over her phone. 'Have I ever let you down before?'

Freddie didn't respond, furiously swiping. 'Oh my god, where did he find even shorter shorts?'

'How have you been?' Briar asked Sierra. 'How's the vet's office?'

Sierra shrugged. 'I quit.'

'Oh, why?'

'I got into this art therapy master's program,' Sierra said. 'I start in the fall.'

Briar turned to Freddie, who definitely should have mentioned this to her, but he missed her glare, still enraptured by Paul Mescal's thighs.

'I'm so happy for you,' Alice said, patting Sierra's shoulder.

'I should be thanking you, actually. If you've taught me anything, it's that higher education is a perfect way to avoid the real world,' Sierra joked.

'Can't avoid it forever,' Alice sing-songed back, opening the trunk of the car.

The final cars arrived together. RJ and Briar's dad came in one car, Noah, Harper and Cook in the other.

Cook beamed at Briar and Alice, pulling them under either arm.

'First summer under ye belt, hen,' he said, shaking Alice by the shoulder. 'How do ye feel?'

'Accomplished, for once,' Alice said, her cheeks were flushed in a way that Briar found adorable.

'She really pulled it off,' Briar said.

'Couldn't have done it without a lot of help,' Alice murmured, glancing around the group. 'You guys have supported me through a ton this past year. I'm so happy you could make it.'

'Alright, alright, save the speech,' Noah cut in, grinning. 'We're losing daylight.'

And they began down the trail.

The night passed catching up around the campfire. With how busy things had been in Briar's life – fitting college applications and trips to camp in between her bartending shifts – she hadn't seen her siblings since the spring.

The twins were back in California, working on a video game together. They refused to tell Briar the concept of the game, since they were superstitious about sharing things before it was finished, but the illustrations Briar had seen in the background of their FaceTimes made her suspect that it took place in a forest. She had also caught Laurel furiously dictating a voice note as she studied some cool-looking moss on their hike to the campsite.

RJ was still in New York, still working on Wall Street, but Briar predicted he was only a few years out from quitting. His therapist agreed that the job was bad for his health, so thankfully Briar wasn't the only one constantly reminding him to look after himself anymore.

At some point, Noah pulled out his guitar and started quietly strumming a tune Briar recognized but couldn't quite place. Harper leaned into his side, her head resting on his shoulder. The picture the two of them made by the fire pit reminded Briar of the final hours of their wedding. In the end, Alice had suggested having it at the camp, and they had gladly accepted.

'Ahem.' Cook cleared his throat, clanking a knife against his tankard of beer. 'I'd like to propose a toast.' They all dutifully raised their glasses. 'To Susan.'

'To Susan.'

'And,' he continued, 'to the entire Elwood family.'

'The Elwoods.'

'And finally,' Cook said, looking at Alice. 'To Miss Alice Hughes, without whom our most beloved camp wouldn't be what it is today.'

'To Alice,' they all cheered, the twins whooping and stomping their feet. Briar couldn't stop smiling, reveling in everyone's collective understanding of how great her girlfriend was.

'Speech!' Sierra called, hiccuping into her cup.

'Speech!' Freddie echoed.

Alice looked at Briar for help, her face glowing red, but Briar just grinned traitorously back.

Alice stood. 'Um. When I came to the US, I thought I'd be back in London by the end of the weekend.' She glanced at the faces around the fire, her eyes resting on Briar. 'I had no idea that I'd still find a home here. I thought I'd lost it forever. Susan gave me a lot of presents over the years, but I think her best one was giving me a good reason to come home and face my mistakes.' Briar reached up to grab Alice's hand, squeezing it. 'I'm so glad to be back in your life,' Alice said quietly. Then she turned back to the group. 'In all your lives.'

'Hear, hear,' Harper said.

The group raised their glasses and drank again, but Briar couldn't stop staring at Alice, at the firelight flickering in her eyes. She was amazed by how much time the two of them had ahead, of how many choices they could make together to build the life that they'd always dreamed of.

Acknowledgements

We wanted this book to be an ode to nature, which has always been a source of comfort in our darkest times, and to the idea that we all need more childlike whimsy in our lives. Summer camp was the perfect backdrop, and we drew on our own camp experiences and others' for inspiration. Much like a summer camp, this book would not exist without many people's efforts. We would like to thank Rebecca and Sam, who gave us feedback on the realism of the camp setting; Natalie, who gave us feedback on the realism of life in academia; and Emily, who just told us the book was great. Thank you to Jennifer, whose real life camp stories were an important part of this one. Thanks to our families, who have been nothing but supportive, and to Madeline's fiancée, Kelly, for hosting and feeding us during many writing sessions. Thanks to our network of other authors, Laura Hankin and Ella Dawson in particular, for showing us the ropes as we set out to write our second book, and to Elizabeth Held for creating spaces for all of us to join together. We would like to thank our agent Kate Rizzo for always seeing our vision and pushing us to pursue it. She kept us sane through every draft and always took our calls when we had hit a wall. Her tireless work, and the work of everyone at Greene & Heaton, has made the process of publishing so much more joyful. And, finally, this book wouldn't be what it is without our editor, Emily Bedford, and the team at Canelo, DK. Thank you for your many wonderful ideas for this book and your belief in the importance of telling queer love stories.